FATAL LOYALTY

a novel

SUE DUFFY

Kregel
Publications

Fatal Loyalty: A Novel

© 2010 by Sue Duffy

Published by Kregel Publications, a division of Kregel, Inc., P.O. Box 2607, Grand Rapids, MI 49501.

Library of Congress Cataloging-in-Publication Data
Duffy, Sue.
  Fatal loyalty : a novel / Sue Duffy.
  p. cm.
1. Coconut Grove (Miami, Fla.)—Fiction. I. Title.
PS3604.U38F38   2010   813'.6—dc22   2010004764

ISBN 978-0-8254-2594-3

Printed in the United States of America

10 11 12 13 14 / 5 4 3 2 1

To my husband, Mike Duffy,
my dad, J. D. Railey,
and the memory of my mom,
Doris Railey.

ACKNOWLEDGMENTS

FOR THEIR CONTRIBUTIONS to this book, I would like to thank the following:

Les Stobbe, my literary agent, for his unwavering support and guidance.

Steve Barclift, Dawn Anderson, Becky Fish, Cat Hoort, and the rest of the Kregel Publications staff for seeing promise in this book.

Florida's attorney general's office, Department of Law Enforcement, and Department of State for critical information on drug trafficking, elections, law enforcement jurisdictions and procedures, and other issues relevant to this book's plot.

Phillip Edney of the FBI's Office of Public Affairs in Washington, D.C., for answering lots of strange questions.

Thomas Landress of the South Carolina attorney general's office for his legal and law-enforcement savvy.

Gail Baldwin for his vivid memories of life at his Stiltsville home.

My children—Kim, Laura, and Brian—for the way they brought me up, for the life lessons we learned together.

My brother, Scott Railey, for his expert knowledge of guns and ammunition.

Faithful friends Carmen Roberson and Nancy Mauney for their objective reviews of the evolving manuscript.

And again . . . my husband, Mike, for his love and wise counsel; and my parents, J. D. and Doris Railey, for a godly home.

PROLOGUE

IN AN INSTANT, his world collapsed, and no one knew it but him. The giddy chatter of students rushing to and from the cafeteria swirled about him as he felt blindly for something to lean against.

Eyes locked on the overhead television screen, Evan Markham backed slowly toward a post in the crowded student union. Just moments ago, he'd been one of them, a Florida State student preparing for exams and the long-awaited summer break. But what he'd just heard ended it all.

He had only glanced at the News at Noon anchorwoman with the glossy lips as he hurried to class. He caught something about a shootout in Tampa, but kept going. As he reached the door, though, he heard a name that stopped him cold.

". . . Leo Francini."

Evan turned suddenly and stared at the screen as the woman switched the broadcast to an on-the-scene reporter. A cold sweat sprang from his brow as he moved quickly toward others gathering before the monitor.

"This quiet residential street in Tampa was the scene today of a bloody standoff between FBI agents and members of a drug cartel run by Miami racketeer Leo Francini," the somber-faced young man announced. "Before the violence ended about nine o'clock this morning, two FBI agents and Francini's son, Donnie Francini, were killed. It is believed that Leo Francini was in the area, though not involved in the shootout. An intense manhunt by the FBI and local police is now underway. A house-to-house search is being conducted in . . ."

Steadying himself against the post, Evan turned to see if anyone was watching him. *How could they know? No one knows.*

Then another name caught him.

"Florida Attorney General Tony Ryborg, visibly shaken by the deaths of the two FBI agents, just moments ago issued what he calls an iron-clad promise to the people of this state, saying, 'Leo Francini will be brought to justice and pay the severest penalty for these deaths.'"

Two hours later, Evan was packed and ready to leave. For where, he didn't yet know. He'd removed all his belongings from the apartment and left a note for the roommate he hardly knew. He hadn't allowed himself to get close to many people, switching roommates often during the three years he'd been enrolled. Still, the guy deserved an apology for the sudden departure.

Evan returned to the student union to close his checking account and put a hold on his mail, evading inquiries about why he would do so before final exams.

As he left the building, he saw her. As usual, she didn't notice him. Andie Ryborg seemed as absorbed in a private world as he was. Only hers hadn't just ended in a gunfight.

One last time, he hung back and watched her. Dark hair fell loosely about her face as she sketched beneath a tree, focused on the gurgling fountain in the center of the green.

They'll find you. Get away!

CHAPTER 1

One month later

A PRIMORDIAL MIST CLUNG to the River of Grass as the old woman boarded the small airboat. Currents of raw, pungent air rattled the high saw grass, stirring its reptile population awake as the eastern sky announced the first rays of morning. The Florida Everglades was a severe and unforgiving landscape. An unwise choice and a person could be swallowed up by the simmering sea of sharp reeds, fangs, teeth, and the even deadlier ways of man. But the woman wasn't afraid. This was home.

With quick, confident motions, she cranked the powerful fan engine looming behind her and latched onto left and right control sticks. The sudden roar of the air blades launched a flock of ibis on their escape from the woman and her solo mission, as if they knew where she was headed and wanted no part of it.

The flat-bottomed boat eased away from the dock, parting reeds, skirting cypress, and gaining speed as its path through the marshy grass flayed wide beneath the force. The old woman tensed at the controls, her anger barely contained. "How dare they?" she growled over the drone of the engine.

Thirty minutes later, she eased back on the throttle and scouted a distant hammock of hardwoods. Certain of her destination, she made her slow, deliberate approach.

Even the beat of the rotors couldn't mask the sudden rifle shot off her bow. She immediately cut the engine and waited. When the second shot fired, she hollered to the unseen gunman, "Stop shooting. Tell Leo Francini I'm here!"

Two men in camouflage emerged from the trees, both waving guns and shouting, "Get away!"

"No! Get Leo!"

"He's not here!"

"Well, who *is* here?"

The men seemed confused. Then one of them left while the other kept the woman in his sights. "Don't come any closer!" he ordered.

She could see his taunting smile and knew he recognized her. Moments later, she was waved ashore and led into a clearing of what had once been a fish camp. Now, the crumbling assembly of cabins was just another base camp for a drug cartel run by the man she was looking for. She'd dealt with him once before and believed it would be the last time. But again, she'd discovered his dealers pedaling their wares in her territory. No one encroached on her turf.

The woman disappeared inside a long, low cabin sprouting enough satellite dishes, antennae, cables, and other communications equipment to mount a war. When she finally emerged, she was dogged by a very plump, very agitated young man shouting apparent obscenities at her in Spanish. Finally, she turned and broke into his tirade. "You remind Leo that we had a deal. And this is what you get when you break a deal with me." She took a few more steps and turned again. "Remind him how eager the FBI is to find him after that gun battle in Tampa—and how many eyes there are in the Everglades. It might not be such a good place to stay."

Without looking back, the woman hurried to her boat, clinging to the hope that Leo's order to leave her alone would hold, despite the rage of the man snapping at her from behind. In moments, though, she seemed forgotten as the men plunged into a fury of de-camping. Orders were screamed, equipment dismantled, inventory loaded onto airboats. The young drug boss managed to execute the frenetic evacuation just moments before a Miami law enforcement team bore down on the camp. An anonymous caller had phoned in the tip, told them where to find one of the cartel camps, and told them she was sure Francini wasn't there.

CHAPTER 2

❧

One year later

THE MAN KNEELING LOW over the grave was watched.

"Why would he bury his wife in a cow pasture?" Jimmy Seibels abruptly asked the older man seated beside him.

Captain Warren Jacobs turned a molten gaze on the brash young officer, who fidgeted nervously in the passenger seat of the black sedan. "You see any cows?" Warren asked irritably.

Jimmy studied the sprawling meadow as if ordered to find something bovine wandering there. "No, sir," he reported, "but that don't mean it's not a cow pasture."

"That *doesn't* mean." Warren corrected, scratching the stubble of gray hair ringing the bald crown of his head. "Did you sleep through English?" He turned back to watch the hillside with its lone headstone. Radio transmissions from the Florida Department of Law Enforcement headquarters squawked from the dashboard.

"All I'm saying is it seems like a man in his position would have buried his wife in a normal cemetery with some fancy monument, don't you think?"

Without shifting his focus from the man he'd come to guard, Warren replied grimly, "There are things you don't know and probably wouldn't understand if I told you." He opened the car door and looked quickly back at Jimmy. "I don't like him being that far from us. Get out and stand near the car. I'm moving closer." His words, like the movements of his lean body, were quick and efficient. The young man obeyed without further comment.

❧

On the distant hillside, a bald eagle swooped low over Tony
Ryborg, who raised his head in greeting. "Hey there, buddy. It's
just me." He watched the great bird lift and dip with the warm
currents that stirred that July morning. It sailed far over the
meadow, then banked slowly and returned, making another pass
over the simple grave.

In eight years, Tony had worn a hard path to that spot beneath
a sprawling live oak tree. From there, the land sloped gently away
in every direction, leaving the tree and the single gravestone
alone on the highest point for miles. It was the place his Jessica
had always retreated to when old demons threatened.

He watched the bird circle lazily above him, then looked back
at the ground.

"I can't stay long this time, Jess," he whispered. "You're free of
it, but I'm not. This battle won't let me go. I just pray it stays clear
of Andie. She's so alone down there."

Glancing across the field, he could almost see his wife and
daughter laughing in fits as he struggled to stay upright on the
old mare they rode through the meadow one summer. The vision
made him close his eyes, draw a quivering breath, and release it
slowly to the wind.

The brisk flapping of the eagle's wings made Tony look up. "If
I believed in such things, Jess, I might think that was you watching me. But even if it was, you still couldn't answer the question
that haunts me: Where were you going that day?"

Soon, he rose and walked briskly away from the grave. He
turned toward Warren, who now stood nearby. "We'll have to hurry."

"Yes, sir," said Warren, falling in step behind the man who, at
fifty-seven, showed no signs of slowing. Warren crossed the field
on full alert, eyes scanning in every direction.

As Florida's attorney general and candidate for governor, Tony
Ryborg pursued one agenda above all others: to wage a head-on
war against drug trafficking in and through his state. Throughout
a legendary career as Dade County sheriff, then FDLE commis-
sioner, and now attorney general, Tony had worked relentlessly
to apprehend and convict drug growers, dealers, and their over-
seas bosses to the fullest extent of the law. When that wasn't

enough, Tony pushed for harsher punishments under new laws. As governor, he would be able to flex even greater muscle against drug cartels from Florida to the Caribbean and South America. He hadn't intended to run for the state's highest office until the law enforcement community, seeing no other candidate with an anti-drug platform, persuaded him to step in midway through the race.

But some people were determined to keep Tony Ryborg out of the governor's office. For years, drug bosses had tried to disarm him with bribes and threats. When that didn't work, they attempted assassination. It was Warren Jacobs who'd foiled that assault, wrestling the attacker to the ground in front of the Ryborg home and taking a bullet to his chest. Thereafter, Tony and his daughter, Andrea, had lived in the shadow of FDLE security.

"Sir, did you reach Manny Alvarez?" Warren asked as Tony settled into the back seat of the car. Manny was the FDLE officer Tony had assigned to look after his daughter, who had recently moved to Miami.

"I did," Tony answered as he opened his briefcase to begin the day's work. "He says everything's okay at Andie's place. But I asked him to step up his rounds down there anyway." As he fidgeted with a sheaf of papers, he added, "It's just a feeling, Warren. An edge to her voice the last few times we talked."

If not for Jimmy Seibel's presence, Warren might have pursued the conversation about Andie. Assigned to protect the Ryborg family during Tony's first term as attorney general, Warren was well acquainted with the playful girl who drew outlandish caricatures of him and taped them to his windshield—the same girl who refused to leave his hospital room for days after he was shot trying to protect her father.

Warren might have reminded Tony that his daughter was undergoing a transition into her new life in Miami. At twenty-six, she was no more the sheltered child, though she had never wanted to be. No more was she in the comfort and security of her family home and the doting presence of her father. The officer might have suggested that maybe the young woman, though passionate about her independence, was just a bit homesick.

As the car bumped along the rugged terrain, Tony put down his papers and stared into the glade of a nearby pine forest. A few early morning rays penetrated the dense canopy and glinted off the cabin's tin roof. Jessica Ryborg's grandfather had built the small home on family land outside Tallahassee, a retreat from his insurance agency in town. But the deaths of both grandparents had left the old place abandoned for many years until Jessica and Tony restored it as their own private getaway. The sight of it stung with memories he could hardly bear.

Tony focused on the front door, tucked in the deep shade of the porch. He wished it to open and the delicate figure of a woman with auburn curls to emerge. *Jessica*, he mourned silently. *Jessica*.

Turning off the rutted lane, the car hit a pothole and jerked Tony back to the moment. Warren sped onto the highway heading to town. *Just like that morning*, Tony still grieved. *Will it ever stop hurting?*

As he'd done so many times before, Tony forced himself back into his work. Without looking up from the surveillance reports in his lap, he broke the silence in the car. "Warren, when we get back to the office, try to reach Manny for me, please. It seems Mr. Francini is on the move again."

Hearing no response, he looked up to see Warren intently studying his rearview mirror.

"Warren?"

"Sir, I'd like you to lie flat on the seat. Right now!" Tony's first instinct was to turn and look out the rear window. But as he did, Warren snapped a command. "Tony, get down!"

CHAPTER 3

᠅

"SWEET CHILD, this is brutal. What are you doing?"

Andie Ryborg flinched at the man's words. "I . . . I don't know what you mean."

Randall Ivy studied her face. "We seldom know our own madness," he said as he glanced back at the painting.

Don't overreact, Andie cautioned herself. *He's just toying with me. He always does.*

It had been a year since Ivy accepted the first painting Andie had brought him and displayed it in his gallery. The rich monotone of a mime performing on a street corner had sold in less than a week. Ivy's Coconut Grove Gallery, one of Miami's finest, soon exhibited another Ryborg oil, a portrait of an old, leathery-skinned woman pulling shrimp from a net. It sold in record time, too, and after that, Andie was sure all of Miami would soon clamor for more of her work. But now, the more she brought to Ivy's door, the less receptive he was. In six months, he'd accepted only one other painting, hanging it inconspicuously near the back of the gallery. It was still there.

Andie gathered her composure. "What do you mean by that?"

He sighed deeply, running bony fingers through his shoulder-length blond hair. "Oh, it's probably a gentle madness. But its toll on your eye is grave. You've lost your seeing."

In plain English, please. Can you do that?

"Do you know you send signals like a traffic light, my dear?" Ivy remarked with amusement. "I can tell by the color of your face whether to stop or proceed. That bright crimson tells me I should go no further. Is that right?"

She'd had enough. "Mr. Ivy, I don't know what you're talking about. But I think it's time I found another gallery to—"

"Not yet, Andie," Ivy interrupted. "You're not ready to move off in any direction until you determine where you are right now." He persisted. "When you first arrived from Tallahassee, you were very sure of yourself and your art. Your talent is powerful, or I wouldn't have taken you into the gallery so quickly. But you've lost that power, that focus. You're not seeing anymore." He picked up the painting she'd just brought in, placed it on an easel, then turned to her.

"Tell me what you see," he coaxed.

She glanced impatiently at him, then at the painting. "Palms on a beach with sailboats in the distance," she said flatly as if the man deserved no answer at all.

Ivy smiled and nodded smugly. "And that's all. It's bereft of feeling. A visual cliché. But it will do nicely in some motel lobby."

Andie abruptly lifted her painting from the easel and turned toward the door. "I'll not impose on you again," she said, her voice tight.

Ivy raised a surrendering hand, halting her escape. "Andie, I've insulted you, and I should apologize. But I think too much of your talent to do that."

When she didn't respond, he continued. "You've changed in the last few months. The attorney general's only child and just like him," he ventured boldly. "That first day I met you, you were full of his force. Sure of where you were going and eager to get there on your own terms. But that force is missing. Gone from your paintings. Gone from your smile. Why, Andie?"

I won't listen to this. "I'm sure, Mr. Ivy, that somewhere in your vast knowledge of my personal life, you'll discover some answer that suits you. Goodbye."

Andie's retreat was swift and cold. She walked quickly to her car, the vintage, black 1968 Mustang convertible she'd driven for six years. She stashed the painting in the back seat, pulled down the top and settled behind the wheel. The July afternoon simmered, relieved only occasionally by a gust off Biscayne Bay, which was where she headed.

The village charms of old Coconut Grove that usually buoyed Andie's spirits eluded her. Navigating along the narrow, twisting lanes of exotic boutiques and cafés fringed by palms, she saw nothing before her but the taunting face of Randall Ivy.

Moments later, she arrived at South Bay Park and eased the Mustang beneath a sprawling banyan tree. She sat a moment, staring into the massive tree's mystifying anatomy. Its low-slung arms reached so far from the mother trunk they had to send down prop roots for support. Those roots could grow as large as the trunk itself, causing one tree to appear as a grove. The wonder of it lifted Andie just enough to see beyond the unpleasant confrontation with Ivy.

She dropped her keys into her pocket and grabbed a sketch pad and pencil from the back seat. Leaving the top down on her car, she got out and walked toward a shaded park bench overlooking a brilliant blue wash of water and sky. Scattered over the bay, sailboats raised their bleached faces to the wind and cut smartly through the swells. *Tell them they're a visual cliché, Mr. Ivy. That they have no business in your world.*

Dropping her paper and pencil onto the bench, she kicked off her sandals and lifted her long, gauzy skirt above her knees, letting the merciful breeze cool her slim, tanned legs. As she turned to survey the park, where wild, mossy oaks shaded a rambling lawn, a sudden impulse overtook her. Barefoot, she walked quickly toward the playground on the other side of the lawn.

A young mother gently pushed her toddler in a low swing. Andie smiled sweetly at them, settled into a swing higher off the ground, and pushed off. The same wind that fed the sails on the bay now rushed at her, catching her skirt and pulling her away.

Andie closed her eyes, pumped as hard as she could, and let the pendulum movement rock her back to peace. The air ran through her hair like cool fingers, separating each strand of the dark, wavy mane. After a while, she opened her eyes and looked around in time to see the young mother hurrying her child toward the parking lot, casting wary glances over her shoulder at Andie.

Don't be alarmed, Andie called silently after her. *Mr. Ivy says my madness is gentle.* She slowed the swing to a stop and got off.

She was almost light-headed when she returned to the bench and picked up her sketch pad. She gazed at the sailboats and thought again of Ivy. *How dare he presume to know me? He knows nothing. Nothing about the threats, the horrid notes.*

A restless energy swept through her, and she had to get away. She decided to drive over the causeway for a long walk down the beach. But as she rose from the bench, she saw movement in the tangle of shrubs nearby. Her pulse flew. It was the old sickening throb she'd known far too long. The commands of those who'd trained her echoed in her mind: drop, roll, and run low to the ground.

But not here. Not now. I'm supposed to be rid of that. She refused to succumb to her imagination. *There's no one there*, she assured herself.

Slowly, defiantly, she walked to her car, the breeze still cool on her bare arms. She looked quickly behind her. *You see*, she told herself, *no one's there.*

Two hours later, Andie rinsed the sand from her feet and left Key Biscayne's scenic shore. Returning to the mainland over the Rickenbacker Causeway, her hair blowing free inside the open convertible, she felt restored. She cruised back into Coconut Grove, this time savoring its every scented nuance, gliding beneath its leafy canopies, past the old, tile-roofed homes draped in bougainvillea, around the hammocks of salt marsh studded with wild herons. Though the Grove was now her home, it was too far from the father she adored—and not far enough from the threat of danger they both knew too well.

It was Tony Ryborg's job to bring the state's offenders to justice. But it was his relentless pursuit of drug traffickers that had made him a target. Too many times, the cartels had threatened him and his daughter if he didn't back off their operations. Too many times, Andie had been plucked from school and whisked to safety.

The latest round of threats to her father, though, had taken a curious turn, demanding Tony Ryborg withdraw from the governor's race. It was the same demand Andie had recently found scrawled in notes left for her. It was the message of her midnight caller. *They'll stop*, she assured herself. *I've outlasted them before. I will again.*

Not far from the old village was Andie's small, tidy house. Wishing to attract no attention to the move from her father's Tallahassee home, she had hunted alone for the place where she would begin the rest of her life. She'd found the two-bedroom bungalow tucked in a stand of royal palms and Australian pines. It was ill-kept, overgrown and exactly what she wanted. The hand-lettered For Rent sign nailed to a tree signaled no real estate agent. Surrounding homes were barely visible through a wild tropical thicket. She'd moved in two weeks later.

Andie pulled into the yard and parked on a bed of pine straw to one side of the house. Before getting out, she paused to admire the sun's final burst through the trees. On the lawn, the play of dazzling light against deep indigo shadows intrigued her. Light and dark so amiably paired. But not so in the world she'd discovered at too young an age. There, light battled the dark. It had to. That's why she wouldn't let her father resign his post, why he must become governor.

But she knew her father's mind: he could dodge threats against his own life but was prepared to withdraw from a battle that threatened his child. He'd already lost his wife to a heart attack when Andie was eighteen. She knew he wouldn't risk losing her too.

But something happened during Andie's junior year at FSU that made him persevere. She had joined a campus ministry to female inmates in a nearby prison. She drew particularly close to a young woman named Claire, whose drug addiction had cost her countless jobs, her home, and worst of all, her child. Claire had been convicted of selling cocaine to support her habit and her two-year-old daughter. Upon the young woman's release from prison, Andie helped her through more drug rehabilitation, found a job and apartment for her, and brought her into the Christian church where Andie and her dad worshipped. There was even hope the woman's daughter would be returned to her from foster care.

Andie thought she had witnessed a miraculous turn-around in Claire's life until early one Sunday morning. On her way to get Claire for church service, an ambulance overtook Andie and stopped in front of the apartment building where Claire lived. Andie watched in horror as emergency personnel rushed into her friend's apartment. She ran in behind them and watched helplessly as they tried to revive the young woman slumped on the floor. But the drug had already done its deed. Claire was gone.

And the dealers who'd supplied her death had surely moved on to other victims.

"Hunt them down!" Andie tearfully begged her dad. "Find them all, and put them away. You can't quit, Dad. I won't let you!"

Andie thought of Claire as she pulled the top over the convertible and turned toward the house. *She would have liked this place.*

The landlord had welcomed and funded Andie's efforts to improve the house. She hired roofers, plumbers, and electricians to make basic repairs and upgrades. A floor refinisher stripped the wide-plank pine floors to their natural color, and Andie repainted all the rooms herself. Dark and grungy interior walls were coated with a soft taupe, then hung with colorful paintings and prints. The dingy yellow exterior became a dusky rose with glossy, black Bahamian shutters.

Her favorite place in the house was the screened-in front porch. She furnished it with second-hand wicker chairs and tables she painted the same glossy black as the shutters. Over the pine floor, she spread a bold Aztec rug of coral, green, and black. Across the ceiling, she strung tiny, star-shaped lights to mimic the constellations.

And everywhere, Andie grew plants. She cleared the tangled yards of weeds, then pruned and coaxed the old growth to new life. On the porch and throughout the house, she draped vines and clustered pots of more plants in different colors and textures.

This was home now. The old place seemed to embrace her, thankful for its rebirth.

Before going inside, she walked to the back yard to check a bed of caladiums she'd just planted in the shade of a ponderous ficus tree. As she suspected, the soil around them was parched from the heat. She started toward the house, where she kept a hose coiled near the back door, and suddenly stopped. The door was open.

Suspended between denial and flight, she stood motionless, staring hard at the door, not willing to believe anyone had breached the security of her home. Her mind seized the first logical explanation. *I must not have locked the door. Sometimes it doesn't close all the way, so the wind must have blown it open. That has to be it.*

Moving slowly toward the house, she heard nothing stir inside.

She eased up the steps and, with one sudden movement, jerked the door open wide. Her hand shot to the switch just inside the door, and the navy and white kitchen she loved to wake up to was flooded with light. Still no sound. Then she thought of the gun. She kept one in her bedroom, which at this moment seemed miles away.

Glancing about the kitchen, she saw nothing out of place. Cautiously, her heart pounding, she moved into the hallway from where she could see into almost every room of the house. She flipped on more lights. Everything was in place, and the front door was securely locked.

This is insane, she scolded herself. *It must have been the wind.* Andie took a deep breath, fighting the nausea of fright. She looked about the house. *God, are you here?*

Since her mother's death, she'd wrestled with her faith. Though her mother had openly praised God for rescuing her from drug addiction, Andie believed it was the ravages of that addiction that had claimed her mother's life at too young an age, just as it had Claire's. For too long, Andie had wrestled with one persistent, angry question: Why did God allow evil to destroy the good?

Yet as she walked through the rooms of her house, she sensed the nearness of him. She still believed that no matter her doubts, no matter what the world flung at her, God was still close.

Steeling herself against fear, determined to salvage her composure, she returned to the kitchen for a glass of iced tea and headed for the front porch. Leaving the door between the porch and living room open, she dropped onto the plump cushions of a wicker lounge. When the trembling subsided, she picked up the phone and called her dad.

"Hello," he answered crisply on the first ring. She guessed he was at the desk in his study, bent over a campaign speech with the cell phone at his fingertips. The primaries over, his strategists were in constant communication with the man opinion polls now placed ahead of the Democrat's candidate, state senator Bill Neiman.

"Governor Ryborg, please," Andie teased.

"Well, he's not in," he played along. "But if you'd like to speak to his boss, I'll page his daughter for you."

"Got that right," she said, momentarily forgetting her fear and resting in the sound of her dad's voice.

"How's my girl?" he asked softly. "No problems?"

She hesitated. *You can't tell him. He's got to stay focused on the campaign.* "Now, Dad, have I reported any to you?" *That's evasion, not lying*, she reasoned.

"I pray you're okay, hon." His voice dropped. "I'm not at all happy about you being so far from me. Things are happening, and I, well, never mind."

"What's wrong, Dad?"

"Nothing's wrong. Has Manny checked on you today?"

"Dad, you said—"

"I said nothing's wrong, honey. Now, please tell me about Manny."

Andie backed off. "Well, the less I see of that hound dog bodyguard, the better." Even as she said the words, she knew they weren't true. Minutes ago, she would have welcomed the sight of the gentle warrior Manny Alvarez.

"He's a medal-of-honor cop, Andie. Give the man his due."

"Well, he's more like a big hairy nanny with no social graces," she said, intent on keeping the conversation light. "He pops in unannounced, raids my fridge, and prowls through the house, dropping little pieces of food everywhere."

"He's doing exactly what I told him to, except for the food thing. Scouting your place and keeping you safe is his job. Be nice to him."

Andie smiled at the father who wasn't there, wishing he was. "I miss you, Dad. But it's time for me to make my own way. I appreciate your concern. I even appreciate Manny, sometimes. Does he really have five kids?"

"All girls. And now he's got you."

His voice was a salve to her. She imagined him as he spoke—the high round cheeks that squeezed his eyes nearly shut when he laughed, the wild gray eyebrows he refused to trim. "They make me look meaner than I am," he'd once told her. "And some people need to think I'm real mean." She closed her eyes and tried not to think how close those people might be. As her dad talked, her mind wandered to the park, to the movement in the shrubs.

"Are you listening to me, Andie?" he asked with mild impatience.

She opened her eyes and laughed, realizing her dad had been telling something in great detail and she hadn't heard a word.

"Sorry, Dad," she giggled and turned to look outside. "I was—" The words caught in her throat. Her hand flew to her mouth, stifling a scream as she dropped the phone.

A man in a mask stared at her through one of the screen windows.

"Andie?" Her father's voice called from the phone on the floor. "Andie!"

CHAPTER 4

ऊ

ALONE ON A SCARRED BEACH miles from the Florida mainland, Evan Markham dug his heels into the sand and waited. The eastern horizon faded slowly into night. In the overcast sky, no stars, no moon would light the point in the sea he'd come to watch. But the signal would flash brightly enough, and he would go.

Evan glanced up and down the beach at the ghostly forms faintly silhouetted against the disappearing light. They were the ravaged remains of Dutch Key after Hurricane Andrew's direct hit in August 1992. The tiny island off Key Largo, just south of Miami, had served as a laboratory for marine biologists from Florida's public universities and private industries. But the squat old buildings had been brutally clawed by winds clocked at more than 175 miles per hour.

Stricken trees still lay where they'd fallen across the now-abandoned habitat. Restoration had been promised, not delivered. There was talk of rebuilding a lab more centrally located up the coast, but none of that mattered to Evan.

He stood up, stretched his long legs, and yawned. There'd been little sleep since he'd arrived in Miami three weeks ago. Though he was just twenty-seven, he felt fatigue as he never had before.

As night fell, waves with bright phosphorus heads rushed against the shore. *Better check the boat*, he thought, and started for the path that snaked through the palmettos to the other side of the island. Several times along the way, he stopped to listen. Few boaters ever ventured onto the island. Still, this was no time for a surprise encounter.

Though the hurricane had torn away the island's old wooden dock, a small concrete pier installed just before the storm hit remained intact. It was there that Evan's forty-foot trawler now waited. Its lines, he was glad to see, were still tightly knotted. On the lee side of the island, the sea was at rest, and the boat rocked gently at its moorings.

Evan boarded the broad, sturdy vessel with the high bow and roomy cabins. *It'll never win any races*, he thought. *But it's solid, and it's home until this is over.* Its name, *Misfit*, made Evan Markham look upon the boat as a kindred spirit.

He entered the cabin and turned on a light, the generator still firing life through the circuits. He checked his watch. *Only ten o'clock. Plenty of time.* He took the steps down to his cabin. There, a small salon, V-berth, and head formed a cocoon he found strangely comforting.

Evan tossed his hat on the bed. He set his watch to wake him at half past midnight, sank onto the sheets, and drifted into a fitful sleep.

At one in the morning, a light rain fell as Evan resumed his vigil on the beach. A half-hour later, he was adjusting the tarp he'd rigged against the rain when he saw it. A quick burst of light in the east. Evan waited for the rest of the coded flash sequence. When it came, he grabbed the halogen strobe light beside him, flashed the all-clear sequence, then raced to the trawler. Moments later, it churned toward the open sea.

It had stopped raining by the time Evan cautiously approached the large fishing boat with the high tuna tower. At a safe distance, he shifted into neutral and swept the deck of the other vessel with his strobe. The other boat did the same to him. When both captains were satisfied of each other's identity, Evan threw out fenders and tied up alongside. After securing the lines, he hopped aboard the other boat and gripped the hand of Leo Francini.

"So, you continue to outstep the law," Evan said as Leo led him into the cabin. "That hole you dug for yourself in the Bahamas must be awfully deep."

"Deep pockets, Evan," Leo corrected. "That's what it takes to keep neighbors quiet, you understand. Great sums of money and the fear that one night they'll wake up to find someone they care about missing." He scratched the stubble on his flat cheek. "Now, tell me what I want to hear."

೪

It was dawn when *Misfit* returned from the rendezvous with Leo Francini, nosing its way through Biscayne Bay toward the Miami River. For weeks, Evan had docked at a small marina north of town, but the dock master asked too many questions to suit him. He knew he had to leave. Intent on finding a secure hideout, he'd cruised the Miami River just days ago and found exactly what he was looking for. Before leaving for Dutch Key, he'd returned to the spot for one more check. For nearly an hour, he'd sat with his engines off, watching and listening for activity of any kind. Now, he was going back to make himself at home.

Approaching the Brickell Avenue Bridge at the entrance to the river, Evan looked up at the handsome boulevard running to and from downtown Miami. Too early for rush-hour traffic, the city still slumbered. Yellow hibiscus fluttered in the ocean breeze. Graceful palms cut swayback silhouettes against a pink sky. In the glassy corporate towers stacked about the causeway, Evan could see reflections of the sunrise behind him. But he was unmoved by its beauty. His mood was dark, residual from two hours of Leo Francini's ranting against Tony Ryborg and those who threatened the Francini cartel.

Far beyond the bridge, past the elegant hotels and pastel villas with sun-baked terraces, the waterfront grew seamy. Industrial warehouses, rusting boat sheds, and rundown apartments lined the banks. Between an engine repair shop overrun by cats and a vacant lot sprouting billboards in Spanish, a small creek wound from the river back to a tangle of trees and little else. On one side of the narrow channel rose a solid screen of bamboo. The other side was a jungle of schefflera, banana, and live oak trees. Evan had discovered an old dock at the end of the creek. The trawler's depth-finder showed ample clearance to navigate the channel all the way to the end. No one seemed to live in the few ramshackle dwellings barely visible through the trees. He couldn't believe his good fortune in finding such a place.

He slowed the engines and turned into the creek, breathing the heady fragrance of wild honeysuckle. A sudden screech made him jerk his head toward the sound. Something orange and lime flashed across his bow. The parrot dived on the intruding vessel several more times, then retreated to an overhanging limb to exchange stares with Evan.

He steered straight for the old wooden dock at the end, hoping its anchorage would hold the big trawler. After tying up, he walked to the end of the dock and studied his surroundings. If all those months in military school had taught him anything, it was surveillance, the practical kind—staking out the commandant's house before a raid on the man's prized watermelon patch or learning the security protocols before hacking into the school's computers to adjust grades.

But there'd been little time for Evan to fully appraise the safety of this location. He knew he should have come after dark and watched each structure for signs of life. He could only hope his arrival in this out-of-the-way jungle didn't alert the wrong people.

He gazed through the trees. Through a break in the bamboo thicket, he saw a tiny cement-block house with its front door open, just as it had been both times he'd visited the spot. Nothing changed. On the opposite bank stood a wood-sided cabin with a wrap-around porch and a small camper parked behind it, grass growing over its tires. It was the bike leaning against the side of the cabin that gave Evan a start. It hadn't been there yesterday.

After studying the house awhile, Evan returned to the boat. In the galley, he slapped together a sandwich and dropped some chips on a plate, but he was too nervous to eat. *Settle down,* he told himself as he pushed the plate aside and headed back to the dock. *There's no one around.*

"Hey you!" a voice called. Evan spun toward the sound.

The short, stocky woman in a purple housedress and fuzzy yellow slippers moved quickly toward him with a fly swatter in one hand and a leash in the other. The rat-like dog at the end of the leash was more dragged than walked down the dock.

Evan gaped at the sight.

"Hey, young fella, what are you up to down here, huh?" Though her words demanded, her face crinkled into a half smile. Evan didn't respond.

"Gator got your tongue?" The woman swatted furiously at a mosquito and yanked at the leash. "Get on up here, Elvis, you sorry excuse for a dog."

By the time she reached Evan, the woman was aflutter with an irritable Elvis jerking backward on the leash. The swatter, now tucked between an arm and her chest, flapped wildly in her face, but freed one hand to present something similar to a handshake. It was more like a quick slide across Evan's hesitantly extended palm.

"My name's Victoria, but that's too highfalutin' given my present station in life, so make it Vic, and what's yours?" As her words tumbled, so did Elvis, right off the dock. But the leash held as he dangled from the neck just inches above the water, flailing and wailing in midair.

"Your name, son. What is it?" Vic ignored Elvis's plight while keeping a firm grip on the leash.

"Ma'am, your dog is—"

"Oh, Elvis pulls that stunt all the time. Just wants attention. Are you in trouble?"

The question caught Evan off guard. And the dog's shrieks were getting weaker. Afraid the tiny animal was choking to death and needing time to answer the abrupt question, Evan leaned over the dock and slowly pulled the dog to safety.

"Well, Elvis found a sucker, I guess," Vic grumbled.

Evan set the little dog down on the dock and stroked its head. He was repaid with a sharp growl and a lunge for his bare leg, but Vic pulled the animal up short before he made contact with Evan's flesh.

"See why I don't care if he dangles there all day?" Vic said. "Oh, I don't mean it. He's about all I got." She looked down at the dog, now curled into a profound sulk. "And what was that name?"

"Evan, uh . . ." He silently cursed himself for giving his real name.

"Evan what?" Vic asked quickly, swatting at a fly buzzing the knot of dyed red hair on top of her head.

"Jackson," he lied.

"Uh-huh. Well, that's a mighty big boat for sightseeing this nasty old river."

"Yes, ma'am. Well, uh . . ." He needed an excuse for being there and quickly. "I'm writing a book, a novel, and . . . uh . . . just need a quiet place away from everything. You know how noisy apartment living is."

The woman eyed him suspiciously.

"Anyway, I thought I'd just hang around here for a while. Uh, do you live close by?"

"That's my place over there." She pointed to the cabin.

Evan studied the old place again and noticed the bike was gone. "Do you live alone?"

Vic ignored the question. "You can make yourself comfortable back here in my private jungle."

"Yours?"

"Every last weed. My husband and I bought the property about twenty-five years ago. Now, it's just mine. He's been dead since '92. Andrew got him good."

"Andrew?"

"You know, that big blow we had down here that knocked us around so bad."

Evan nodded and waited for the rest of the story.

"The hurricane, son. Ever watch the news?"

"Oh, yes, ma'am. So what happened to your husband?"

She drew still and gazed into the water. "That's a story for another time. Right now you've got a book to write. So get to it. Elvis and I will be seeing you, Mr. Evan Jackson." She glanced quickly from him to the boat. "Mighty nice boat for such a young fella." She caught his eye for a second, then walked away, dragging the still-pouting Elvis back up the dock. "Oh, Elvis, you're not hurt. Serves you right for being so ornery and . . ." Her voice trailed off as she disappeared through the trees.

She could be trouble, Evan warned himself.

He boarded the trawler and went below. He needed sleep before the night's work. As he drew the curtain over the starboard windows, he caught a flash of purple across the water. Vic had just dismounted her bike and leaned it against the side of her cabin. She retrieved Elvis from the basket on front and set him free to run. Then she looked Evan's way, her hands on her hips.

After a while, she clapped her hands for Elvis to come, and the two of them went inside. Evan pulled the curtain completely over the windows and sprawled across the bed.

Two hours later, a sharp rap on the side of the boat snatched him from a deep sleep.

It came again before he could scramble from bed. Fears of police swarming over the dock triggered a rush of adrenaline. He lunged across the cabin toward the port-side window, yanked back one edge of the curtain and looked up at the dock. A pair of fuzzy yellow slippers filled the window.

"You in there, Evan?" Vic hollered, banging loudly on the boat.

"What have I done to myself?" he moaned aloud. "Just a minute," he called irritably.

"Well, hurry up. This stuff's getting hot."

What? Evan slowly climbed the steps and opened the door.

"I thought you'd like some chilled mango to feed your brain," Vic said, brushing past him as she boarded the vessel uninvited. "Got my own tree, and there's nothing better on a hot day like this." She glanced around the galley, then peeped into the cabin below. "Don't see any writing going on here."

Evan drew a long breath, debating how firm to get with this woman. "Now look. You just can't—"

"Oh, yes, I can," Vic interrupted. "You're on my property, and I don't think your name's Evan Jackson. For that matter, I'm not so sure you're even thinking about writing a book. It wouldn't be any of my business what you're doing if you weren't parked in my back door. But you are. So tell me the truth about yourself, or get on out of here."

Evan glared at her. Her words stung him hard, and he didn't know why. She was just a crazy old woman. "I'm leaving right now, so please get off my boat."

He looked her straight in the eye, and despite her harsh words, he saw something he hadn't seen in a very long time. Compassion.

"Where will you go?" she asked simply.

He didn't answer. He didn't know.

Vic gathered up her purple skirt and sat down. "Take a seat, Evan, or whatever your name is."

"My name *is* Evan, and I asked you to leave this boat."

"Yeah, you did. And I asked you to sit down. I got something to say to you, and it won't take long. Then you can go."

Let her talk, then get out of here! Evan sighed loudly as he dropped onto a bench seat opposite the woman.

"You're in trouble. I know it. I'm not clairvoyant or any of that nonsense. I've just been around enough to read trouble on a person's face. And it's all over yours."

Evan rolled his eyes and looked out the window. *One more minute and I'm kicking you off this boat.*

As if reading his thoughts, Vic quickly added. "A curious thing happened after Hurricane Andrew hit."

Evan glanced back at her.

"While some lost their lives, others got new life handed back to them."

He looked curiously at her.

She continued. "Old hurts and troubles didn't matter anymore. Staying alive did. Neighbors who used to squabble over silly things rushed to each other's aid. People who thought they didn't need other people found the kindness of strangers a mighty comforting thing."

"Excuse me, but what are you getting at?"

"Well, son, I think you're in a storm. And before I get to liking you too much, I'd like to know if you plan on dying in it."

CHAPTER 5

꒜

"**WARREN, JUST BECAUSE** you can't track down that car, I'll not have your men following me everywhere I go," said Tony Ryborg, seated at his desk and shuffling through a stack of documents awaiting his signature. It was almost five o'clock, quitting time for most in the capitol complex, but not for the attorney general, who often worked until nine or later. The man with no one waiting for him at home.

"Sir, it's *because* there's no trace of the car that I'm ordering higher security," said Warren Jacobs, standing ramrod straight before Tony. "And the next time we visit the hill, there'll be at least one more car with us."

Tony looked up from the papers and stared at Warren, the man he most trusted with his life. Relinquishing his privacy had never been easy for him.

"If they'd intended to harm me, they would have," Tony insisted, then turned his attention back to the papers as if dismissing the matter. "It was just punks out joy riding on a country road."

Warren shook his head. "I don't think so, sir. The way they sped up on our tail and stayed there was tactical. It was a wide-open road. They could have passed at any time, but they hovered, then all of a sudden shot to our left and kept pace with us."

"Just punks," Tony repeated without looking up.

Warren didn't waver. "The windows were tinted, and we couldn't see who was inside. We traced the plates to a salvage operation, an auto graveyard, sir. Stolen plates. But no theft reports on that make car. It just disappeared after it sped away from us. Even the backup I called in couldn't find it. It was definitely tactical, sir. And maybe it wasn't their intent to harm you. Just scare you."

"Well, I'm not scared!" Tony pounded his fist on the desk and stood up. "After all these years, don't you know that?"

Though he didn't respond, Warren's gaze was steady on Tony's suddenly flushed face.

"The Leo Francinis of this world, hard as they've tried, will not threaten me out of this or any other office. And they won't tie me into some mealy-mouthed knot of nerves!" Tony walked briskly to the window and looked up at the network of tree limbs. Their leaves fluttered in the sunlight, casting flickers of shadow against the pane. *There's a gentle world out there somewhere,* he told himself.

He watched two children turn somersaults on the lawn below, their mother hovering protectively. He could hear the carefree squeals of the young. *They're so vulnerable. So trusting.* And Tony Ryborg, candidate for governor, protector of the people, turned back to Warren. "Do what you must."

"Thank you, sir." Warren seemed to relax, and Tony regretted raising his voice.

"Now, what's the report from Manny?" Tony asked, returning to his desk.

Warren smiled broadly. "It seems our Miss Andie is no easier to handle than you are, sir."

"Just full of yourself today, aren't you, officer?"

"Well, sir. You do know what I'm talking about. She's always been iron-willed. I told Manny that, and now he believes me."

"But he has nothing to report?"

"He's a good man, sir. He'd alert us immediately if he thought there was a problem."

Tony picked up a report and let it drop to his desk. "But there is a problem. This is the workup on a bust last night in South Miami. It was a Francini operation. Another grow house. And where there's one, there's a whole nest of them operating in neighborhoods where kids run out to play on their swing sets next door."

Hydroponic marijuana, grown without soil, had become the drug du jour, and Florida was second only to California in the number of "grow houses" cultivating it. Fifteen times more potent than common marijuana, the hydroponic variety had an average street value of five thousand dollars a pound and was almost an equal trade with cocaine. A grower could move into a house in the suburbs, cover the windows, install elaborate grow lights, and cram every room full of plants. Such operations were far less detectable than growing common marijuana in the open—and far more lucrative.

Tony was pushing new legislation for tougher penalties on those who grew hydroponic marijuana, who owned the houses where it grew, and, especially, those who kept children in grow houses.

"How many arrests?" Warren asked.

"Three. But guess who tipped us off?" Tony wasn't looking for an answer. "A kid selling chocolate bars for his church choir. Is that not divine justice?"

Warren settled into a chair opposite Tony's desk, appearing ready for more of the story.

"While the grower left him standing at the front door long enough to get money, the kid looked around, noticed all the plants, and later told his dad. And guess what dad does for a living?" Still no pause for an answer. "He's a cop."

"Sweet," Warren said. "I hope the kid got his money before the bust."

"Officers found about five hundred hydro plants and twelve chocolate bars, bought and paid for, the reporting officer notes." Tony smacked the table with his hand. "If a little kid can bring down one Francini operation, surely all of us big guys can take out the whole cartel."

Tony grew sullen. "Why can't we do that, Warren?" He returned to the window. "You see that woman down there with her kids?" Warren walked up beside him and peered at the lawn below. "She's watching them like a hawk with her wings spread over her babies, because she knows there's a snake headed for the nest. Leo Francini's the snake. He's just waiting for that moment when her back is turned, when those kids get a little bigger, a little fatter with money and daring. Then he'll slither up next to them and waggle his wares, entice them to try a little weed, snort a little powder. He and his kind will tell them it's what all the cool kids do. 'Don't you want to be cool and fly high for a while?' they'll ask."

Warren watched as the young mother finally gathered her children and walked away. "No one's fought to protect those kids harder than you have, Tony."

"Not hard enough. Francini's back in business."

"But the man's not around," Warren added. "He hasn't been seen since shortly before his son was killed."

Tony mulled that over quietly. "But he's out there. Just one of the heads of the snake, but the biggest, ugliest head. And we've got to crush it."

Tony took off his glasses and rubbed his eyes. "Warren, I'm going home early tonight. I've got a speech to write for the Orlando stump next week. And a young lady in Miami to catch up with. By the way, tell Manny to double up his rounds at her place. I'll prepare her for it." He shoved files into his briefcase and grabbed his coat.

Warren took the radio from his belt and snapped orders into it. Then he turned to Tony, "An officer is pulling up behind your car now, sir. He'll follow you home. Have a good evening."

Tony didn't feel like arguing. "Fine. See you in the morning." His mood grew melancholy as he drove from his reserved parking space at the capitol. He usually skirted the Florida State campus on his way home, but this evening, something drew him back to the old bricks of his alma mater. Even with a security detail in tow, he wandered a few of the lanes, past dorms pulsing with the ebb and flow of students out of class for the day. *How many have already been bitten by the snake?* he brooded. *How many minds gone bad?*

As Tony drove away, the memory of a long-ago night returned to him. It had been during his senior year at FSU. A sociology major headed to law school, he had volunteered one afternoon a week to help the staff at a local drug rehabilitation center.

His second day on the job, he had processed men and women of all ages into the eight-week residential program. Some had been court-ordered to the facility. Some referred by physicians. Others were nearly dragged there by parents or spouses desperate for help.

His Friday shift was over, and he was preparing to leave for the big homecoming weekend on campus. As he stored the day's admissions file in a drawer, a young woman approached the desk.

He glanced up ready to inform her that the office was closed, but the sight of her checked his words.

Though one eye was swollen shut and matted hair clung to a bruised face, she held her head high and announced in a barely controlled voice, "If you don't admit me to this place tonight, I won't be alive tomorrow."

Tony knew little about drug addiction, but he knew it didn't keep regular hours. He returned the file to the desktop and invited the girl to sit down. Seeing that wasn't an easy task for her, Tony went quickly to her aid. As her knees buckled, he caught her around the shoulders and waist. There seemed nothing to hold on to beneath her thin dress but bone.

He lowered her gently to a chair and called down the hall for help, but none came. As the girl sat shivering, he grabbed a blanket from a nearby cabinet and wrapped it around her. He poured hot coffee for her and, again, peered anxiously down the hall.

"You don't know what to do with me, do you?" she asked, looking intently at him as he helped her grip the cup. He sat down awkwardly beside her, embarrassed by her question.

She was so small and wounded. How could the tough football player be so incapable of helping her? "I guess not," he admitted. "I'm still pretty new here, and . . . uh . . . I—"

"And you haven't seen too many people like me," she interrupted. Then she did something unexpected. With a trembling hand, she reached to touch his cheek. "I'm so sorry," she whispered, then slowly withdrew her hand. He felt her eyes take in his neatly clipped hair, the pressed shirt, the college ring on his finger. "You can't understand, can you?" she asked weakly. "This evil hasn't touched you and I hope it never will." Tears suddenly clouded her eyes. "But it's destroying me."

Then she asked something he would never forget. "How do you know when you're dead?"

He knew then there would be no homecoming weekend for him. How could he revel in a game when someone like her barely clung to life?

"What's your name?" he asked her.

"Jessica."

CHAPTER 6

ANDIE PLUNGED HER GLOVED hands into the sandy soil beneath the ficus tree. The faint breath of early morning stirred against her as she separated clumps of caladiums. Some turned creamy faces lightly etched in chartreuse toward her. Others nodded vividly in pinks and reds. They reminded her of her art students at Dade Community College, faces lifted toward her, casting their colors in directions she showed them.

Then she thought of another face, the masked one that had appeared at her porch window just a week ago. The sudden thought of it made her lay down her spade and sit still in the grass. That night, she had tried to smother her scream as she dropped the phone, leaving her father frantically calling her name. Her first impulse had been to chase after the man, who quickly disappeared. Instead, she flipped on the outside lights, searching for signs of him, then retrieved the phone and lied. "Dad . . . uh . . . it's okay," she had almost whispered, trying to steady her breathing. "I . . . just saw a snake on a tree outside. I've . . . I've got to get it out of here. Can I call you later?" She'd almost hung up on him as she raced to check locks on all the windows and doors, especially the back one, and grab the gun from the nightstand. She'd sat with it in her lap all night, taking two calls from her father, looking for assurance that she was all right. She'd convinced him she was, though she knew better. For the rest of the night, she prayed. They were whispers to a Savior she sometimes didn't understand. Still, she called to him.

But not Tony Ryborg. She would not jeopardize her father's commitment to his race for governor. It was in the state's highest office he would wield the heaviest blows to the drug cartels ruining so many lives. But if he knew someone was stalking her, harassing her, Andie felt sure that he'd give it all up. That's what they wanted, whoever they were. Their message, no matter how it was delivered, was always the same: "If your father wins the race, he'll lose his daughter."

After her mother had died, Andie had watched her father's confidence erode. She would not speed that process.

The wind chimes above her jingled softly in the breeze, and Andie raised her face to them. To her, they were her mother's voice. She remembered them hanging outside the kitchen window and how much her mother delighted in their harmonies. Because her father was a light sleeper, though, her mother awoke sometimes to find the chimes lying stilled on a back porch table. She finally packed them away.

Andie had hung the chimes in her Coconut Grove yard before unpacking anything else. Now, to their soothing accompaniment, she returned to the matter of caladiums, plucking a fresh clump from the ground. As she tugged gently to separate the bulbs, a voice caught her from behind.

"Hey, Andie!"

A low groan escaped from her as she turned to greet Manny Alvarez. The hefty FDLE officer moved across the yard like a Hummer, his eyes sweeping the property. "What, no breakfast ready for me?" he called just before he tripped over a rake and rolled into a sitting position on the ground.

Fighting to contain a fit of laughter, Andie ran to help him. But when he opened his mouth to pick grass from it, she doubled over into near hysteria, wallowing in the relief of it.

"I hate to see you so worried about me," Manny said in a pretend sulk. "But I think I'm going to be okay."

Wiping tears from her eyes, she turned back to face him and said, "Of course, you are, you big nanny." She helped him from the ground. "I'll fix some breakfast for you." She led the way to the back door, and even the chilling thought of it standing open that night she had returned from the gallery didn't penetrate the contentment of pure silliness.

Manny followed her into the kitchen and lowered himself onto a barstool, wincing slightly.

Andie raised her eyebrows at him. "I believe you did hurt yourself, big guy."

"Naw, I just did that to make you laugh," he said.

"Sure you did," she said, grinning. "Want some pancakes?"

"Not really. I just ate a half dozen doughnuts. Thought I'd stop by and take a look around."

"A half dozen? That explains why you're having trouble walking."

"Yeah, yeah," he said, fingering the lock on a kitchen window beside him.

"Manny, you were just here yesterday, you know."

"Well, get used to it, kiddo. You're part of my job description, and I like to get paid." He winked at her as he got up and started his tour of the house and grounds. Then he searched her car.

She was eating a bowl of cereal when he returned to the kitchen.

"You been working outside near the front porch?" he asked casually.

Andie stopped chewing, then swallowed and looked up at him. "I . . . uh . . . might have. Why?"

"There's a set of prints out in the dirt. Want to come take a look?"

Andie sighed, feigning exasperation. "Manny, I'm in the yard all the time."

"Okay. But do you mind if I take a look in your closet?"

"What on earth for? Oh . . . wait a minute. You're going to check the bottoms of my shoes, aren't you?"

Manny shrugged. "It's what I do best."

Don't act like you're hiding something, she cautioned herself. "Go ahead," she said, studying the contents of her cereal bowl.

After a few moments, he returned to the kitchen. "Mind if I take these outside?" He held up an old pair of her sneakers.

Andie waved him toward the door.

While he was gone, she poured out the rest of her cereal, no longer hungry. *One call from him, and Dad will do something crazy.*

Manny came back in through the front door. "You know that door was unlocked?"

"Yes, Manny. I walked out to get the paper this morning."

"Always lock it when you come in, okay? I'll sleep better at night." He returned the shoes to Andie's closet and rechecked the

windows on his way back to the kitchen. "You might be right,"
Manny reported. "Those shoes could have made the prints. It's
hard to tell since they're not real fresh. But the length's about
right." He cocked an eyebrow at her. "You've got some long feet,
girl." Ignoring Andie's glare, he kept going. "You haven't heard
anything outside the windows, have you?"

Andie honestly told him she hadn't. The man in the mask
had appeared as silently as he had disappeared. Every night after
that, she'd listened for his return but had heard nothing.

"Okay, I'm out of here. You got classes tomorrow?"

"This afternoon," she replied.

"Not according to the schedule," he countered.

"Manny, I changed my Tuesday–Thursday class schedule,
bought a different brand of toothpaste, and cut my hair. Sorry I
forgot to file a report with your office." She regretted her rude-
ness. "I'm sorry, Manny. I know it's your job. I'll give you my
new schedule."

As she wrote, Manny paced in front of her. "It's not the job
thing, Andie. You're Tony Ryborg's daughter, and if the whole law
enforcement community knew you were in Miami, you'd have
guys with guns and badges hovering around you day and night."

Andie frowned at him.

"Besides, you're like one of my kids," he said as he turned to
leave. "Sassy and in need of a good whipping." He winked again
and left through the front door, stopping on the other side to lock
it with his own key.

The silence in the wake of his leaving made Andie suddenly
ache with loneliness.

⤳

The afternoon shower arrived as it always did during South
Florida summers—on time and over quickly. It struck as Andie
parked outside Dade Community College. She reached for the yellow umbrella she kept in the back seat. Not finding it, she pulled
on a long painting smock she'd left in the car and dashed through
the downpour.

It was the first week of fall semester, and the halls were filled with students waiting for the rain to subside.

If she took time to dry off with paper towels in the bathroom, she'd be late for class. So she walked into Studio C, dripping and apologizing to a few students already setting up their easels and paint boxes. A young man named Travis brought Andie a hand towel he kept in his backpack.

"Here ya go. You can mop up with this." He grinned shyly at Andie, then left her to her task.

She patted her face dry, careful not to smear what little makeup she wore. Then she ran the towel through her hair, curly like her mom's, coal dark like her dad's.

Next, she peeled away the wet smock, thankful the sleeveless blouse and cotton capri pants beneath were fairly dry.

As she removed her soaked sandals, she glanced up to see Travis watching her. She felt the color rise to her face and neck and regretted this little scene she'd created in front of him. She smiled nervously. "Thank you, Travis. I'll wash this and return it to you."

"Anytime, Miss Ryborg," he said, still watching her.

The class was now full. It was the second time it had met, and Andie was pleased to see most everyone had returned. Her landscape-painting class had filled quickly the last two semesters. She'd been fortunate to land a spot on the faculty so soon after arriving in Miami. She attributed that to the master of fine arts degree she'd earned at FSU and the recommendations from its faculty. And she couldn't disregard the hearty thumbs-up Randall Ivy had given her—before she "lost her seeing," that is.

In her third semester at the community college, very few knew who she was, whose daughter she was. She worked hard to keep a low profile. Randall Ivy had scolded her for refusing to attend an open house at his gallery. "It would help sell your paintings," he'd insisted.

"My paintings speak for themselves," she'd argued. "My standing beside them makes no difference."

Ivy's response had been, "That's where you're wrong, my dear. You underestimate the marketing power of a beautiful woman."

Andie taped a large poster of a Grecian temple ruin on the studio wall and turned to face her class. "What do you see?" she asked them.

"Big cracked stones and weeds," said a girl in tight jeans and a Grateful Dead T-shirt. Several others laughed.

"I see form and texture and light," said a boy whose blue eyes sparkled above a bushy beard.

"Isn't that the set for an Elton John concert?" someone else offered.

Andie rolled her eyes and grinned. "Anyone else?" she asked.

"I see man's futile attempt to pacify the gods." The voice came timidly from the back of the room. All heads turned. Andie moved closer to see an elderly woman she hadn't noticed before. The woman stood near the door, clutching a small purse and nothing else.

"I'm sorry, ma'am," Andie said. "I didn't see you come in." She stared at the tall, striking woman whose pure white hair was caught up in a bright blue clasp. Over long black pants, she wore a flowing tunic splashed with different colors. "Did you just enroll in this class?" Seeing no art supplies, Andie wasn't sure the woman had the right room.

"Yes. This morning."

"And your name?"

"Thea Long."

"Well, Ms. Long. We're happy to have you. You're here for the landscape course, right?" Andie hoped her questions didn't embarrass the woman.

"I'm here to learn the things you know," the woman told her.

What an odd way to put it, Andie thought.

"Well, I hope you enjoy our class. Uh, you'll need some supplies."

"Oh, yes. Perhaps you can tell me what to bring next time?"

"I'll be happy to." Andie returned to the front of the class and continued the study. Thea Long took a seat and listened quietly, her eyes never leaving Andie's face.

Because hers was the last class of the day for some students, Andie often lingered with those who wanted to keep working on their paintings. By the time she left the building, it was dark. She used to welcome Miami's warm, velvety nights, the ones that swirled with heady vapors. They had been interludes for resting and conjuring new images to splash upon her canvases. But now, the dark did cruel things behind its mask. She could succumb to them or dismiss them. This night, she willed them gone. Defiantly, Andie pulled back the top on the Mustang, exposing herself to the night. *I will not be afraid.*

The bay air caressed her as she entered the Grove, and she refused to think of anything but the coming autumn's promise of cooler days and a fresh start at a new painting. She had allowed fear of what or who lurked near her to displace her art. Finally, she had faced the truth of what Randall Ivy had told her. It hurt to admit it, but he'd been right. She *had* lost her seeing. Her paintings *had* become clichés. But now, she thought only of renewal. *Things are going to change. I will regain control of my life.*

As she turned onto her street, she was thinking about Thea Long. *Why had she come to an art class with no supplies?*

When she turned into her driveway, her headlights picked up something yellow leaning against the door to the screened porch. She backed into the street again and trained the high beams directly on the door. It was her umbrella, the one she'd reached for but hadn't found earlier. She was sure she'd used it the day before and left it in the car. Why was it now on the front steps? Her mind raced with possibilities. Had it fallen from the car into the yard and a neighbor left it on the porch for her? But she had no neighbors who would offer such a gesture. There were few houses on her street, and everyone kept to themselves. Had Manny placed it there? But he had a key to her house. He would have left it inside or at least on the porch.

She kept staring at the umbrella, unwilling to approach it but knowing she must. Wishing she'd turned on the outside lights before leaving the house, she set the parking brake on the Mustang, still partially in the street with its lights full on the porch. Her hand flew to the glove compartment where she kept Mace and a flashlight. She grabbed both and got out of the car. She listened for a moment, then, glancing quickly about her, walked slowly toward the house.

Climbing the steps toward the door, she didn't notice anything unusual about the umbrella, which was closed and upside down. When she picked it up, though, it fell open. Cradled inside was a small, framed photograph of her father, the one she always kept on her nightstand.

In an instant, she knew. Knew that inside her house this moment was a message waiting for her. *Please, God, make the messenger be gone.*

With what felt like ice water flooding her veins, she opened the screen door and entered the porch. She stopped to listen but heard nothing inside the house. She moved toward the front door, which she was certain she'd locked before leaving for class. When she reached for the knob, she saw the door wasn't even closed. It was happening again.

Numbly, no more feeling left inside her, she swung the door open wide, stepped inside her house, and almost robotically turned on the lights. Every painting had been removed from the walls and stacked on the living-room floor. The furniture had been overturned.

She nodded slowly to herself, conceding that her tormentor would not be letting her go. With no thought of the gun in her bedroom, she moved slowly toward the kitchen, as one in a nightmare who must run but can't. The contents of cabinets were strewn over the floor, and water ran in the sink.

In the guest bedroom, all her linens had been dumped onto a bed, and lamps lay on their sides. But when she entered her bedroom, the nightmare paralysis disappeared. At the sight of a "Tony Ryborg for Governor" campaign poster streaked with red paint and nailed to the wall above her bed, Andie screamed and ran from the house.

As the Mustang lunged to life and sped down the street, a figure moved in the woods behind the house.

CHAPTER 7

THE MUSTANG SHOT DOWN the winding lanes of the Grove. Andie drove in a blind panic, eyes darting to and from the rearview mirror. No one there, yet. Over the scream of the engine, she cried, "God, go with me!"

She raced from the Grove, heading west for the busier U.S. 1. *Easier to lose them in traffic*, she reasoned. After a few miles of weaving lane to lane, watching for the same pattern in rearview headlights, Andie finally slowed and pulled into a crowded gas station. She parked to one side and watched. No movement in her direction. It was time to put the top up on the Mustang and roll up the windows. Time to hide. Andie looked in the rearview mirror, but this time at herself. The eyes wild, the mouth drawn and hard. She almost laughed. *And this is me in control of my life.*

She looked around the gas station and saw a father pumping gas into the family van, a mother waiting with young children inside. Andie couldn't stop her tears, hot mournful tears for the mother she'd lost, for the desperation of this terrifying night. And nowhere to go.

I can't go back there. She picked up her cell phone. *One call to Dad, and it would be over. He'd gather me home and protect me.* She looked back at the family in the van. *But who would protect them? For my sake, Dad would give up the battle, end his campaign, his job, and we both would fail them.*

Just then, the phone in her hand announced an incoming text message. It was Manny checking in. She stared at the phone. *I need you, Manny. But telling you is the same as telling Dad.* She leaned back and imagined something even more troubling: her dad bent over a second grave on the hilltop. *That would destroy him.*

Andie rolled down the window on the old car and inhaled. A salty whiff seemed to revive her. Salt healed, didn't it? She breathed in more, and her pulse slowed, her mind cleared. Something almost palpable stirred in the air about her, soothed her. "Lord," she whispered. "is it you?" She rolled up the window again as if to prevent his escape. "I want to believe you're here. Mom said you would never leave us, but you left her dead in an airport, all alone." Fresh tears brimmed in her eyes. "Why did you do that? I don't understand you." She watched the van pull away, its taillights growing dim. "Now, where do I go?"

Just then, the cell phone rang. Manny again, and no text message. Andie quickly blew her nose before answering. "I'm sorry, Manny."

"Do I need to send a platoon to find you?" he asked irritably. "You know the drill. If you don't text back within ten minutes—make that two!—I'm sending up a chopper."

"I'm sorry, Manny. I just got caught up in, uh, other things."

"You got a cold?"

"Uh, yeah, I think I do."

"Is that all? You need anything?"

I wouldn't mind seeing your big clumsy self right now, Andie wanted to say. "Just a good night's sleep," she answered instead. *But where?* she wondered.

"I think I'll make rounds at your place tonight."

No! You can't go there! Andie quickly composed herself. "Manny, everything's fine. I'll see you in a couple of days, okay?"

"Righto. But you work on your answer-Manny skills, you hear?" The conversation was over.

Andie started the car, not knowing where she was going. Maybe a hotel out of town. After that, she'd find a hiding place, then convince her dad she was safe. She had no idea how to pull that off.

Some things at the house she'd risk returning for—her mother's chimes, photographs, her paintings, some clothes—but not tonight. She'd also gather her art supplies from her studio at the college. *The college*. Andie recalled a couple of bunks in a remote teacher's lounge in the art department. She'd heard that some students had slept there during all-nighters to finish their studio projects.

Though the thought of sleeping alone in an empty school was just a little less frightening than returning to her violated house, Andie hurried to get there before the doors were locked for the night. Her mind fogged over with the uncertainties of the coming day. If she fled, how far? Who would teach her classes? How long would the money she'd saved sustain her? And how would she explain a sudden departure to her dad?

In the parking lot, Andie noticed a few people leaving the library. One of them caught her eye. It was Thea Long. *She's still here?* As Andie drove beneath an overhead light, Thea seemed to recognize her and waved. Andie returned a quick wave and kept going, focused only on her mission. *No time to socialize.* But when she noticed Thea seemed to be waving her back, Andie stopped. *I don't have time for this.* But there the old woman stood. Groaning to herself, Andie turned the car around and pulled up next to Thea and rolled the window down. *A few quick words, and I'm gone,* she promised herself.

"Thea, you're here awfully late," Andie offered.

"I'm glad I was. I got to see you again." The smile spread quickly, and even in the haze of artificial light, the woman's handsome features stood out to Andie.

"Were you taking a night class?" she asked.

"No, just studying in the library, dear. But why are you here at this hour, Andie? Is everything all right?"

Why did she ask me that? Andie scrambled for an answer, but none came. She couldn't even speak. The lump that rose in her throat wouldn't let her. Andie turned away from the woman and fought for control.

"Andie, would you like to join me for a cup of hot tea?"

Andie looked back at the woman as if she'd just spoken in a foreign language. "What?" she asked weakly.

"I'd like to help with whatever has distressed you," Thea said. "Will you let me?"

Andie stared hard at this woman she'd just met, a stranger offering help in this treacherous hour. *How could that be?* Still,

Andie mustered strength enough to repel the offer. "You're very kind but I have to go before . . . I mean . . . you can't begin to understand what—"

Something in Thea's eyes stopped Andie. The old woman reached inside the car and gently touched Andie's shoulder. "You're trembling, and I don't know why. But I can take you where it's safe. And we'll figure out what to do."

Safe? Andie looked incredulously at the woman. *Why did she use that word? What if I was upset because I'd just lost my cat or argued with a friend? Why* safe? Andie repeated the word silently to herself. *Is there even such a place?* She thought of the lonely bunk in the deserted school, then searched the face of Thea Long. The confident set of the chin, the eyes that saw things they couldn't possibly see. *How could she know what's happening to me? She's just a kind, maybe lonely old woman who needs to be useful to someone.*

"Thank you for your offer, Thea, but I can't—"

"Is someone following you?" Thea asked directly.

"Wh . . . why would you ask me that?" Andie's polite demeanor was unraveling.

Thea removed her hand from Andie's shoulder. "I've known all kinds of fear, Andie. I know its signals and the way it changes a person. You aren't the young woman from class this afternoon. Something has frightened you."

Andie's mouth fell slightly open, but Thea kept going. "You're leery of me. You think I might be a little daft. But I think you need a safe harbor, and I have quite a nice one. I'd like to take you there." She didn't wait for Andie to object again. "We should leave here quickly, I think. My car is that blue Volkswagen. Will you follow me?"

An almost imperceptible nod of Andie's head was all it took. With surprising speed, Thea dashed to her car, and in seconds, it was moving. Before Andie could process what had just happened, she fell in behind the VW. For the second time that night, she had no idea where she was going.

Back on U.S. 1, Andie followed Thea north, still watching for any persistent headlights behind her. After a couple of miles, the little blue car turned east and wound through neighborhoods bisected by long, palm-studded canals, the homes growing more sumptuous nearer the shore. When it seemed they would surely drive straight into Biscayne Bay, Thea Long signaled a sharp right turn at the edge of a marsh. She followed an open road bordered by frangipani and ficus trees, their long limbs casting shadows over the moonlit road.

After a short distance, she signaled a left turn and slowed almost to a stop before a high, coquina-rock wall running parallel to the road. Andie watched as a black, wrought-iron gate opened slowly and the blue car entered a dark, curving lane. Hesitantly, Andie followed, suddenly anxious about her surroundings. *I have no idea who this woman is, and I'm following her into . . . what is this place?*

Overhanging trees made a tunnel of the driveway, but every few yards, a low Malibu light kept the cars on track. Soon, they drove onto a vast expanse of lawn that ran straight to the sea. Here, the moonlight danced over the water and skipped across sprawling gardens, sprinkling just enough light for Andie to follow where Thea led: to a stately, plantation-style home flanked by white columns, each one underlit as if it were a historic obelisk.

Thea stopped in front of the home and got out, motioning Andie to join her. Though its front porch was lighted, the interior of the home was dark except for a lamp Andie saw in the front hall. It cast a fractured amber glow through the prisms of cut-glass windows on each side of the door.

Who is this woman who speaks so humbly and lives like a queen?

At Andie's obvious surprise, Thea laughed softly. "It's not my house, dear. It belongs to my former employer. I was his family's housekeeper for nearly forty years. Make that head housekeeper. There was a whole staff of servants to the Blaker family."

"But you still live here?"

"Not in this house. The Blakers' son, Thad, and his wife own it now, though they're only here a few times a year. They live in Italy." Thea turned and motioned. "I live there."

The estate stretched over a point in the bay, the land curving into the currents on three sides. On the north side, the water pooled into a cove. It was there that Thea pointed. Andie saw a tall, narrow structure bathed in the artificial glow of a spotlight.

"Follow me," Thea said.

Back in their cars, the two women turned off the main drive to the house and followed a sandy lane to the cove. Andie pulled up next to Thea on a parking pad of crushed shells, tires crunching a loud notice of their arrival—to no one, Andie hoped. She got out of her car and stood before what she guessed was a boathouse. It was built of pale, almost shimmering stone that plunged three stories to the water. A blue-tiled roof rose to a steep gable. Walking to the edge of the bank, Andie looked down at the base of the house and saw a wide, overhead door closed tightly at the waterline.

"When I retired, Thad gave me this old boathouse," Thea said from behind her. "Since he didn't plan on living in the family home full-time anymore, he didn't need this. He'd rarely used it since his parents died, anyway. He didn't care for boats the way they did and sold all of them but the old racer. It's still locked up below."

Andie looked back at the door to the boat shed. "Do you know how to drive the boat?"

"Oh my, yes. I had an uncle who ran a shrimp boat out of the Keys. As a teenager, I used to co-skipper that old clunker during summers. My uncle taught me navigation rules, how to read charts and plot a course, even engine maintenance. Years later, I hauled the Blaker children all over this bay in one boat or another."

What an unusual woman, Andie thought. But then, so little of her own life had been usual. And now, it was even preposterous.

Andie listened to the rhythmic lapping of the tide against the shore. In the broad reach of the spotlight, she scanned the far end of the cove, seeing nothing but the dark outline of the mangrove. Thea's earlier words returned to her. *A safe harbor.* She looked back at Thea. "This is an amazing place."

Thea nodded. "You need something to eat, I think. And some sleep. Let's go inside, and I'll get your room ready."

My room? I was just her art teacher for a couple of hours, and she's giving me a room in her home? Why?

Thea led the way up uneven stone steps to a bright red door set deep in the wall. She threw two deadbolt locks before opening the door. When she turned on the lights, Andie took a few steps inside and stopped, her mouth falling open. The room was full of stunning art. Vivid colors sprang from paintings on the walls. Sculptures of animals and trees, lots of trees, framed the space. Spread over a terra-cotta tile floor was a brightly colored rug loomed in an American Indian pattern. A collection of crude pottery was displayed inside a soaring pine hutch made from what looked like hand-planed wood and dowels.

"Thea, is there any end to the surprises you have for me this night?"

The old woman chuckled. "Feel free to look around. I'll just take care of a few things in my bedroom." She waved a hand toward a room off the living room. "Then I'll get the loft ready for you." She looked hesitantly at Andie. It seemed she wanted to say something, then changed her mind and left the room.

Andie moved closer to the paintings. Most of them were of children at play. They were all original, the brush work free and loose. And they were all by an artist named Joch, just one name written lightly at the bottom of each work. A name unfamiliar to Andie.

While Thea readied the upstairs room, Andie headed toward the kitchen where she'd noticed some whimsical face pottery. She passed near Thea's bedroom and stopped to glance inside. An old blue and white quilt covered the bed, and the walls were clad in an old-fashioned blue and white toile paper. Andie was about to move on to the kitchen when something caught her eye. One of the walls in the bedroom was blank, unlike the rest of the house, except for two picture hooks a couple of feet apart. The wallpaper had faded around whatever had hung there. Hung there until recently, Andie suspected. Perhaps in the last few minutes.

CHAPTER 8

❦

"DID YOU GET THE CAR?" Leo Francini asked.

Evan nodded. "It was just where you said it'd be."

Leo ran a wary eye up and down Evan's lanky frame, then locked on the handsome young face. *Something about this kid I just don't like. He's soft. Scared of something.* Leo glanced into the void about them. In this dark hour on the ocean, he noted that nothing stirred. Nothing but the nervous eyes of Evan Markham.

"Have a beer," Leo urged. "You look tense. What's the matter?"

Waving away the offered can, Evan responded, "Nothing. Not a thing. I think I've pushed her to the edge. You should have seen how she tore out of there last night."

The two men sat alone on the back deck of the fishing boat. The crew was below, engaged in a raucous card game and yelling playful obscenities at each other.

Leo rubbed his bony face and fastened his eyes on Evan. "I'm counting on this to work. You understand?"

"Yes, sir." Evan fidgeted with the keys to *Misfit*, which at that moment was tied up alongside the fishing vessel Leo used to slip into American waters. He could sail from his hideout in the Bahamas and return the same night. He'd never been stopped, never searched by authorities of any kind.

"Let the big man tremble for what I can do to his child." Leo fairly exalted in his confidence. "Let her run to him in terror, then watch him fall to his knees and plead for my mercy." In the filmy wash of the anchor lights, Leo saw something flicker across the younger man's face, something that suddenly loosed the strong jaw line and Leo knew. *I've sent a boy to do the devil's work.*

Even so, Leo was too proud to acknowledge weakness in his newest recruit. He resolved to train him harder. "We will demonstrate that we can reach her any time we choose, Evan, no matter how hidden she thinks she is."

Leo leaned forward in his chair, watching Evan still nervously working the keys in his hands, the steady jangle of them persisting in its warning to Leo. "But one thing concerns me."

The keys suddenly fell silent.

Leo noted the quick shift of Evan's jaw. "I see no letup in his campaign. After all the harassing and threats, she should have carried our message to him by now. You see, the beauty of this little plan of mine is that not only do I boot Ryborg off his train to the governor's mansion, but I'm banking he'll hang it all up and flee with his little girl and a horde of security."

"What about all the times you've threatened him before?" Evan asked, squaring his body toward Leo.

"You doubt me?" Leo shot back.

"I just wonder why you think Ryborg would bend to you now when he never has before." Evan seemed intent on holding his ground.

That pleased Leo. *Maybe I'm wrong about him.* "I see hope in you, Evan. You ask questions, and you learn. You'll never rise in my organization unless you do. So I welcome even your doubts."

"I'll learn," Evan said dryly.

Leo clapped his hands loudly and threw back his head, gazing at the few stars shining that night. "You just might do that, but—"

Just then a man jumped from inside the boat's cabin, a gun in his hand. "You okay, boss?" he hollered.

Evan jumped at the sudden intrusion. He seemed about to leap from his chair when Leo reached to restrain him. Leo clamped a hand over Evan's forearm, noting the strength of the muscle that bulged beneath. It amused Leo to see the boy react so physically.

"Yes, Miguel. Go back inside."

As the man returned to the cabin, Leo nodded in his direction, then looked at Evan, who had settled back in his chair. "That's what you want, Evan—people around you who can get the job done. Know what I mean?" He looked hard into Evan's eyes, meeting no resistance, no backing away from the thinly veiled taunt. After a moment, Leo added, "But we're going to work well together, you and I. This is the future for you. And now, I'll answer your question." He popped open a cold beer from the cooler by his chair.

"Tony Ryborg isn't the man he used to be. His wife's death snuffed out a lot of his fire. Then his daughter up and leaves him to be some reclusive artist in the Grove. He's been damaged."

"So why is he running for governor, and why is he such a threat to you in that office?"

"More fine questions from my new field agent." Leo took a long draw from the can. "Ryborg's running because others are pushing him to. They still think he's the man to end our business with the good citizens of Florida. Ever since he was Dade County sheriff, he's been on our tails, driving hard and cracking his whip at us. The threat in him being governor is this: on his worst day, Tony Ryborg can rip us into more shreds than anyone else. I tried to stop him cold before, and it backfired."

"The assassination attempt?"

Evan seemed more relaxed now, eager to learn. "That stirred up every cop in the state. They went nuts trying to shut us down. I lost some of my best men. We all did."

"We?"

"The other cartels. None of our guys could sneeze without being locked up. We had to disappear and wait out the storm." Leo stood up and walked to the rail of the boat. "No, it's best we get at him through the girl," he said staring into the water. Then he cut his eyes toward Evan.

"But that's not advancing as quickly as I'd like. There are a few others I could send to help you. A woman I've done business with before. She's fearless, if a little unorthodox. And then there's Ray."

Evan stood quickly and joined Leo at the rail. "What do you mean?"

Leo noted the hard edge on the question. "A guy named Ray Dingo could lend you a hand."

"I don't need any help!" Evan snapped.

Leo glared at him, then relaxed. *Well, well. Temper. I like that.* "Ray's a little too ruthless sometimes, but he always gets the job done. I'm not sure your tactics are getting through to Miss Ryborg. It might be time for something a little more persuasive."

"Like what?" Evan took a step closer to Leo, who just shrugged.

"Oh, we could leave that to Ray."

Evan rounded boldly on Leo. "I said I could do the job, and I'll handle it, Leo. Alone. You keep this Dingo guy away from me."

Leo smirked. "You mean, away from her?"

"I mean—"

"I know what you mean." Leo cocked his head to one side and smiled. "She's a looker, isn't she?"

"What?"

"Maybe you don't want to see her get hurt, is that it?"

Evan lunged at the challenge. "You're dead wrong!"

Leo lost the smirk. "You'd better watch yourself, boy."

Evan seemed to stumble over his thoughts. "I . . . I just like to work alone. That's all." Gripping the rail with both hands, he looked toward his boat. "Just let me do my job."

Leo restrained his anger, choosing another tactic to deal with the kid's insolence. After a long throbbing silence, he calmly walked back to his chair and sat down. "How's your mother, Evan?" he asked with little expression.

Evan spun around and shot a forbidding look at Leo. "We don't talk about her. Part of the deal, remember?"

"Sure. Okay. I guess you don't want to talk about college either."

"That's over."

"Yeah, but you sure did want it for some reason."

"Why are you jerking me around, Leo?"

"Because I want to be sure you're with me. You see, I'm not real convinced you're here to avenge Donnie's death. You two weren't much in the way of friends. So why are you here?"

Evan hesitated for just a moment before replying, "Money, right?"

Leo laughed and got up. He walked to the rail again, his stride confident, almost a swagger. He untied one of the lines holding *Misfit* to the side of his boat and handed it to Evan. "His name's Dingo," Leo said with finality. "Watch for him."

CHAPTER 9

∽

DINGO! LEO SUSPECTS something or he wouldn't threaten me with that guy. Or maybe he's just trying to prove who's boss. He's playing a game. But so am I.

The ocean lay flat and gray as slate in this hour before dawn. *Misfit* eased its way toward the channel to the Miami River and home. *Some home,* Evan brooded. *A broken-down dock in a dead-end ditch. And that nosy old woman.*

An image of the FSU campus sprang to mind, and he knew why. That's where he'd been happiest, relatively. It was far from Tennessee and his mom's hawk-eyed family. At school, he was free of their watchful, distrustful eyes, their unfailing pity. He knew they expected little from him. That's why he'd worked at the lumber mill all those years after high school. But he showed them. The scholarship to FSU took them all by surprise. No one had known he'd applied.

But something else drew him to the university in Florida's capital. Andie Ryborg. Like him, she'd tasted the world's bile. It had spewed over her and her family, but they hadn't run from it and its horrid stench as he had. They'd wrestled with it, even wiped it out sometimes. Other times, it had infected her spirit. He knew that, just as he knew other things about her he shouldn't. He'd watched her sit alone beneath a tree on Landis Green or at the back of a coffee shop, always reading or sketching—always alone and watching who was near. He ached for what he saw in her eyes. At times, they seemed to waltz upon her canvas, then suddenly flare if someone came too close. Eyes of fear.

He watched her through the lens of guilt. For all the years he'd done nothing to halt the violence, for all the times he could have summoned the law and ended it all, he mourned. But this time, he had stopped running, cowering. He would do whatever it took to protect even one. Even one young woman who didn't know he existed.

A salty spray kicked up from the bow and flew in Evan's face. He wiped his eyes, then ran his hand through the errant clumps of damp, sandy hair. In this peaceful hour with few boats adrift, he welcomed the solitude, the brief reprieve from his dreadful mission.

Nearing the creek off the river, he slowed his engines, turned, and headed down its unruly path. Moments later, he was snugly tied up at the dock. The big wad of yellow paper taped to one of the cleats didn't surprise him at all. It had Vic's brand of communication all over it. He took it below and read it:

> Come tap on my door when you get back. Doesn't
> matter when. I've got something to show you.
> Vic

Evan sighed and looked out the window toward the old cabin. There she was in the muddled yellow of the porch light, waving to him already. *Just suck it up and go*, he told himself. *Maybe it's food.*

He'd never been inside her house, but it was exactly as he suspected—a wild, domestic concoction of incomprehensible things. Rabbit ears from a fifties television and a rusted Red Flyer wagon sat on top of a scarred bookcase, which held no books. Instead, an assortment of early model, electric, table-top fans were crammed onto all three shelves. Some, it seemed to Evan, carried their original dust.

"Impressive collection, Vic. You must be proud." Before he could stop it, a full-toothed grin spread across his face and wouldn't let go of him.

"Well, aren't you gracious as all get out." She turned to the little dog who danced at her feet. "Isn't he, Elvis? We're so glad our little home causes him such amusement." She turned back to Evan. "You might also be interested in my pre–Civil War collection of bedpans."

With that, Evan had to walk outside to compose himself. He thought maybe he should keep going, certain he was no longer welcome inside. But it had felt so good to laugh again.

"Oh, be quiet and come back here," Vic commanded from the doorway. "You're not the first one to make light of my interest in peculiar antiques." She paused. "Like myself."

Evan cleared his throat, straightened his face, and reentered the house. He chose a seat at the tiny kitchen table and crossed his long legs as if settling in for the next round, which came in an unexpected way.

"I thought you might like to see what killed my husband."

Whoa! You could get whiplash from a conversation with this lady. "Vic, uh, I don't know if I'm up for this."

But she'd already pulled the thing from a nearby cabinet and held it in front of Evan. "Pretty, isn't it?" A long, thin shard of emerald green glass lay across her two open palms. "It doesn't take a mighty thing to slice through an artery, not if it flies into you at 160 miles an hour."

Evan stared at the glass, studying the full length of it but not touching it.

"Go ahead and pick it up if you want to," Vic coaxed. "It's clean, of course. Right after I pulled it from his neck, the rain washed every trace of blood from it. It's been in that box ever since. Fact is, you're the first person I've shown it to since the coroner."

Evan was helpless to understand what she was doing. He pulled away from her and the proffered instrument of death.

"I don't mean to upset you, Evan. That first day you tied up out there, you asked me how he died. I told you I'd tell you about it sometime. I decided it was now."

"Why?" he demanded, his defenses back on full alert.

Vic returned the shard to its unceremonious cardboard box and put it back in the cabinet. "Let me make you a café Cubano. You'd like that, wouldn't you?" She didn't wait for an answer, nor did she seem ready to supply one to his question. She busied herself with a shiny, new-looking espresso machine Evan found incongruent with the rest of the dingy, outdated cabin.

"You can't live in Miami without crossing all kinds of cultural borders," she said by way of explaining the sleek machine. "A Cuban friend of mine gave this little gizmo to me last Christmas. If you haven't tried the sweet elixir of a café Cubano yet, hold on. And I hope you weren't planning on taking a nap anytime soon. This stuff will jump-start you into next Tuesday."

Evan watched in silence as she added sugar and coffee to the machine and hit a few buttons. As the apparatus whirred to life, she pulled down a couple of demitasse cups and saucers. "My friend says you have to drink Cuban coffee in these tiny little things you can't get a finger through. I don't think your body could stand a regular cup full of this brew, but I frankly don't see why you can't pour just half a cup, do you? And why are you so quiet all of a sudden?"

"You haven't answered my question."

"Oh, right. We'll get there. First, I want to know how your novel is coming."

Evan fumbled for an answer. "It's, uh, going slowly. Why?"

"Just wondered how you get much done when you're gone so much."

Evan bristled. "Research," he said. And that was all.

"Is that right? Research, huh?" Vic locked eyes with him, then looked away. Throwing up an arm and pointing out the window, she said, "By the way, that old, squat building up there where you park that little car of yours is where Roger, that's my husband, and I were supposed to ride out the hurricane. For the few of us who live in this rangy part of the river, that seemed the safest place to go. Just an old warehouse for the guy down the way who fixes boat motors. No windows, low sturdy roof, all cement block and up there on that little rise above the river. Perfect. But not for Roger."

"So what happened?" Evan asked, surprised at his own interest.

Vic looked at her lap and smoothed the faded cotton of her housedress. It was pink with little blue flowers and snaps up the front. This morning, she was barefoot.

"Hurricanes are wicked, Evan. But so are lots of things. Some things we can fix. Some things we just need to run from. But my

Roger never knew the difference. He thought he could set everything right all by himself. He ran a Dade County halfway house they hid out in some groves, away from polite society, he used to say. He'd get those folks fresh from prison or some rehab center, clean them up, get them jobs, even sent some back to school. He thought he was the only one who could fix them. And he didn't flinch when the old vices that got them into trouble to begin with surfaced again. He fought them all. There was just about no one he wouldn't go head to head with, even the suits down at city hall. And he fought them all by himself."

Evan didn't move in his chair.

"We'd lived through hurricanes before and came out okay. Roger treated them like anything else he thought he could stand up to. But when Andrew reached the coast and revved his engines up to class five, he wasn't the least bit intimidated by my scrawny little husband."

That drew an unbidden smile from Evan, but one that quickly disappeared.

"We'd tied up the boat real tight to the dock and some trees out there, lashing it down with extra lines. That boat was his passion, just behind me, you understand. It was his baby, the only one we'd ever had, and nothing was going to mess with it. We thought it was safe back in this little hurricane hole.

"So when we headed for the warehouse, Roger felt good about things. Not for long, though. The wind came screaming at us quicker and harder than we'd ever seen it. Pretty soon, we heard a tree land hard not far from us, then another one. Roger jumped up and opened the door, which nearly blew off its hinges. Everyone screamed for him to shut it. He did, after he yelled to me, 'The boat!' and ran outside."

"What did you do?" Evan asked, his voice rising slightly.

"I tried to follow him, but the folks there, a few neighbors and others I barely knew, held me back. They knew better than Roger did that just outside that door was a killer none of us had one whit of power over. And they weren't going to let it get me too."

"So . . . what happened to Roger?" Evan had fallen hopelessly into the story.

"During the eye, we ran to the dock, which, by the way, hadn't been touched, nor the boat. And we found him. We dragged him back to the warehouse just before the other wall of the eye slammed into us like it'd never left." She stopped a moment, as if to catch her breath, then kept going.

"You know, standing over Roger down on the dock, that glass sticking out of his neck and his blood drained out of him, the sky was real peaceful and blue. The giant had roared, and my little David, without a slingshot or stones, raced out alone to face the enemy. But the enemy won and went away. It came back, though. It always comes back." Her gaze fell hard on Evan. "Doesn't it?"

Evan stared back, struggling with how, or if, to answer. *What does she want from me?*

"Well, here now. Our coffee's ready." Vic got up to pour the strong-smelling brew.

"I'm sorry for your loss," Evan finally offered.

Vic set the cups down on the table and, still standing, cocked her head at him. "Do you remember what I said to you that first day we met? That I knew you were in some kind of storm and wondered if you planned on dying in it?"

Slowly pushing the coffee aside, Evan rose from the table, having no more desire to be sociable. But that didn't stop Vic.

"You see, Evan, you can't kill giants all by yourself. Roger thought he could, and all it took was a little old piece of glass from someone's shattered lantern, a random projectile hurled at magnum-force, to destroy him."

Evan squared his shoulders and held Vic's gaze. "I'm not David or anyone else you can think of. I'm just a guy needing to get away for a while and write a book." A necessary lie, he reasoned, though telling it made him queasy. Lying hadn't been a problem for him before. Why now? Maybe he was weary of doing it, of faking a new identity. Faking a life. Or maybe it was because just now, he saw an earnest caring in Vic's eyes.

He shifted his weight to the other foot and took a deep breath. "Look, Vic, I'm grateful for you letting me tie up at your dock. I've offered to pay you, and you won't let me. But that doesn't give you entrance into my head. Nothing does. So if it bothers you for me to be here, I'll move on."

Vic looked thoughtful for a moment, then suddenly changed gears. "I didn't mean to get your dander up. Well, maybe a little bit. Just trying to do what I seem to do best—meddle. I've made a pretty good living doing that."

Evan raised his eyebrows.

"But you stay on here awhile longer, if you like." Vic stooped just then to look under the kitchen table. "Elvis! Now where did that varmint get off to? Well, anyway, Elvis and I kind of like having you for a neighbor.

"You never know when we might need each other."

CHAPTER 10

WHEN ANDIE AWOKE in Thea's boathouse that first morning, she struggled to place where she was. But as quickly as the frightful night before came clawing back to consciousness, what she saw from her bed dispelled it, at least for a while.

Lace curtains fluttered at an open window filled with ocean blue. Rising on one elbow, she squinted into morning light that blew in on a wisp of the sea, its vapors filling the room, and she breathed them in. Lightheaded from a merciful sleep, she drifted to the window and looked out. Bay waters spun a web of blue-green currents. Three floors down, those same waters gently patted the stone house. The peaceful cove lay curled against the lattice of a tangled mangrove swamp so dense Andie couldn't see into it. Peaceful, yes, but she still searched its twisting limbs and the wide sweep of water, seeing no one about. *Will I ever be free?*

The spell was broken. For all its ethereal charm, this refuge wasn't far enough away to protect her and her dad. *I have to leave.*

After a quick shower, she pulled on the same wrinkled shirt and capri pants she'd worn yesterday. Thea had loaned her a nightshirt, which she now folded carefully and left on the bed. The smell of sausage and waffles grilling met her on the stairs, and she flashed back to Saturday mornings in Tallahassee when her mother had cooked extravagant breakfasts for her and her dad. Later, Andie would take a plate or two out to the *ninjas.* That's what she called the FDLE officers who often camped in an unmarked car outside the family home. The frequency of their surveillance depended on the intensity of chatter on the drug-world network, and any mention of the name Ryborg.

Shaking off the bittersweet memory, Andie greeted Thea with unmasked gratitude. "You've been incredibly kind to me, Thea, and 'thank you' just isn't enough. When I get back, I'd like to give you private art lessons. Free, of course."

Thea turned quickly from the waffle iron, alarm in her eyes. "Where are you going?" she asked abruptly.

Her reaction surprised Andie. "I can't stay here. This is your home, and I won't intrude." *Or expose you to danger.*

"But something, or someone, is troubling you, dear. And surely you can stay until we, I mean you, resolve the matter."

Andie studied the woman. Only seven in the morning, and already the soft gray hair was neatly swept up in the same enameled blue clasp. She was in pressed blue jeans and a crisp, white linen blouse. "Thea, you're a beautiful woman, do you know that?"

The compliment elicited an awkward smile from Thea and a slight flutter of her hands. "Oh, listen to you. What a sweet thing to say to one who's almost eighty. But I suspect you're deliberately changing the subject. I'm concerned about where you'll go and what you'll do if you leave here. And I don't even know what trouble will follow you."

Don't tell her.

"Thea, I'm going to Tallahassee to spend some time with my dad."

"The attorney general?"

How did she know?

Something flashed in Thea's eyes. Andie saw it before the woman could mask whatever it was. "It's not a common name, you know," Thea offered, her voice tentative. "And there are 'Ryborg for Governor' posters everywhere." She turned from Andie and busied herself with the waffles.

Andie stared at the back of the woman's head, not satisfied with that answer, an answer to an unspoken question, at that. Still, this woman who'd taken her in deserved as much information as Randall Ivy did. There was no telling how many he'd bragged to about his latest "find" being the only child of Tony Ryborg.

"Yes, he's my dad," Andie finally confided. "But the fewer people who know that, the better."

Just then, Andie glanced at a big gray jar with the laughing face of a jester emerging from one side, as if the clay had slapped him in the face and dried.

Thea turned to see Andie studying the piece and gestured toward the rest of her collection of face pottery. More jars, pitchers, and bowls, each carved with a different facial expression, were lined up along the backsplash of a kitchen counter. "Characters, aren't they?" Thea remarked. "They're sort of like family."

"Tell me about your real family," Andie encouraged, eager to shift the attention from herself and needing to know more about this woman.

Returning to the sausages, Thea spoke almost in cadence with the cooking, the turning and patting of the meat, a practiced rhythm. "Oh, there aren't many of us left now. My parents are gone. I have one brother, a niece, and a nephew who still live on the reservation."

"Reservation?" Andie couldn't hide her surprise.

Thea scooped sausage patties from the pan onto a plate and blotted the excess grease. "I'm a Miccosukee Indian," she said without looking up.

Andie's eyes grew wide.

"All my family lived on a reservation in the Everglades. I did, too, until I was seventeen."

Andie's surprise turned to delight. "Oh, I've been there! At one of those reservations when I was in high school. My mom and some of her friends took a bunch of us kids to the Keys, and we stopped on the way to visit the village. Though I think it was more like a visitor center."

A smile creased Thea's face as Andie grew more animated, as if still a child.

"It was spring, and we'd gone to watch the Green Corn Dance. What a thing to see! Such an ancient custom with all the bright costumes. The dancers. That pounding music, so hypnotic. I talked about it for weeks."

Barely pausing for breath, she continued. "I climbed inside a chickee, where one family lived. It was high off the ground so the air could ventilate from underneath and—"

"And keep the wildlife out," Thea chimed in.

"Yes! I remember the gators and snakes. But most of all there were these magnificent paintings. They almost throbbed with color and movement." All at once, Andie rushed into the living room. "The children!" she exclaimed, pointing to the paintings on the walls. "They're Miccosukee, aren't they?"

"Every one of them," Thea said, her eyes sliding from one canvas to another.

"Is the artist Miccosukee too?"

"Yes. You like the paintings?"

"They're extraordinary. The imagery is so powerful. You can almost hear their voices. Do you have children?"

It was as if a sheer veil dropped over Thea's face, screening some of its light. She looked down at the dish towel she carried and slowly wiped her hands. "I never married," she said finally. "No family of my own." A pause. "But I sure had a time chasing after the two Blaker children. They filled my days with lots of motherhood."

Andie was sorry she'd charged so clumsily into the question, sorry she hadn't noticed the absence of family photos about the small home. No mention of children or husband. But then, she'd only known this woman for less than twenty-four hours.

"Let's eat our breakfast on the terrace," Thea suggested brightly. Andie agreed eagerly.

After the breakfast dishes were cleared away, Andie returned to the terrace with the last of her coffee. She scanned the waters beyond the cove, out where the wild Atlantic calmed itself before entering the tidal sanctuary of Biscayne Bay. Boat traffic was mild that morning, not even a freighter on the horizon. She was surprised at how clearly she could see the stilt houses from this vantage point.

"Lovely, isn't it?" said Thea, rejoining her.

Andie nodded distractedly. "You know, I've never seen those odd little places up close." She pointed toward the wide-open waters of the bay, at the seven cottages raised high on cement pilings in the straights off Key Biscayne. "They're just out there in the middle of the bay as if they'd fallen from the sky."

"There used to be a whole colony of them," Thea noted. "About twenty-seven back in the sixties. The earliest ones were built in the thirties on barges; then they started drilling into the sea-grass beds for more permanent structures."

"Not so permanent, I hear."

"Right. Between fires and hurricanes—Andrew took out seven of them—that's all that's left. And there's a fight to preserve them, between private citizens who claim the houses are part of folk history versus the federal government who thinks they don't belong in Biscayne National Park."

"Who lives there?"

"No one, anymore. People used to lease them from the state before it deeded the seabed beneath them to the federal government back in the eighties. They were mostly weekend getaways. Some were the ill-repute kind with lots of drinking and gambling going on day and night. Others were family style, with children everywhere. The Blakers leased one of them for many years. I went out there quite often with them. The kids would jump right off the roof into the bay." Thea seemed moved by the memory. "It's a strange place, especially at night. Even with others in the same house, I felt like I was alone in a faraway world."

Andie grew still, her thoughts racing ahead. Far away. Only a boat can reach it. No one lives there.

Andie couldn't linger anymore, not even in this tucked-away refuge. It had occurred to her that Manny might get to her house before she could straighten the mess. If he found it the way she left it, well, she just couldn't let that happen.

An hour later, she thanked Thea for her hospitality, apologized for the hasty departure, promised to keep in touch with her, and sped away.

At the bungalow, Andie pulled up close to the back door where she could load her things from the house, but she remained in the car until she was satisfied no one was around. Even a peaceful, light-filled morning could hide an assailant.

Slowly, she unlocked the door and slipped anxiously into the kitchen, then the hallway. If more damage had been done, she couldn't tell from the looks of the mess remaining throughout the house. Quickly, she righted the overturned furniture, returned linens to their drawers and closets, and picked up the scattered contents of the kitchen. She carried the paintings she would take with her to the car and re-hung the rest. Then she headed to her bedroom. The sight of the blood-red poster nailed over the bed made her gasp as if seeing it for the first time. She quickly snatched it from the wall, wadded it, and threw it in the back of her car, from where she would toss it into the nearest Dumpster.

Later, she had finished the restoration and changed into clean clothes. She packed her mom's wind chimes, more clothes, and the gun. She was backing away from the house when a black sedan turned onto her street. *I knew it!*

"And where are you headed on this lovely, allergy-packed morning?" Manny asked from the open window of his car, blowing his nose loudly. They were stopped in the street for what Andie hoped would be a quick conversation.

"I'm going home for a few days, Manny. I want to surprise Dad, so please don't tell him."

"What about your classes?"

Andie hesitated. She'd planned to call Manny once she left Miami. "They called in a substitute."

"And you were going to let me know about this, right?"

"Right."

"And this is the kind of advance notice I get?" There was a long sigh from inside the Mustang. "Oh, go on and have a good time," Manny relented. "I'll keep an eye on the place."

Heading north on the Florida Turnpike, Andie knew she wasn't just going home for a visit. She was fleeing. Her solo life had fallen into someone else's hurtful hands. She was running home, the only safe place she knew. Or was it?

In the distance, an image rose from that point where the road narrows to infinity, where all things are possible, but only one is the way. It was the image of a lone house on stilts surrounded by open water.

CHAPTER 11

"THEY'RE NOT ANY SAFER in the schools than they are in the street," Tony was heard railing into the phone. "Predators are after them on the Internet in their own homes! The governor of this state must be our children's number-one defender out there where they live. It's not a job to be done from inside a stranglehold of legislative committees stacked one inside the other like a set of Russian dolls that don't do anything but look pretty. What's that? My opponent? He'll have to speak for himself. But when you reach him, ask him about the child pornography bill that was sent to his committee two years ago and if anyone there has the foggiest idea what happened to it."

"That's the fourth reporter to call this afternoon," said Freda Tavers, special assistant to the attorney general.

"That speech Tony gave to the Florida Chamber of Commerce this morning lit a fuse in the opponent's camp," Warren quipped. He was at his usual post near Freda's desk outside Tony's open door. "I wish you could have heard how he took down Neiman and his cronies in the senate. He challenged them to get out from behind their desks and into the streets to see what FDLE is up against." Warren nodded his head with obvious pleasure.

"Warren, you out there?" Tony called from inside his office. He had ended his phone interview with the *Orlando Sentinel* reporter and had turned from campaigning back to his real job, as he saw it. Becoming governor had never been in his plan book until others had convinced him the state needed more muscle at the top. His blend of tough cop and legal warrior was the perfect fit, his supporters had claimed. Grooming him for the campaign trail was a different challenge, though. "Sir, yes, you must give speeches and kiss babies, much like you didn't do when running for attorney general," his campaign manager had informed him. "If every cop and teacher in the state hadn't voted for you, you might not have won."

"Coming, sir." Warren hurried inside.

Moments later, the two were pouring over maps of the Bahamas. "While the FBI was running an undercover gig here near Freeport, they turned up some interesting data on a couple of missing islanders from Andros," Tony briefed. "The local police have no clues to their fate, but one of them was an American charter captain who the feds discovered had done some business with Francini."

"They still running their op down there?"

"Yeah, something unrelated to drugs, but now they're after this too. Just giving us the alert." Tony rolled up the maps. "I'm taking these over to—"

"You're not going anywhere right now." The voice came from the doorway.

Warren whirled around as Tony shot up from his chair and stared as if what had just appeared before him was an apparition.

Andie Ryborg's eyes glistened as Tony tossed his glasses across the desk and rushed toward her. "Andie!" His voice quavered, and without another word, he gathered her up in his beefy arms and hugged her hard.

"Dad, I'm so glad to see you." She was almost limp in his embrace.

Then Tony held her at arm's length and frowned. "Honey, are you all right?" He tried to imagine what had brought her home so unexpectedly.

"I'm okay, Dad. I just had some free time and thought I'd surprise you."

"Well, you sure did that." He looked at Warren, who was moving in for his turn at a greeting.

"You're just as pretty and unpredictable as ever," Warren told Andie as he squeezed her shoulders.

Tony turned to see Freda watching the reunion from the doorway. "Freda, did you know about this?"

"Maybe a minute before you did, sir. And we already had our hug." She looked at Andie and winked. "Can I get you anything?"

Andie shook her head. "Thanks, Freda. I'm fine."

Tony couldn't take his eyes off his daughter. As she chatted with Warren about his kids and Freda about her gardening, Tony was intent on Andie's face. No one knew her like he did. *She's so thin.* He listened to her talk. *And something's missing from her voice.*

Soon, Warren left, and Freda returned to her desk. Seated together on the sofa in his office, Tony and Andie talked about many things—her painting, the little house in Coconut Grove, and the weeds overtaking her mom's flower beds at the family home. The subject soon turned to the campaign.

"I've got three months to swing the undecided votes, Andie."

"Aren't you campaigning in Orlando next week?" Andie asked.

Tony nodded. "I'm even doing a Mickey thing with the ears at a tourism convention there."

"No way." Andie looked dumbstruck.

"That's what I told my campaign manager. He still believes it's going to happen, though. Me at the podium addressing two thousand hospitality managers from around the state with mouse ears to make me look like a regular guy."

"What does he consider irregular?"

"Good point. But he's trying to counter Bill Neiman's claim that I'm just a tough ex-cop with nothing on my mind but settling scores with hoodlums. That I don't know or care enough about the everyday, law-abiding citizen just trying to make ends meet."

"The voters will see through that smoke, Dad. And I'll help them. I'll go to Orlando and campaign with you. But I won't do the mouse ears."

Tony laughed and patted her hand.

"Maybe we should tell them about Claire," she added. Then hesitantly, "And about Mom."

Tony's smile suddenly disappeared. "No, Andie. We won't bring her into this."

"But they should know why chasing drugs off the street is so important to you. Mom would agree. You know she would."

Tony squeezed her hand. "She might, honey. But I won't tarnish her memory to get elected." He looked into the deep pile of the rug as if something lurked there, then turned back to her and added, "And you know I don't want you campaigning with me in Orlando or anywhere else. The less you're seen, the better. I won't expose you to my enemies any more than I already have. I couldn't bear it if they turned their wicked intents on you."

Andie grew still. "Don't worry about me, Dad. I can take care of myself." She quickly jumped up from the sofa and offered him her hand. "Come on. Let's get out of here and go eat something we shouldn't."

Tony let her pull him up, his face softening into an amused grin. "Remember how I used to show up at your dorm at night and we'd go to Jerry's Restaurant for strawberry pie?" He lifted his eyebrows a couple of times.

"Oh, yeah. I see where this is headed. Okay, but don't you think we should eat dinner first?"

"You got it," he said. They turned out the lights and closed the office door. Warren was waiting next to Freda's desk. "Andie and I are going to dinner," Tony announced. "Just the two of us." He looked pointedly at Warren. *Surely I can have dinner with my daughter without someone watching over us. Just leave us alone tonight.*

Warren nodded agreeably, but the glance he shot Tony's way signaled something different. "Enjoy your dinner, sir." His demeanor softened as he turned to Andie. "It's just like old times having you here, girl. You're sure you don't want to come home and find some nice math professor to marry and give your dad a bunch of snotty grandkids?"

"Nice try, Warren," Tony said. "Maybe we'll get her back one day."

Father and daughter left in separate cars, agreeing to meet at Jerry's. As Tony pulled from his parking space and merged with downtown, rush-hour traffic, he looked in his rearview mirror, knowing what he'd see. Warren's black sedan was only two car-lengths behind him.

On the way to the restaurant, Tony thought of the Orlando campaign speech coming up and the conversation with Andie. *No, I won't tell them about Jessica. That was our private pain and I'll not drag it into the light for all to see.* Tony stared into the old Mustang's taillights and drifted back to that last day with his wife.

It was a Monday morning at the cabin.

"Honey, your eggs are getting cold," Jessica had called. "Hurry up."

Tony had rushed into the kitchen and plopped his briefcase onto the worn oak table. He slipped his arms around his wife and squeezed. "We needed this weekend, didn't we?" he said, nuzzling her neck with kisses.

She clung to him. "We need lots of them."

He finally released her and sat down to his breakfast. "I'm sorry I've been away so much."

"Don't apologize," she said, joining him at the table. "It's your job, and when you have to go, Andie and I understand. But you're right, we needed a weekend alone."

"Did Andie take her car to school this morning? It needs a complete overhaul, you know." He gulped his breakfast. "Why won't she let me buy her a new one?"

"That old thing is an art form to her, Tony. 'Just humming with soul,' she says."

"Well its hum is off key and badly needs a tune-up."

Jessica smiled and took a last sip of coffee. She started to get up from the table, then paused and turned serious eyes toward her husband. "Tony, I . . ."

He glanced at her. "What is it, Jess?" He shoveled the last of the scrambled eggs into his mouth.

She hesitated another moment. Then as if dismissing a trivial concern, she reached for his empty plate. "Nothing. We'd better hurry. We both have many things to do today."

Later, they locked the cabin and lingered on the porch. Once more, Tony drew his wife into his arms and kissed her. "I won't be late tonight," he said, turning the collar of her coat up against the early chill. "Maybe we can take a walk after dinner."

Without waiting for a response, he grabbed luggage and loaded both cars. She had driven to the cabin ahead of him on Friday, wanting time to walk the fields and read alone beneath the live oak tree on the hill.

He followed her into Tallahassee and returned her wave as she veered off the highway toward their home in the suburbs.

He continued on to his office near the capitol, noticing the dogwoods had just begun to bloom. Then he remembered something Jessica once said: "Some say the dogwood blossom is symbolic of the Easter message—its pure white stained by the Savior's blood, its four petals depicting the cross. When I see it, though, I don't feel the sadness of death. I see the promise of life that goes on."

He'd planted a white dogwood tree for Jessica near the kitchen window, but just now couldn't recall seeing any blossoms on it.

When he turned into his reserved parking space, the sign tugged at him. Attorney General, it read. He stared at it for a moment. *Lord, you've brought me from an abandoned infant to this. Don't let me fail you.*

After a moment, he glanced at his watch and hurried from the car. He knew the morning's appointments calendar would be full. Freda Tavers, his administrative right hand and the woman he'd called "the Warden" for over twenty years, scheduled everything but bathroom breaks for him. He stopped at her desk to retrieve messages and endure another cocked-eyebrow appraisal of his tie.

"Go ahead, Freda. Say it again because I might not have understood it the first hundred times." A tight-lipped grin creased his face as the portly woman with a mischievous glint in her eye scanned his attire. Because she'd worked for him since he was sheriff, she'd earned certain rights, she'd declared.

"Okay, I will. There's a law against bad ties in this state, and as attorney general, you should be the first to uphold it. Aren't you ashamed?"

"Are you through?" he asked.

"As finished as that tie, sir."

"Fine. Then we can get on with the less important matters of the day." He winked as he walked away, headed for his cavernous, mahogany-walled office. The morning went swiftly. His docket seemed to replenish itself by the hour, filling with cases such as unsolicited mailings of prescription drugs by a major pharmaceuticals company, a dance studio scheme bilking senior citizens, Medicaid fraud, and the thing that gripped him hardest and wouldn't let go—narcotics trafficking.

Just before noon, Tony was meeting with two state legislators when Freda appeared at his office door.

"Sir, I need you to come with me, please."

"In a moment, Freda, we're about to wrap this—"

"No . . . sir," she said nervously. "You must come with me *now*. I'm sorry."

Only then did Tony hear the break in her voice. He searched the familiar face, its eyes wide and pleading, and rose quickly from his chair.

"Freda, what's the matter?" he asked as he approached her.

Without answering, she ushered him into the hall, closing the door behind them. She led him into a nearby conference room and closed the door. Warren Jacobs was waiting inside.

"What's going on?" Tony demanded of them both, a foreboding rising inside him.

"Tony," Freda said, dropping formalities, "something has happened to Jessica. I . . . I don't know how to tell you this." She looked quickly at Warren, then back at Tony's clouding face. "They think . . . she had a heart attack. She's . . ." Her words choked.

"She's gone, Tony." Warren spoke the words with merciful finality, barely containing his own emotion.

But Tony seemed not to hear him. He only stared into Warren's eyes, the flickering within them like a phantom video of Jessica waving goodbye to him from her car just hours ago. The image ended suddenly as Warren took Tony's arm and tried to pull him into a chair.

Tony jerked away. "What do you mean she's gone? What does that mean, Warren?" he demanded, his voice shrill. "To a hospital? Is that where she's gone?" Tony turned toward the door. "I have to go."

Before Warren could reach him, though, Tony stopped and looked back at Freda. For a torturous moment, he studied the drawn, ashen face of his trusted aide, then asked, "Is Jess dead?"

The nod of her head was slight, but her words were finally clear. "They said it was quick. I'm so sorry."

"Who is 'they'?" he demanded.

"The paramedics," she answered, not taking her eyes from him.

"Paramedics where? Where did this happen?"

"At the airport," Warren reported.

"The what?" Tony was suddenly filled with hope. "Jess wasn't at the airport today. It's not her! It's a mistake!"

He rushed to his desk, grabbed the phone and dialed his home number, certain his wife would answer. But it was her taped voice, cheerfully welcoming the call and inviting Tony to leave a message. "Jess, honey, call me immediately. There's been a terrible mistake, and I need to know you're—"

Freda laid a gentle but firm hand over his and took the receiver from him. Few people would have been allowed to do that. "Tony, her identification was on her. And a close neighbor of yours was at the airport. He said it was Jessica."

"They found a ticket to Asheville, North Carolina, in her purse," Warren said.

Tony lowered himself slowly to his chair, struggling to make sense of it. "I told her I'd be home for dinner and that we'd walk," he recalled numbly. "We said goodbye, and that was all."

As Freda and Warren hovered nearby, Tony leaned over, rested his head in his hands, and wept. In his tortured mind, he returned to the world he'd just left that morning, at the cabin where they'd eaten breakfast together and talked about oil changes. Just hours ago, he'd held her. Suddenly, he lifted the lapel of his coat and buried his face in it. She was there. The scent of her lingered where she'd embraced him. Where she'd pressed against him to kiss him goodbye. How could he have known?

Finally, Tony stood and wiped his face, now drained of color. "Freda, get Andie out of school as quickly as you can and bring her to the house. Tell her nothing about this. I'll be waiting for her."

He turned to Warren. "Follow me home. Then you can take us to . . . to Jess."

Tony entered his house as if treading on hallowed ground. Would Jessica appear to him there? Would he hear her voice? He thought of the answering machine and headed for the kitchen.

He saw the note propped on the counter as soon as he entered the room and rushed to it.

Tony and Andie,

Welcome home, my loves. Please don't be angry
with me, but I had to leave for a couple of days. It's
a secret mission. A surprise for you, Tony. I nearly
gave in and squealed it to you this morning, but I
was afraid you'd think me foolish and convince me
not to go. So I just sneaked away. Something we'd
punish you for, Andie.

When I return, you won't believe what I have to tell
you. Maybe then you won't be upset with me. I love
you both dearly, and always will.

See you tomorrow night,
Jess

Having completed a quick inspection of the house, Warren joined
Tony in the kitchen. "What's that?" he asked, pointing to the note.
     Tony handed it to him and walked to the window. The dog-
wood was in full bloom.

જ

His head throbbing, Tony slowly surfaced from the grueling
memory. Drawing in a ragged breath, he refocused on the road
ahead. He couldn't recall anything about the last few miles he'd
driven and was grateful to see Andie still ahead.
     Lord, is she safe?
     Stopping behind her at the next light, he saw her staring at
him in her rearview mirror.

CHAPTER 12

ॐ

A BANYAN AND PALMETTO thicket on a moonless night is the blackest veil. Behind its enfolding dark, Evan crouched just yards from Andie's back door. In this hour before midnight, she would return, if she was going to. She always did after class and a few private hours in her studio at the college. But there had been no sign of her in five days. Even that big cop had stepped down his patrol of her house. A call to the college and Evan had discovered a substitute was teaching her class. For how long? he'd asked the woman in administration, but she wasn't sure.

Through the windows of Andie's house, Evan had noticed paintings missing from the walls. An open door revealed a near-empty closet. And the chimes were gone. *It worked! And now this lunacy can end.*

Evan would confirm to Leo that Andie Ryborg had fled back to her father's protection. Surely one of Leo's men—they were everywhere—would confirm her return to Tallahassee. Surely the dominoes would then fall as planned. A terrified daughter threatened by unseen assailants would force Ryborg to comply with their demands. He'd leave the race, maybe even retire. Maybe he and Andie could move to the mountains and live in the peace they deserved.

Evan should have been glad. He could end his charade as a common hoodlum and leave Leo's world for good. But alone in the dark of this forsaken wood, this sad hiding place, he felt little relief, only remorse for what he had done, for the emotional wounds he'd inflicted on an innocent young woman. Now she was gone, and the loneliness he'd endured for so long was suddenly unbearable. *But she's safe now. I've managed to snatch one victim away from Leo.*

As Evan stood to leave, a beam of light swept over the back yard and into the trees near him. Evan flung himself to the ground. The light sliced like a blade over his head, then cut toward the house. He raised his head enough to see a man with a flashlight approach Andie's back door, which Evan knew was locked. The man then went to each window and flashed a quick beam inside the rooms. When he passed beneath the corner spotlight, Evan could see that it wasn't the cop. He was pretty sure he knew who it was.

Dingo. Well, you can just crawl back into that snake pit you came from because she's not here. The job's over.

⌁

As he pulled away from Andie's house, Dingo reached for the vibrating cell phone beside him, noting the caller. "Guess the kid was right, Leo," he announced. "Looks like she's gone. And know what?"

"What's that?"

"I'm real disappointed. I had plans for the luscious Miss Ryborg."

Leo didn't respond immediately. "You enjoy your job too much, Ray."

Laughter gurgled in Dingo's throat as he flipped the phone shut and tossed it on the seat. Reaching into the duffle bag on the floor, he fingered the sheathed stiletto blade and smiled to himself.

CHAPTER 13

ॐ

KNEELING IN THE DIRT, Andie pulled weeds from her mother's caladium beds, regretting that her own probably sweltered in the oppressive heat of a Miami August. *But they'll survive longer than I would in that house.*

Alone in the garden of this home where she'd grown up, where the dogwood tree still bloomed its radiance each spring, it should have been easy for Andie to believe that nothing could harm her. Easy to remain here with her dad. She could teach at the university and paint in the studio her parents had outfitted for her over the garage. She could take care of her dad and keep the weeds out of her mother's garden.

But they always came back. No matter how lovely the garden, the weeds still attacked. *An assassin could still ambush your father in the front yard of his home.*

Andie sat back on her heels, and tears, too long behind the barricade, gushed down her cheeks. She let them flow like a spring over parched ground. *God, why do you let these things happen to us?*

She removed her gloves, wiped away the last of her tears, and went inside. She'd been home a week, and until that moment had rested in the false security of mere distance from her tormentors. Though she didn't know how far away was far enough.

Resisting the urge to visit a few of her professors at the university, she stayed close to home. She cleaned, gardened, cooked, and mostly stayed out of sight. She'd ventured out only once to the grocery store, an uneventful yet pleasant trip that lifted her spirits—until the next day when she went to the mailbox by the street. As she reached inside the box, a car slowly passed in front of her, its two male occupants staring at her. She glared at them, and they sped away.

Though she did nothing to encourage it, men often let their gaze linger on Andie. That day, after rushing inside the house and locking the door behind her, she told herself that what had just happened was more of the same. Still, she remained indoors the rest of that day and was relieved to see her dad's headlights in the driveway that evening.

Andie dropped her garden gloves in the laundry room and went to clean tear-streaked dirt from her face. But as she passed the open door to her dad's bedroom, she glanced at the old keepsake box he kept on the dresser. It had been many years since she'd explored its contents. Isabel Ryborg had made it for her son. The flat wooden box was covered in news clippings of Tony Ryborg's exploits on the playing fields of his youth. His mother had laminated the box to protect the newsprint heralding her son's many honors. She'd died just two months before Jessica Ryborg did.

Andie went to the box and lifted its lid. She pulled out a small album of photos taken on her parents' honeymoon. Her mom looked so frail, and Andie knew why. Her parents had married just a year after they'd met. It wasn't until Andie was in high school that her mom told her about that first night in the rehab center. And for that, Andie loved her even more.

In a pile of certificates and framed awards, Andie saw the pale blue envelope. Her throat grew tight. It was the note her mother had left them that last day. Though Andie could recite its words by heart, she pulled it out and read again: ". . . When I return, you won't believe what I have to tell you."

Tell us what, Mom? What was in Asheville?

Fresh tears stung, but Andie would have no more of them. She quickly replaced the note in its envelope and returned it to the box. Then she spotted something else, something she had played with as a child, and she welcomed the sight of it. She picked up the small, brightly painted gourd and rattled the dried seed pods inside. Someone had made the toy for her father when he was a baby.

Andie imagined her dad sitting alone on his bed, pulling items from the box and slowly examining each one, reliving parts of his life. He'd often spoken of his childhood with two doting parents. A child's Bible inside the box had been their gift to him when he was baptized. She'd seen him read it often throughout his life. Andie opened it and read: *To our son, Tony, God's gift, brought to us in such a special way.*

She remembered the night her dad explained that "special way" to her. She had come home from school and told her parents how sorry she was for one of her sixth-grade classmates who had been adopted. After dinner, her dad told her why she shouldn't feel sorry for the child—that he, too, had been adopted, and had been loved as much as any child could be.

He explained that just hours after his birth, his real mother gave him to Isabel and Paul Ryborg. In dismay, Andie asked bluntly, "But who are your real parents?"

He didn't know, he told her. It was many years before she understood that he didn't want to know. His parents were Isabel and Paul Ryborg, he said, and that was all he needed to know. She finally accepted that.

Andie replaced the lid on the box and returned it to the dresser, wondering how often her father visited the cache. At that moment, she wanted desperately to stay in this home she loved, full of memories that wove a tapestry both light and dark. Here, she could tend the father who'd given so much to so many and nearly died doing it. But the best thing she could do for him, she believed, was leave. *They can find me even here,* she feared. *Maybe they already have.*

Besides, if she suddenly announced she was moving back, he'd demand to know why.

I have to go back.

CHAPTER 14

ༀ

THE TEXT MESSAGE READ: Tomorrow Sweetwater 5 at 8 a.

Evan stared at the small screen, not believing the message's implication. *Brazen fool,* he fussed. *You dare them to catch you.*

The Sweetwater docks were too short a hop upriver to take *Misfit.* Evan drove the compact sedan Leo had provided weeks ago. Heading west alongside the river, he passed a series of small-cargo terminals. Snug to the docks were freighters receiving containers bound for the Bahamas and the rest of the Caribbean.

Evan knew about the seaports and docks in Florida, especially those on the Miami River. He knew that while food, clothing, small appliances, and used vehicles were loaded onto the ships, other things were offloaded. Things like narcotics and illegal aliens.

Some freighters would tie up at the river's docks much longer than it should take to load their cargo holds and depart. Evan had read that in a recent grand jury report, customs officials claimed that the purpose for such delays was to wait for the right moment to unload the contraband, when eyes of the Coast Guard, DEA, FDLE, immigration, and port authorities weren't watching.

He turned off the road at a rusted tin sign reading *Sweetwater* and searched the waterfront for dock five. The old crone of a boat anchored there looked like many junk freighters up and down the river. About two hundred feet long, pocked and gangly, but riveted tight as a fortress.

Dock workers buzzed about the ship, their cranes swinging multi-ton containers from shore to ship. All eyes fell upon Evan when he emerged from the car. He knew why. Watching for law enforcement was a practiced commodity. Many dock workers knew that their early warnings would be well rewarded by those slipping contraband onto U.S. soil.

Ignoring their collective glare, Evan hurried up the gangway and boarded the vessel near its helm. A hard-bodied man in a tight-fitting black T-shirt and camouflage pants appeared immediately from a doorway near the stern of the ship and approached. With his salt-and-pepper buzz cut and military swagger, the man, though much shorter and older than Evan, seemed to have cast himself in the image of a B-movie action figure.

"Hey, college boy," the man called with no pretense of a greeting. "This way." He motioned back the way he'd come, and Evan followed. The man's size and frame matched the silhouette of the one Evan had just seen prowling around Andie's house. *Got to be Ray Dingo.* Evan imagined the man's rough hands on Andie, throwing her into the trunk of a car. He wanted to crush the man and throw him to the concrete dock below. *Get ahold of yourself!*

The man stopped in front of a closed door and turned toward Evan. "I was ready to finish the job for you, you know. Good thing I didn't have to, wouldn't you say? She's too pretty to mess up."

Evan tightened his fists at his sides but managed to keep a passive face.

"By the way," the man said with a cocky grin, "I'm Ray Dingo, but you probably guessed that."

Evan shrugged. "Sounds like a cartoon character." He brushed past Dingo, opened the door, and stepped into a dimly lit, squalid room that smelled of diesel fumes and cigarettes.

"Surprise," called Leo Francini, raising his hand but not budging from his metal chair.

Evan laughed at him. "No surprise at all. You've always fancied yourself the daring gangster outwitting the feds."

"The kid's got a mouth," Dingo snarled, following Evan into the room.

Evan ignored him, but Leo shot Dingo a reproachful glance. "I think you'd better get back to your watch," Leo commanded, and Dingo immediately left the room.

Evan glanced around, surprised at the apparent lack of protection for the notorious drug boss. "Where's your army?" he asked.

"The whole crew is my army," Leo replied quickly. "You didn't think I'd enter U.S. waters alone, did you? Not after what happened the last time I was here." He lit a cigarette and stood, walking to a small window by the door, silently watching the activity on the dock.

Evan remembered that day in the FSU student union when news of the Tampa shootout erupted from the television screen. "Where were you when Donnie was killed?" he asked.

Leo turned a smoldering eye on Evan. "Where were *you*?" He moved away from the window and squared off with Evan, his jaw jutting forward, his eyes hard. Something fired inside them, and Evan knew he'd overstepped his bounds.

Then at once, the malice drained from Leo's face, but Evan couldn't read what *was* there. As if he'd simply fast-forwarded over a disagreeable passage, Leo emerged on the other side, ready to move on. He stepped back from Evan and gestured toward his surroundings. "You ever seen one of these things up close?"

"Never wanted to." Evan didn't care what Leo thought of him anymore. He just wanted to leave the man's world and never look back. Andie had been gone eight days now, and Evan planned to disappear that afternoon.

"I'd take you on a tour, but the captain would prefer I stay out of sight. Even though I own this ship."

"You're kidding." Evan said. "You own this thing?"

"I can see you're impressed." Leo grinned with mock satisfaction. "I knew you would be. She's a house of mirrors. Nothing is what it seems. Hidden compartments everywhere. False ceilings and floors, hollowed walls. She's a smuggler's dream. You know, there's more to us than grow houses. We do a nice little import business with the coke trade in South America. Wouldn't want anyone to interfere with that. I take exception to people who meddle with my business, you know."

"All too well," Evan allowed.

"Some I let off, like the old dame in the Everglades who shut down one of my little camps out there. She and I had this agreement I didn't live up to, and she just ran me right out of her territory. Darnedest thing I ever saw." Leo shook his head and smiled. "It was laughable. But others don't make me laugh."

The first glimmer of suspicion clouded Evan's face. "Why are you here, Leo?"

"To congratulate you. Our fair young maiden has run home to Daddy. We've seen her there, tracked her. She appears to have moved in. Works in the yard, gets the mail, takes long walks through the neighborhood."

A chill ran through Evan. Something Leo had said came back to him: "We can get to her anywhere, anytime we want."

"Who's watching her in Tallahassee?" he asked casually.

Leo eyed him closely. "And why do you need to know that, hmm? Afraid someone might get too close to her?" Leo seemed truly amused. "You're more transparent than you know. It's a good thing your days with the lovely Andie are over. An unwise dalliance there might have tripped you up, and I have other work for you to do. Maybe something offshore next time. Would you like that?"

Evan managed to present a believable face. "Sure, Leo. Anywhere you say." *But first, you have to find me.*

Leo returned to the window and looked out. "Dingo's not real bright, you know. Says things he shouldn't. Just not a people person." He chuckled. "He'd rather kill than make polite conversation." Leo turned to look at Evan. "But he kills for *me*, and that's all that matters. So be careful around him. You see, you're both valuable in your own ways. And I'd hate to lose either one of you to a silly disturbance. Understand?"

Evan did.

"Back to my question, Leo. Why are you here?"

Leo laughed. "You're a pit bull. Latch on and never let go." He sat back down and invited Evan to join him.

Evan eased onto a metal bench beside a wall hung with rows of life preservers. He heard footsteps at the door; then it opened. Dingo stepped inside, running a hand over his square head. "The truck's ready," he announced to Leo, then shifted his gaze to Evan. "College boy going with us?"

"No. Evan's staying here for a while." Leo looked firmly at

Evan as if to reinforce an order. "Then he's coming to the island. He needs to see what he's been missing."

Evan remained calm. *That's not going to happen.* But he needed to keep the conversation on an even keel. "Where are you going?" he asked.

Leo seemed to study every nuance of Evan's expressions and body language. "There are things you don't need to know, Evan. You did your job and did it well, I hope. But I'm not sure. I have to *make* sure."

What does that mean?

"There's a bigger picture you can't see right now," Leo allowed.

"Yeah," Dingo pitched in. "And people you can't see."

Suddenly, Leo turned on Dingo. "That's enough! Get out!"

The outburst stunned Evan. Dingo slinked from the room and shut the door. Leo composed himself quickly. "He doesn't know what he's saying half the time. Another reason to ignore him."

But Evan couldn't ignore what had just happened. Something was up, and he had to know what. *This thing isn't over!*

Leo busied himself with a duffle bag. As he bent to tie it, Evan caught a glimpse of metal just above the man's ankle. Another gun would be at Leo's belt. There always was.

"We'll be back in a couple of days," Leo said, his voice clipped. "Then we'll leave for the island. You can follow in your boat, so gas it up and get ready. I won't have time to wait. Oh, and use this." Leo reached in his pocket and tossed a cell phone to Evan. "Pre-paid and the only way you can call to and from the island." With that, Evan was dismissed.

An ill-formed urgency rose in him. But he didn't know what to do with it. He didn't know what the thing he feared looked like or from what direction it was coming. As he drove along the river road, his mind tumbled questions. *What if Tony Ryborg doesn't drop out of the race? How will they "make sure" he does? Who are the people I can't see?*

CHAPTER 15

~ঌৎ~

ANDIE COAXED THE OLD MUSTANG down the driveway of her father's Tallahassee home. She'd cranked the car only once since arriving over a week ago, and it was sluggish. *Come on, old girl. We've got a long way to go.*

Her dad had left that morning for a week on the campaign trail, starting with Orlando. Now, it was time for her to go too. She'd felt eyes on her. That day at the mailbox was deliberate, though she'd tried to convince herself otherwise. Later, while walking, she'd noticed a car parked in two different places along her route, its lone male occupant too intent on studying a map. Too quick to turn his head away as Andie passed. She'd raced between houses, cutting through back yards on a dead run until she reached home. She'd slammed the dead bolts in place on all doors and knelt beneath a front window, watching. And praying.

She'd begun to read the Bible again and was stunned at how clearly it spoke to her present turmoil, how God's Word counseled and encouraged her. But it was at times such as this, cowering on the floor before a real and present danger, that she felt his hand come upon her, bracing and comforting. Could she trust that hand to save her from this evil?

As she pulled into the street, she stopped and looked back at the house. She nodded silent approval of the weeded and groomed beds and unconsciously thumbed the tips of her nails. Their worn and jagged edges were testament to her days working the soil of her parents' home. Idling in the street, she ran a painter's eye over the lawn. Its broad stroke of green filtered deep into the shade of early morning, all the way to the serenity bench her mom had placed beneath a canopy of mature crape myrtles. Andie searched that spot as if her mom might suddenly appear on the plain teak bench, propped to one side with a book or a bowl of beans to snap for supper. That's what the evening meal was still called by Southerners like Jessica Ryborg.

Andie loved to hear tales of her mom's childhood. "Oh, we were all just a bunch of fiddler crabs scurrying over the sand and playing our music all day long," Jessica Ryborg had once told her daughter. Now, as Andie drove away from the house, she remembered one of those lazy-day talks with her mom.

"You know, my daddy was a banker, and mama, well, she sat out on the big front porch a lot, sipping on things," Andie's mom said as they sat on the bench one afternoon. "Our maid did all the work in the house and didn't seem to care what my brother and I did with our time."

"What *did* you do, Mom?" Andie coaxed.

"Every chance we got, we ran down to the beach, picking up friends along the way," Jessica Ryborg answered. "You never got to see my family's old place there on Mobile Bay, but it sat on a point where the bay swam into the ocean. I never wanted to be any place else in the world. Down there in the warm sand and that cool, green water, catching fiddler crabs and moving their little pinchers like they were violins playing great sonatas or hillbilly music for their dancing friends. My parents hated hillbilly music."

"When did you go to school?"

"When we weren't on the beach. One time, though, we skipped school to sneak into the old fishing pier down the beach from our house. It had been nearly demolished by a hurricane but was still standing. My brother, Ted, got the bright idea that we could row out to the end of the pier and climb up into the old dance hall at the end. Only the place had begun to lean like it would slide off its poles and into the ocean at any moment."

"Weren't you afraid to go there?"

"Sure we were. That's why we went. Big risk, big thrill. We were dumb kids who thought no matter what we did, God wouldn't let anything bad happen to us. Our friend Billy said so, and his dad was a preacher. So on Billy's word, we dragged our rowboat out of the shed we kept behind the dunes, threw in a rope ladder from Billy's tree house, and set off for the pier, just the three of us.

"It was so easy. We just rowed out to the end of the pier at high tide, when the boat would be closest to the underside of the dance hall. We tied the boat to a cross beam. Then Billy, in what we thought was a stroke of genius, attached hooks to the end of the rope ladder and hurled them over the big board running underneath a hole in the side of the hall. The hooks caught on the board and we climbed the ladder."

Andie clung to every word. "Then what?"

"We turned on the little transistor radio we brought and danced to the Beach Boys! I mean we were laying down some feet on that old floor and singing to the fish."

"No one heard you?"

"There was not one soul on that beach . . . until the whole building suddenly collapsed into Mobile Bay! Then there were a bunch of people out there."

Andie's mouth dropped open, and her mom laughed so hard she could hardly finish the story. "It would probably have killed us, but we jumped clear of it the first moment we felt it move."

"Were you hurt?"

"Just splinters and jelly fish stings. Nothing bad. We even got our pictures in the paper. And I honestly believe that was the proudest my dad ever was of his kids. He called it a harebrained stunt and wished he'd thought of it himself. It was one of the few good times I remember having with my dad."

"You didn't like your parents, did you, Mom?"

"Oh, I loved my parents. But they didn't love *being* parents. They never knew that I adored violin sonatas. Or that my brother belonged to a secret gang at school. The day Daddy died, he and Mama had been in Europe for a month, and in all that time, we only talked to them twice, once when my brother was expelled from the private school we went to and the other time when I got a fish hook in my finger and our maid didn't know what to do. But one day, someone from Daddy's office in Mobile called our maid and told her Daddy had suffered a heart attack in Westminster Abbey and died right there in Poet's Corner. My dad hated poetry, too."

As the old Mustang headed south from Tallahassee, Andie remembered a much later time when her mom led her to the bench to talk. "Darlin', there's something about my life you don't know, and I think you should." That's when Jessica Ryborg described the years leading up to the night she met Tony Ryborg.

"After Daddy died, Mama sent me and my brother to live with her sister in Tallahassee. Mama had become an alcoholic and couldn't take care of us anymore, not that she ever had. But we knew we weren't wanted at my aunt's house. She had three kids of her own, and though I'm sure Mama sent her money, she was glad when Ted and I, after several years, moved out on our own. We got an apartment together, and our friends were our family. My grandparents had died by then.

"I started dating a guy who told me that cocaine was a thrill. He said nothing bad would happen to me if I tried it, and I suddenly remembered what my friend Billy had said before we rowed out to the pier. I guess I thought God would take care of me again. And he did, but this time, he didn't save me until I'd nearly drowned in drugs."

Andie cried, and her mom comforted her but kept going. She told her about the night at the rehab center and the long years of recovery. "Andie, I think God waited so long to heal me because I didn't think he could."

҂

It was late afternoon and Andie was just a few hours north of Miami when her cell phone rang. Andie didn't recognize the incoming number.

"Andie, are you okay?"

"Oh, Thea, yes. I'm fine." Andie remembered giving Thea the cell number before she left Miami.

"Are you almost home?"

I don't know where that is, Andie wanted to say. "You mean Miami?"

"Yes. But more specifically, here."

Andie had planned to check into a hotel until she could make more permanent arrangements. "I can't do that, Thea. I have to—"

"You have to go someplace besides your house, right?"

"Well, uh . . ."

"The code to the gate is 3589. I've cooked a duck in orange sauce for dinner. I'd be honored if you'd join me." Hearing no response, Thea added. "Please don't feel pressured, Andie. If you have someplace else to go, then I'm glad for you."

The thought of checking into a lonely hotel room squeezed like an ice-cold hand.

"I might add, Andie, that there's a security camera at the gate and the whole circumference of the property is wired, even the beach."

There seemed nothing else for Andie to do. "Thank you, Thea. I'll see you in a little while." Andie couldn't put a finger on what disturbed her so about Thea. As kindly as she seemed, something was simmering just beneath the surface. Against her better judgment, Andie refused to entertain such notions.

That night after dinner, Andie and Thea sat on the terrace. "The sky is such a cobalt blue this time of evening," said Thea as she leaned back in her chair and studied the heavens. "Soon, it will turn black. But as the beautiful color is overcome by darkness, something extraordinary happens." Andie turned her gaze from the sky to the face of Thea Long. "A billion sparkling diamonds pop through the veil, and the blacker it grows, the brighter they shine." Thea turned a gentle eye on Andie. "And you know what? They were there all the time."

Something gripped like a vise inside Andie. Thea was quiet as she looked back at the fading horizon, but Andie kept watching her. *A most unusual woman.*

"Would you like a piece of key lime pie?" Thea asked brightly as she rose from her chair. "I have two trees just there by the cove that give me the juiciest fruit."

Andie obliged. "I'd love that, but let me help you." She followed Thea to the kitchen, as if pushing off from any reminder of her troubles, if only for a little while. She knew, though, that in the morning, she would have to leave for a place where no one could find her. As much as a stilt house in the middle of the bay appealed to her, the process of applying for an artist-in-residence lease would take a couple of months. That's what the ranger at the Biscayne National Park headquarters had told her when she called from Tallahassee.

But just then, she thought of someone who might help her. *Randall Ivy could pull strings for me, if he would. I didn't leave there on great terms, but it's worth a try.*

As Thea sliced into the pie, she asked, "Andie, would you like to go with me into the Grove tomorrow morning? I have just a bit of shopping to do at the market. We wouldn't stay long."

Andie quickly weighed more options. *I do need to visit Ivy at the gallery. Maybe I can afford an hour or two before I drop into a hole somewhere and pull a lid over me.*

"Perhaps, Thea, and then I have to go."

The old woman seemed suddenly agitated, her hand shaking as she lifted a slice of pie to Andie's plate. "Let's not talk about your leaving right now, dear. We're having such a nice time."

Thea led Andie to a comfortable living-room sofa, where they settled down to enjoy their pie. "Do you think it's a good idea for your dad to be running for governor?"

Andie's fork froze in mid-air. She gaped at Thea but saw only the campaign poster above her bed, dripping red paint, its message brutally clear.

"Did I say something to upset you, dear?"

Andie couldn't read the woman's face, couldn't dismiss suspicion. But it was crazy to imagine this woman had anything to do with what was happening to her. *It was just a harmless question.*

"No . . . but I . . . uh . . . think I'd better get some sleep, Thea."

"You'll go with me to the market in the morning, then?"

Andie stared at her for an uncomfortable moment, then forced herself to say, "For just a little while."

CHAPTER 16

ॐ

ON AN EARLY FRIDAY-MORNING flight to Orlando, Tony sat
with Warren in first class. Other FDLE officers and reporters
were nearby. A local security detail would meet the plane and
escort the candidate to the dedication of the new Orange County
Courthouse in downtown Orlando. Tony was scheduled to
address a gathering on the front steps of the building about nine
o'clock that morning. It would be one of many public appearances before returning to the capital days later.

The last stop on Tony's swing through the state would be a
long-awaited debate with Senator Bill Neiman Wednesday night
in Palm Beach. But it was Monday morning's address in Miami
Beach that Tony believed would most impact his campaign.
Though delivered during a state medical convention at the Excalibur Hotel, Tony knew the local media would turn out in force,
allowing him to reconnoiter the tricky labyrinth of South Florida
voters, long considered Neiman's stronghold. His family's string
of hotels and restaurants took root in Miami in the sixties and
spread throughout the region. Besides that multi-faceted corpo-
ration and the family villa on Star Island near Miami Beach,
Neiman also inherited his family's penchant for local charitable
causes. It was his high-profile championing of the elderly and
minorities that had won the hearts of voters.

The political terrain of Miami Beach was daunting. Within
quaking distance of the high-octane South Beach nightlife were
the sagging retirement hotels where so many elderly, fixed-
income residents from the North sat in folding chairs lined up on
front porches, mostly women holding big black purses on their
laps and watching the parade. South Beach pranced day and
night to the undulating rhythm of the young and expressive. How

many different ways can you decorate the body? The women of the porches kept count.

Other worlds unfolded inside lavish condos and stucco mansions lining the long ocean boulevards, where the wealthy rode their fortunes and worked their tans and golf games.

"Know what you'll say in Miami Beach, sir?" asked Warren, seated next to his boss.

"You mean besides, 'Give us your tired, your overworked drug dealers yearning to slither through South Beach'?" Tony regretted his snide comment that slipped out too quickly.

"Way to be the jolly Republican in a Democratic land," Warren quipped. He and Tony Ryborg had traveled through so many years together, theirs was an easy bond that glided back and forth between formality and familiarity.

"I'm working on 'jolly.' Give me time."

Later, Tony tried to study his remarks for the Orlando crowd but couldn't stay focused. He leaned toward Warren. "Something's up with Andie," he said in a hushed voice. "This whole week at home, she barely left the house. I don't think she touched her paints. She had almost nothing to say about her classes or if anything else had sold at the gallery. And when I asked about her house, she acted like she had to think hard about something to say. She used to bubble over about that little place." Tony looked out the window and nodded confirmation to himself. "Something's up."

"Well, you'll be down there soon enough," Warren said. "You'll see for yourself what life is like for her now. Oh, and by the way, Manny will meet us at her house for a little briefing. I know Andie resisted when you told her there'd be more security around her. But she'll have to get used to it. And, you'll need to prepare her for what Neiman's camp is getting ready to hurl your way." Warren hesitated. "You know, about Jessica."

Tony clenched his teeth. It was the involuntary response to any mention of Jessica Ryborg's battle with drugs. It had never been a secret, though little had been made of it through Tony's long career in law enforcement. But now, Neiman strategists were looking for anything to tarnish the motivations of one of Florida's most respected public servants.

"Tony Ryborg would be a one-track, drugs-only governor," Neiman recently declared in a small, town-hall meeting in the Panhandle. Then he oozed compassion for "the late Mrs. Ryborg's unfortunate habit" declaring it a guarded secret. "But the hard-working people of this state need a governor looking out for them, not just his own personal vendetta." It was the first time he'd dug into the Ryborg family's history, but Tony knew it wouldn't be the last.

He nodded grimly, acknowledging but not responding to Warren's coaching. He was suddenly adrift in his own private world, hardly noticing when Warren got up to confer with his security team.

Left alone, Tony focused on the cloudscape beyond his window. Cirrus clouds like a flock of white gulls floated against a vaporous mountain billowing into frothy peaks. Then the mountain changed, slowly reconfiguring into the head of a giant, its face clearly defined until even that image morphed into a ghost ship sailing at twenty thousand feet.

Shape shifters, Tony thought. *Now you're this; now you're that. You're Tony Ryborg, son of a math teacher and his wife. Before that, you were someone else's son. Someone who didn't want you, even before they knew you.*

Again, the haunting questions surfaced unbidden. They came anytime they wanted, relentless and pointless: Who is Tony Ryborg, really? Who begot him and what happened to them? Was I supposed to be someone else?

Even as he asked that last question, he knew the answer, had known it for a very long time. *No. God, you have molded me, even in the womb of a stranger. I am who you made me to be and have gone where you have led me. I haven't liked places you've taken me. But I've never doubted that it's you who drives me, who keeps me from the hands of my enemies. Steady me now. And please, hold onto my child. Make her as sure of you as I am. Somehow.*

When the plane landed, Tony was whisked into a caravan headed along an unannounced route to downtown Orlando. At the courthouse, Warren and local FDLE officers escorted him to the front lobby of the imposing structure. A growing crowd spread over the front steps of the building and into the street, which was blocked off to traffic. The governor's race was entering the home stretch. As with most races or games of any kind, the final moments tick loudest.

When Tony stepped from the building, the sunlight caught him full in the face as the crowd erupted in applause. Suddenly, affirmation swept through him like a warm tide, and he beamed, not with pride but with resolve. More than ever, he knew his purpose.

Cutting a strong figure at the podium, his broad shoulders straining at the seams of his old blue suit (paired with another tie Freda had threatened to run through her shredder), he cast aside prepared remarks intended for the whole state to hear, and spoke only to those gathered. He singled out some he knew in the crowd with a special greeting, commented on the rising cost of Disney tickets and the need to clone Interstate 4 and disperse its racing horde. He invited those who'd brought breakfast bags from surrounding office buildings to find a shady patch of grass and settle down with their food. He even asked one woman what that good-looking stuff was she was eating and where he could get some when he left. The people warmed quickly to his affable manner.

❧

In an alley across the street, hunched low in a panel truck with the windows down, two more listened attentively, one of them risking everything to be there. In a ragged T-shirt, a painter's cap, and dark glasses, Leo Francini waited. It was the closest he had ever come to Tony Ryborg.

"I want to hear it myself," he gloated to his driver, Ray Dingo. "I want to inhale the same air Tony Ryborg does before and after he drops the bomb that he's quitting the governor's race."

But it was taking too long. Uniformed officers were about to make another pass in front of the alley, and Tony Ryborg was still talking about the fragile citrus industry, prescription costs, Medicaid fraud, and gang violence.

"Get it over with, man," Leo growled and pulled the cap lower over his face. "Tell all the good people you're pulling out and running for cover." He pumped his fist. "You watch, Dingo. This is gonna be good."

᠅

After a few more comments on taxation and Central Florida's galloping tourism, Tony Ryborg paused and scanned the faces before him. A light breeze rustled the fronds of nearby royal palms, sending them clattering against each other like muffled chimes. He looked up and stared at them for a long interval, his mind churning. *Should I do this? Is this the moment?* Some standing in the crowd shifted their weight, grew restless, even embarrassed for what seemed sudden confusion in the man at the podium.

Though it seemed that Tony had reached an impasse in his speech and didn't know where to head next, at that moment, he decided exactly where he would go. *Andie was right. I have to do this, and do it now.*

He turned back to the crowd and drew in a steadying breath. "If you'll grant me a few more minutes, I'd like to tell you something I rarely talk about. It's personal. But I look at you all gathered here, and I understand that what I'm asking is personal to you. I'm asking you to let me lead you to safety."

Tony paused another moment, then dove in. "My wife died of a heart attack not long after our twenty-seventh wedding anniversary. When we married, she was addicted to cocaine. She'd also shot heroin, and the night she stumbled into the drug rehab center where I worked was the night I fell in love with her. Until that night, she'd fought her battle with drugs alone, but not anymore. We married, and I crawled through the terrors of addiction beside her. With God's help, we chased the dealers and the demons from our lives. But they're still out there. More now than ever. Listen to this:

"There are nearly eight hundred thousand drug addicts in our state. The number of eighth-graders shooting up with heroin has tripled. The average age that a child first experiments with drugs is ten. Cocaine-related deaths outnumber homicides. As much as eighty percent of all crime in our state is due to illicit drug activity. And a mom can stroll her toddler down the street of her neighborhood and suddenly be caught in the middle of a gun battle—over drugs!"

⌁

Inside the panel truck, Leo slammed his fist against the dash. "You must be insane! Don't you know what I can do to you?"

"Watch it, Leo," Dingo warned. "Cops are everywhere, and guess who they'd love to catch. Let's get out of here."

"No! We'll see this to the end."

⌁

Tony kept rolling. "From other podiums, I have been declared one-track, interested only in settling a private score, and not caring about the issues that concern you most. Well, what I have just told you should concern you plenty. Not because it happened to me and someone I love, but because it can happen to you—and to your eighth-grader.

"That's why you're not safe. That's why as attorney general, I've waged war against those who would dare contaminate your children with their poison." He paused before his final statement. "If what happened to my wife makes me mad enough to stop it from happening to you and your family, I honor her memory by staying the course and leading you to safety." With that, Tony stepped from the podium, managed a weak smile, and mouthed a thank-you because he couldn't speak anymore. Emotion caught in his throat, and he just slipped away with Warren and three other officers. But they only made it to the door of the courthouse, halted by the thunderous, persistent applause. Tony turned awkwardly, surprised by the crowd's reaction to the hard things he had said. He gratefully acknowledged their cheers, gave a simple wave, and disappeared into the building.

Immediately, television reporters jumped before live-feed cameras, spouting refrains from what they called the most galvanizing address of the Ryborg campaign.

꒰ꜛ

Leo slowly raised the dark-tinted window and leaned back in his seat, his eyes narrowed and locked on the place where Tony Ryborg had just stood.

"Go!" he ordered.

꒰ꜛ

The panel truck headed south down the Florida Turnpike, the driver careful to remain under the speed limit. It wouldn't do for the Florida Highway Patrol to pull over two of the state's most wanted criminals.

A cell phone rang inside the truck. "Yeah." A pause. "Give us a few hours." Leo dropped the phone in his pocket. "He wants to meet at the Lauderdale condo."

"Why don't we just pull into the police station and announce ourselves?" Dingo growled. "That condo is smack in the middle of everything."

"Close your mouth and drive."

Just hours after Tony Ryborg refueled his race for governor with a speech the whole state was buzzing about, the truck left the turnpike and headed east to Ft. Lauderdale and the Intracoastal Waterway. From sand flats strewn with Spanish bayonets and scrub palmettos, the land spread itself under the cover of concrete all the way to the ocean. Seedy strip malls gave way to the tony shops and restaurants of Las Olas Boulevard, enclaves of executive suites, and the posh residences that line the storied canals of the Venice of Florida.

Dingo turned into a driveway overhung with bougainvillea and pulled into a parking garage. He and Leo got out, but only Leo entered the low-rise condominium building.

While he waited, Dingo walked to the back of the building, which fronted on the waterway. Tied up at the seawall was a gleaming white yacht named *The Blonde*. Dingo walked down to it, admiring its opulence. He took a seat on a nearby bench and, for almost an hour, watched a parade of more mega-yachts, cruisers, sloops, and sport fishermen with towers as high as the upper stories of the condos behind him parade along this boastful stretch of the Intracoastal.

Soon, though, voices caught his attention. He looked up to see Leo and a man whose back was turned to him standing on an open balcony of the building behind him. The man was a foot shorter than Leo, slim and bald, with just a fringe of blond hair encircling his head. He wore a sedate, gray-tone business suit, but his hands were animated, darting about him like angry birds as he spoke. From three floors down, Dingo couldn't hear what either man was saying, but he knew it wasn't an amiable exchange.

A few minutes later, Leo called to him from the side of the building.

"So, what's up?" Dingo asked when they got in the car.

Leo was agitated. "Get the guys in Tallahassee, and tell them to grab the girl if she's still there. And do it now! Bring her to the island, and I want her in one piece!" Leo stared at the road ahead, oblivious to the surge of noontime traffic around them.

"She's got to make a special appearance in a video we're going to send her daddy."

CHAPTER 17

☙

EVAN CALLED THE COLLEGE Friday morning to see if Andie had returned to her classes yet. When told she hadn't, he was relieved. *Good! Don't come back.* Though Evan suspected she wasn't safe in Tallahassee either. He could only hope to hear that Tony Ryborg had withdrawn from the race and would be leaving Florida for good, taking his daughter with him.

That night, Evan drove to Andie's bungalow for one more check, hoping there would be no sign of her. He found the house as he'd seen it last. Still, he was uneasy about what he'd heard. There would be no escaping Leo now. Evan would have to remain close to uncover these unseen people.

The next morning, Evan awoke to the sound of a dog barking on the dock. Then he heard a voice he'd come to dread.

"Evan, you awake?" Vic pounded on the side of the boat.

Evan pulled the pillow over his head.

"If you are and just don't want to talk to me, that's okay. I just thought you'd like some fresh food from the market."

After a moment with no reply, she added, "Watermelon, peaches, some Canadian bacon, and eggs. Sure would taste good, don't you think?"

Evan opened the cabin door and stuck his head out, squinting against an obtrusive sun.

"Oh, there you are," Vic chirped. "Well, aren't you a sight with your hair all scrunched up like that. Why don't you get yourself dressed, son, and come with me."

Evan eyed the irrepressible woman standing before him, dressed in yet another from her vast collection of housedresses—this one bright green with a scattering of pink flamingos, each balanced on a single leg. *Where does she get those things?* Evan allowed himself a long, frustrated sigh, which seemed to have no effect on Vic.

"By the way, Elvis just peed on your bow line. Hand me a bucket, and I'll rinse it off."

Evan glanced down at the small dog and the yellow fluid soaking into the neat coil. "Don't worry about it," he grumbled. "The rain will wash it off this afternoon."

Vic looked up at the cloudless sky, then back at Evan. "Well, what do ya know. The boy's talking like a native after just a few weeks. You bet it's going to rain, just like it always does—about two o'clock. Course, we'll be back from the market long before then, if you're coming. Hurry up and decide."

It was the prospect of fresh fruit that hooked him. Grocery shopping was almost impossible since Leo had forbidden him to use the car for anything but his assignment. "We don't need anyone tracking that car back to the boat," Leo had said.

Evan had been living on canned goods, heating their contents in the galley. A few times he'd pulled into a drive-through for as much food as he could store on board. But leftover burgers and fries, even heated, turned his stomach.

Leo won't be back for a while, from wherever he is. "Okay, give me a second," he told Vic.

Soon, Vic and Evan were bouncing along the gravel road through her property, Vic gripping the old Dodge Dart's steering wheel as if it might fly from her hands. "Which store are we going to?" Evan asked as Vic finally pulled onto Flagler Street headed for I-95.

"No, son," she corrected. "We're going to the open market in Coconut Grove."

Evan stiffened. "I'd, uh, rather go to a store around here."

"Well, you can't get your feet massaged at Winn Dixie. Don't you know that?"

"You . . . what?"

"Your feet. Ever had anyone massage yours? There's a young lady at the market who gives foot massages for five dollars a pair."

"No, Vic. I'm not interested. I'd just rather stay close to the boat."

But she persisted. "That boat's not going anywhere. And we'll be back in a jiffy. You sit tight and let old Vic take care of things." They were going to Coconut Grove, and that was that.

From Flagler Street they turned onto I-95 heading south to Dixie Highway and the familiar jumble of commerce lining both sides of the road. That much hadn't changed since Evan moved from the city twenty years ago.

While continuing a lengthy tale of how she came to own Elvis after finding him wandering near the river a few years ago, Vic turned onto South Bayshore Drive, which hugged Biscayne Bay on its way to the Grove. A profuse shelter of palm, frangipani, ficus, and water oak spread their protective limbs along the avenue, sometimes touching to form a seamless awning over the road. The bougainvillea and hibiscus were rampant. As a child, Evan hadn't paid much attention to flowers, but today, they seemed to flash at him from deep shade like fireflies in the night.

Tuning out Vic's story, Evan retreated into his private thoughts. As they drove, he watched longingly as people who seemed so carefree walked their dogs, jogged, and bicycled through cool, green neighborhoods. He heard children on a nearby playground and turned to see mothers push their young in swings. Gentle rays of sunlight caught innocent young faces lifted toward the sky. Evan was glad for them but couldn't watch anymore.

"Well, here we are." Vic's announcement spilled from her long story about Elvis, the details of which Evan never heard.

"Looks like a good crowd building," Vic noted as she parked under a spreading ficus tree. "Happens every Saturday."

Evan wondered at the strange sight before him. A small, open field was a hive of activity. Scattered across the worn grass were makeshift displays of things Evan couldn't identify from the car.

"Let's go." Vic grabbed a couple of paper grocery bags from the back seat and handed one to Evan. "Here, take this. Folks here don't always have bags for you."

"What is all this, Vic?" Evan asked, taking the offered bag and climbing from the car.

"It's a good excuse for a folk festival is what it is," Vic said as she slammed the door shut and waved her arm before her. "By noon, this whole place will be swarming with the darnedest mix of humanity you ever saw, and if I didn't need a bit of food, I'd come here just to watch what goes on." She paused a moment. "I do that, you know." She cast a fleeting look at Evan. "I watch people."

As Evan turned to look at her, she hurried back to his question. "Every weekend, people bring the special things they grow or make to this market." They were approaching the first booths. "Look over there. There's some star fruit, and I won't be leaving here today without some. Over there is the man who makes goat's milk fudge. Come on, let's get us a sample."

Evan hesitated before entering the tangle of shoppers. He scanned the crowd. No familiar faces. Certainly no one would recognize him after all this time, he told himself.

Vic plunged into the crowd, motioning Evan to follow. Head slightly down but eyes constantly roving, Evan caught up with her. "All the fruits and vegetables are over there under the trees," she told him. "If you like handmade jewelry and incense and all that hippie stuff, it's out there in the middle. See that guy with the parrot on his shoulder?" Evan nodded, staring at the young man with long dreadlocks. "He carves the prettiest little birds and fish out of basswood, then strings them up into mobiles. Go take a look. In fact, why don't you just explore this place on your own, and we'll meet back at the car in about an hour."

Evan was ready to leave then. "It won't take me that long to buy a few things, Vic. How about twenty minutes?"

Vic frowned at him. "You're a nervous one, Evan. Make it forty-five."

Vic turned and walked away, but another woman soon stopped her. Evan watched as the two women exchanged animated greetings. Then Vic turned to him with a bright smile, took the other woman's arm, and led her toward him.

In no mood for lying his way through introductions and chatty conversation, he quickly sidestepped the advancing pair and headed for the fruit stands, not bothering to look back at what he knew would be another bewildered look on Vic's face.

He bypassed the star fruit and the fudge and stopped at a table of oranges arranged pyramid fashion. Flipping open the bag

Vic had given him, he bought half a dozen and moved along. He soon added bananas, mangoes, and strawberries to the bag. Then he smelled roasted turkey. A few booths down, an old man in a tie-dyed shirt and overalls was turning the birds on a spit over an open fire. Sandwiches of the fresh, hot meat with melted cheese on warm homemade bread were being served. Evan's mouth watered as he approached the booth. He bought two sandwiches and a bottle of water and found a quiet place beyond the crowd to settle down for a serious meal.

Later, he gathered up a few brown eggs and a small loaf of sourdough bread. His bag close to overflowing, he looked about for Vic. It had been only thirty minutes, but maybe she was ready to go, he hoped. He passed a steel drum band playing and swaying in the sunshine. Not far away, he noticed people queuing up in the shade. He went to investigate, chomping on an apple as he strolled along. He had to admit he was grateful for this unexpected interlude. A playful breeze tossed the scent of jasmine at him, and he paused, lifting his face to capture every intoxicating puff, then continued toward the loose line of people.

He saw a young woman with frizzy brown hair standing at the end of a long table. On top of the table was a single mattress covered in a paisley-print sheet. A pillow sat at one end, and nestled onto it was a familiar head with its knot of red hair.

Evan couldn't help himself. A wide-open smile spread across his face as he drew closer. Then he heard Vic say, "Now Darlene, remember to be careful around that old bunion of mine. But you can just go to town on the rest of my ugly feet. They plan to get up and do a little jig after you've worked the kinks out of them."

Completely forgetting himself, Evan stood in the midst of onlookers, shaking his head and smiling at what peculiar leading had brought him into the company of this even more peculiar woman.

After a few moments, Evan noticed a man selling puppies nearby and went to see. *The last thing I need, but doesn't hurt to look.*

The man's radio was blaring country-western music that Evan thought incongruent with the surroundings. He peeked into the box and saw five squirming balls of black fur.

"Full-blooded Labs," the man announced, coming alongside Evan.

Evan nodded. "I just want to look at them." He leaned over and stroked the fur of one. "I used to have a Lab."

"They're the most loyal of beasts, you know," said the middle-aged man dressed in jeans and an Army-green T-shirt. "What happened to yours?"

"My brother shot him," Evan said without looking up.

The man gawked at Evan. "He did what?" he shrieked.

Evan wasn't about to go where this conversation was leading. "Find them all a good home, sir." He was about to move on when the music ended and the radio news announcer said: "A speech by gubernatorial candidate Tony Ryborg created quite a stir in Orlando yesterday." Evan froze. "What began as just another campaign speech ended with the attorney general divulging his late wife's battle with drug addiction"—Evan held his breath— "and an impassioned cry for support in fighting, quote, 'those who would dare contaminate your children with their poison.' Here's how the candidate ended his speech . . ." The broadcast had caught the attention of a few other bystanders, who drew close enough to hear Tony Ryborg's own voice declare: "If what happened to my wife makes me mad enough to stop it from happening to you and your family, I honor her memory by staying the course and leading you to safety."

Evan couldn't believe what he'd just heard.

"Here, buddy," the man with the puppies said, a look of profound sorrow on his face. "You take one of these little fellas home with you. No charge."

Evan looked blankly at the man. "What?" Then he quickly remembered their last exchange. "Oh, no, sir. Thanks, but I have to go."

His mind raced as he dashed away. *Is Ryborg a complete idiot? Do threats against his daughter mean nothing to him? Leo won't stop at anything now.* Evan rushed back to the massage table for Vic. She was gone. He spun around to scan the crowd for her, still scrambling for what to do next. *I've got to get to Tallahassee. But Leo will be back soon. He'll be looking for me.*

A live reggae band had cranked up on the other side of the field, and many were drifting that way. Evan hurried in that direction, pushing past more vendors and milling shoppers. His arm ached, and he realized he'd tensed into a stranglehold on the grocery bag. Switching it to the other arm, he searched the heads of those gathering before the band until he found the right one. Just then, Vic turned around and saw him too.

"Evan," she called. "Come listen to this." She was swaying like a chubby palm in a housedress when Evan reached her.

"Vic, I have to go." He was almost breathless.

"Well, don't you have a minute to—"

"No! I have to go *now*!" he said too forcefully.

Vic blanched. "What's wrong, Evan?"

"Nothing. I just have to get back to the boat. I . . . I've got to catch a plane in just a little while."

"Well, why didn't you tell me sooner? Come on."

With Vic trailing close behind him, Evan pushed back through the crowd. Just as she'd said, it had doubled since they arrived.

"You keep the darnedest schedule," Vic observed, trying to keep up with Evan. "Where are you off to?" Her voice trailed behind him.

"Just . . . stuff, Vic," he called over his shoulder. "I won't be gone but a—" Something caught his eye. The flash of a face. He turned and, without a word, shoved the grocery bag into Vic's free arm and plunged into the crowd. Moving slowly, carefully, he followed something he wasn't sure of—until Andie Ryborg stepped in front of him.

She only glanced at him as she passed. He didn't move, his eyes riveted on the back of her head. Suddenly, she looked back at him, a flicker of recognition in her face.

Do something! he commanded himself. But he didn't know what, not until she turned and hurried away from him. And then she was gone.

No! Don't go! There was nothing else left for him to do. He hollered, "Andie!" and bolted after her.

CHAPTER 18

❦

"THEA, WE HAVE TO GET OUT of here!" In a panic, Andie grabbed the old woman's arm and pulled. *The face. I've seen him before. Where? Why did he look so hard at me?*

Thea resisted. "Andie, what's the matter? Who is that calling you?" She tried to look behind them, but Andie kept tugging her forward.

Then it came again. "Andie!"

"Hurry, Thea! I'll explain later." She urged Thea along until they cleared the market grounds and crossed the road. As they started down the sidewalk, she glanced back to see the man break through the crowd and run into the street, looking frantically in all directions.

Thea's car was a block away. *We'll never make it.* "This way," Andie cried, and they darted down a narrow alley between two buildings. Andie knew it led to the park, where there was usually a policeman on patrol. They had just reached the edge of it when they heard an urgent voice behind them.

"Andie! Don't go back to the house!"

That brought her to a halt. She dropped Thea's arm and spun around to face the man. "Who are you?" she screamed. "What are you doing to me?"

But his face held no aggression. Only pleading. "I'm trying to protect you from—"

"Stop right there!" came the commanding voice of a woman with both hands on a gun aimed directly at the man.

He whirled toward the voice. "Vic!"

The woman spoke directly to Andie. "Ma'am, I know I don't look it, but I'm Special Agent Vic Shay, FBI." She flipped out her badge.

The man's mouth fell open, but no words came.

The strange, gun-toting woman in the housedress kept talking as she patted down the bewildered man. "And I don't know who this young man is, not really. I sure like him a lot, but he's got some awfully nasty friends." Finishing her search of him, the woman looked at the man. "Didn't I tell you I made a living at meddling, Evan? This is how I do it."

Andie struggled to understand what was happening. "I don't know who either one of you is." She glanced quickly at Thea and took her hand. They were backing slowly away when two gray sedans suddenly jumped the curb and lurched to a stop near the woman who claimed to be an agent.

"Mornin' boys," she called as four plainclothesmen with drawn guns jumped out and restrained Evan, though he was offering no resistance. "Ma'am," the woman said to Andie, "meet some of FDLE's finest."

Evan finally found his voice. "Vic, you don't know what's going on!"

"Well, let me tell you what I do know," she said, lowering her weapon. "I know I saw some of Leo Francini's boys hanging around your boat while you were gone a couple of days ago. I just happen to have some history with that bunch. That made me want to follow you last night, all the way to a certain bungalow in Coconut Grove, where I watched you stalk about in the woods behind, then peep in the windows. According to my quick-search friends at the bureau, the bungalow is leased to this young lady here, I believe."

Vic turned to Andie. "Ma'am, I know who you are. And your father. From what I know about Francini's threats against him, you can understand my concern about this young man's surveillance of your home."

A low guttural sound rose from deep in Thea's throat. Andie turned toward her. The older woman seemed suddenly dazed. "Thea, what's the matter?"

Vic rushed to Thea's side. "Ma'am, do you need medical assistance?"

"No. I . . . I'm just concerned for Miss Ryborg's welfare."

"Well, ma'am, we all are. But are you sure you're okay?"

"Yes, certainly," Thea insisted, lowering her eyes.

Vic watched her a moment, then apparently dismissed her as a concern. The agent seemed ready to resume her charge and rounded on Evan. "I brought you with me today for one purpose. When we left the market, I was going to drive you past Miss Ryborg's home and make you tell me what you were doing there."

Just then, Andie rushed at Evan. "How do you know where I live?" she wailed. One of the officers took her arm and gently pulled her away from Evan, who now silently stared at the ground.

"Answer me!" she screamed.

Slowly, Evan raised his eyes to hers. Andie saw something in them she didn't understand.

"I'm so sorry," he whispered.

"For what?" she snapped. But she knew. "It was you! You're the man in the mask!"

Evan flinched as if she'd slapped him.

"You're the one who ransacked my house! You took away my life!"

"No!" Evan finally answered. "I'm trying to *save* your life!"

The force of him made Andie step back. Another officer quickly grabbed his arm and started to haul him to one of the cars.

"Wait!" Evan shouted. "Vic, I beg you to take her in and guard her. They'll come for her—if they're not already here!"

Vic glanced at the growing crowd of curious onlookers, then back at Evan. "One question: Where did you go early Thursday morning?"

He hesitated a moment, then looked her straight in the eye. "To see Leo Francini."

Vic spun toward the officers. "Get 'em out of here quick! All of them!"

CHAPTER 19

As the **FDLE** sedan raced along Dixie Highway, Andie and Thea sat in the back like two hostages. In the car behind, Andie could see Vic and Evan in the back seat. She seethed at the thought of him, at how he'd tormented her. *So why is he now warning me? About what?*

Something troubled her even more. *I've seen him somewhere.*

Just then, the car slowed, and Andie watched as two more sedans just like theirs took up positions in front of them. She twisted in her seat to see another sedan abruptly jump into place behind them and still another pull up alongside, matching their pace.

"Don't be alarmed, Miss Ryborg," said the driver. "We called for escort to headquarters, just in case."

Andie looked stricken. "Thea, I'm so sorry I dragged you into this."

But Thea was strangely quiet.

"Miss Ryborg," said the driver again, "I'm Lieutenant Paul Rivera, and this is my partner, Lieutenant Bill Levitt." The officer in the front passenger seat turned to shake hands with both women, smiling reassuringly at them. "I just want you to know that it's our privilege to take care of you and your friend, Miss, uh . . ."

"Long," Thea supplied, her voice strained.

"Thank you, ma'am. Anyway, Tony Ryborg is law enforcement's best friend in this state, and you can rest assured we'll be taking good care of you. You'll be under guard twenty-four/seven."

This isn't happening. "Can we do this without telling my dad?"

The two officers exchanged curious glances. Then, Lieutenant Levitt turned to face her. "At this point, miss, Tony Ryborg has already been notified."

Then it's over! He'll quit the race, quit it all . . . because of me. And he'll be furious that I hid all this from him. Then she thought of Manny. *After he gets through yelling at me, he'll feel like he failed me. It seems I have the honor of being everyone's problem.* She glanced at Thea, who was staring out the window. *Hers too.*

"Thea." No response. Andie touched the woman's arm. "Thea? Are you okay?"

"Oh, yes. I'm sorry, dear. What did you say?"

"I asked if you were feeling all right."

"Of course."

"You deserve to know what this is all about, or as much as I know, myself. Then you need to distance yourself from me."

Almost in the same breath, Andie asked Lieutenant Rivera, "Do you see any reason why Miss Long can't return to her home? She has nothing to do with any of this." Though some elusive voice within her cautioned that she couldn't be sure of that.

"It's all right, Andie, I don't want you to be alone."

"That's best, Miss Ryborg," Lieutenant Rivera advised. "Besides, we'll need to ask Miss Long some questions."

Thea visibly stiffened. "What kind of questions?"

"Just about what you saw and heard this Evan character say," Lieutenant Rivera said.

"Oh," Thea answered lightly.

"And your background," he added.

Andie sensed the old woman's body tense. "I won't let them keep you long, Thea. Then you can forget all about us Ryborgs."

By the time they arrived at FDLE headquarters, Andie had told Thea why she had escaped to an anonymous life in the Grove and how that had failed—nothing the two officers in the front seat didn't already know by now.

When the motorcade arrived at headquarters, Andie and Thea were ushered into a large conference room and questioned. Andie divulged everything about the harassment and why she'd kept it a secret.

Later, a guard was posted at the door, even inside police head-quarters. A female officer named Sergeant Cleo Banks was dispatched to offer any assistance the women might need. Coffee, sodas, and sandwiches were brought in for them, though neither one was hungry. Andie went to the window and looked out. In the street below, people walked about in the open, some with briefcases, some with iPods strung about them. An elderly couple sat on a bench and shared food from a bag. *Just normal life. How extraordinary to be so . . . ordinary.*

"Miss Ryborg, please make yourself comfortable," said Sergeant Banks, a square-bodied woman, her light brown hair clipped short, sensibly. Andie had no problem believing the gun on the woman's hip also fit comfortably in her hand. "Feel free to curl up on one of the sofas and take a snooze if you like," the woman offered, though her tone was sharp and official. "Miss Long, I'll need you to come with me, please, and bring your identification."

"Where are you taking her?" Andie asked defensively.

"Just down the hall for questioning. I'll bring her right back."

"It's okay, dear," Thea said, pulling her wallet from the quilted backpack she'd carried with her to the market. "They're just doing what they must. Why don't you do as she suggested and get some sleep?"

Andie smiled weakly. *How can you sleep when you're hunted?*

When the door was closed, Andie crumpled onto a sofa, her head in her hands. She'd never felt so isolated in her life, so weary of being afraid. She slipped out of her sandals and tucked her legs up under her long, linen skirt as if rolling herself into a ball. Maybe she could just disappear into the cushions. *But what about Dad? They'll get tired of dallying with me and go straight for him. Again.*

The burden fell heavy on her as she sank into a corner of the sofa. In the chill of the air-conditioned room, she began to shiver inside her thin, sleeveless shirt. She glanced at Thea's open backpack on the table and noticed some kind of garment stuffed inside. She got up and pulled a light, silky wrap from the bright blue pouch, and with it tumbled Thea's keychain. Andie picked it up and noticed the small, clear acrylic frame dangling from it. Inside was a plain piece of parchment. On one side was a simple drawing of a cross composed of hundreds of tiny nails. On the other side were the words:

     No power of hell, no scheme of man,
     Can ever pluck me from His hand.

Andie gripped the little frame so hard its corners dug into the palm of her hand, and just then, she remembered something her mom once told her: "If you ever doubt how much you're loved, just see the nail holes in his hands."

Nothing stirred in the room, but something had changed. She looked back at the words *no scheme of man,* and she knew: *not even this one.*

Drawing Thea's wrap around her, Andie returned to the sofa and drifted effortlessly into sleep.

CHAPTER 20

AS THE DOOR SWUNG OPEN and Evan—still in handcuffs—filed into the conference room with Vic, FDLE chief Frank Manette, Lieutenant Romera, Manny Alvarez, and Thea Long, Andie Ryborg awoke with a start. She pulled the wrap tighter around her. Evan caught the movement, and guilt burned.

"Well, it seems we've caught the secretive—I might even say deceptive—heroine of this story asleep," said Manny, who'd been summoned to headquarters by the chief. The man charged with guarding Andie didn't appear pleased with himself or her. His expression seemed a mixture of embarrassment that he'd failed to detect Evan's stalking, scorn that Andie had hid it from him, and relief that she was, so far, safe.

"Let's all gather around the table, and if you need something to drink, better grab it now because Chief Manette's ready to roll with this," Vic announced. "Right, Frank?"

With a curt nod to Vic's flamingo housedress, Chief Manette observed dryly and with apparent familiarity, "Agent Shay, I trust the circus performer who got *your* luggage will return your clothes soon." Without another glance in Vic's direction, he added. "Now, please, let's sit down. Miss Long, since you are a witness, you may remain."

Evan glanced furtively at Andie as they took seats on opposite sides of the table. He tried to read her expression. *She's got to hate me.* But he couldn't see anything but fatigue and strain in her face, the skin too pale, the familiar contours unyielding as stone.

Chief Manette and Vic took either end of the long table. Thea settled quietly next to Andie. Manny and Lieutenant Romera sat on either side of Evan.

"I'd like to draw Miss Ryborg into what we've gleaned from our questioning of Mr. Evan Markham—not Jackson, as he'd led Agent Shay to believe." Turning to Andie, "You have a right to know what Mr. Markham alleges about his assaults on you and your property, Miss Ryborg. However, the FDLE and FBI are running key points of his statement through a variety of data banks for confirmation."

Chief Manette continued in his crisp, dry manner. "The short of it is this, Miss Ryborg: Mr. Markham says he was once associated with Leo Francini's cartel, but that he disenfranchised himself from it many years ago. How many, he wouldn't say. Mr. Markham hasn't been entirely forthcoming. But he has told us that—"

The door opened. Tony Ryborg swept into the room, accompanied by Warren Jacobs.

"Dad!" Andie stood quickly and went to him. As his powerful arms encircled her, everyone but Evan and Thea rose to their feet, a gesture of respect to one of their own who had become an icon of law and order.

Evan's pulse raced. He'd never seen the man up close. Only from a distance had he watched Tony Ryborg defy those who wanted him out of their way. Evan had been captivated by the strength of the man, the grit of his convictions. But now he wanted to scream at him: *Why did you ignore the threats to your own daughter!*

Chief Manette welcomed Tony, who stood with one protective arm still around Andie. *Anyone looking at her now, even some in this room, would think she was a weak, helpless Daddy's girl,* Evan thought. *But that's not her.*

Approaching to shake Tony's hand, Chief Manette said, "Tony, I'm sorry you had to visit us under these circumstances. But I'm glad you're here. We were just beginning to lay out the scenario we've uncovered from this young man's testimony." He motioned toward Evan, who, for just a second, met Tony's steely glance. "Now, you and Miss Ryborg both can hear it."

Tony greeted the assembly, his eyes falling on Thea, who seemed suddenly ill at ease. "Ma'am," Tony offered her in greeting.

"Dad, this is my friend Thea Long." Andie took his arm and led him to the woman.

Thea hesitantly offered her hand. As he gripped it, she said in a strangely formal way, "It is my privilege to meet you, Mr. Ryborg, and to be of service to your daughter."

"We're both grateful to you, ma'am," Tony responded and released her hand.

Tony pulled a chair to the table opposite Evan. Warren stood a few feet behind Tony with a clear view of the door, his holstered weapon exposed.

"Go ahead, Frank," Tony said, his eyes now leveled at Evan.

"For the last few weeks," Chief Manette began, "Evan Markham has been harassing Miss Ryborg. He's left notes in her car and at her home, calling her late at night, warning that if you didn't give up the governor's race, something terrible would happen to her or you, or both. He once appeared at a window wearing a mask and—"

Tony looked at Andie with haunted eyes. It seemed something had just occurred to him. "Was that, by chance, the snake in the tree you had to chase off?"

"I'm sorry," she answered quietly.

Evan looked at them curiously. *She didn't tell him?*

Chief Manette continued. "He has sat outside her house in the dark and watched her comings and goings. He has invaded her home in Coconut Grove and tampered with her personal effects. And just before her recent trip to Tallahassee, Mr. Markham vandalized the home, turning over furniture, damaging her paintings, and leaving one of your campaign posters splashed with red paint."

Evan could hardly bear to listen. He'd stolen only one glance at Andie, enough to see her head tucked, her face splotched red. He had done this to her and couldn't stand anymore.

"That's enough!" he cried. Manny and Lieutenant Romera both made a move to restrain him further, but Chief Manette waved them off. Evan had already told this man *why* he'd done these things. Now, Evan was determined that he, not the chief, would tell Andie.

He looked across the table at her and saw her brace against him. "You may never understand, but I beg you to try," he implored, his eyes holding hers. "Leo Francini hates your father. He hates him because your father's a good man and Leo isn't, because Tony Ryborg has the means to destroy Francini and all the others like him."

Evan noticed that Tony Ryborg had moved forward in his seat. When Evan looked back at Andie, he was almost afraid to push her further, but he had to. "He told me he would force your dad to abort his campaign. He knew threats to him wouldn't work. He'd tried that before. So he targeted you. I knew the kind of person he would send to frighten you enough to send you running home for protection. I knew that person would most likely do more than frighten you. He would hurt you. So I pretended to join Leo's cartel and made him send me instead."

Andie's face was now full on Evan, searching. "Where do I know you from?"

Evan recalled how she looked at him at the market. *She did recognize me. But how? I was always in the background.* "You don't know me."

But Evan watched as she appeared to piece together a memory puzzle. "Yes, I do. At school, at FSU. In the cafeteria. I caught you staring at me. And another time on Landis Green. It's vague, but I can see your face then." Her eyes bore into him. "Why were you watching me?"

Evan answered simply, "To keep you safe."

Andie cocked her head. "Why was that important to you?"

Tony suddenly straightened in his chair. "Mr. Markham, why should we believe you? How do we know you weren't stalking my daughter under Leo Francini's orders even at FSU? And that now you've been caught, you've concocted this tale of devotion to her welfare?"

Why can't he understand? "Leo won't stop, Mr. Ryborg. Since the threats to Andie obviously didn't persuade you to exit the race, he—"

"Did you and the mighty Francini ever consider the possibility that my daughter was stronger than either of you?" Tony spit the words. "That to run home crying to me was the last thing she'd ever do?"

Evan's eyes darted back to Andie. "Why didn't you tell him?"

"I won't let him quit!" She looked hard at her dad.

She suffered that alone? Didn't tell anyone what was happening to her? How can that be? Where does that kind of strength come from? Evan didn't understand.

Just then, a cell phone rang. It was in Chief Manette's pocket, but it didn't belong to him. It was the one he'd confiscated from Evan. As the chief retrieved it, Evan announced confidently, "It's Leo. Slide the phone over here, hit the speaker button, and don't anyone even breathe." Chief Manette shot a look to Tony, who nodded approval.

Everyone at the table turned off their phones and fell silent. Warren rushed outside the door to keep anyone from entering.

Manny held the phone in front of Evan, who answered it flatly, "Yeah."

"Where are you?" Leo demanded.

Evan took a chance. "At the boat. And you?"

"Leaving U.S. soil. A change of plans. I sent a couple of guys looking for you last night. Where were you?"

"I checked the girl's house to see if she'd slipped back into town." They were never to utter a name on the phone.

"And?"

"Not there."

"Good. Then the capital boys shouldn't have a problem."

"With what?"

"Evidently you didn't hear the big man's speech. He's not budging, so his kid's all ours."

Andie made eye contact with no one.

"What do you mean?" Evan watched Andie, her head bowed and still.

"We're going to grab her and keep her with us for a while."

Andie's head came up, grievous eyes on Evan.

"Then what?" he asked as Chief Manette scribbled a hurried note to him that read: *Where?*

"Oh, we've got a little video planned that will make her dad drop to his knees."

"At the island?" Evan asked, nodding to Chief Manette.

There was momentary silence on the other end. Then, "Yeah, the island."

"How do you know she's in Tallahassee?"

"I told you we've been watching her."

Andie shot a look at her dad, reluctant confirmation on her face.

"But I want you to stay put until we've got her. There's something else I . . ." Leo paused. "Never mind."

"What else is going on?" Evan pressed, his eye on Tony.

"You're asking a lot of questions."

"You once told me that was the only way I'd rise in the organization. Ask and learn, isn't that right?"

Leo chuckled. "Your point, kid. But this time, the less you know, the better."

"I don't understand."

"You will." Leo hung up.

Tony got up and paced. He looked back at Evan, then at Chief Manette. "Please remove the cuffs from him, Frank." That done, Evan massaged his wrists, then pulled himself closer to the table, resting his hands on top to demonstrate he had no hostile moves to make.

"Sir," Evan began, but couldn't finish.

"Just a minute, Evan," Tony said. "After what I just heard, I'm real close to believing your story. Close enough to know we've got one thing to act on immediately—hiding Andie." Evan watched Tony's ramrod demeanor soften for just a moment as he looked at his daughter. "This doesn't mean they've won," he told her. "I promise you I'm not going to quit."

Andie's eyes glistened.

"Frank and Manny, we'll need a safe house for her and heavy guard. For as long as it takes." Then Tony turned to Evan. "Now, where is this island?"

"Some remote cay on the fringe of the Bahamas. I'm not sure where. I've never been there, and Leo's always tight-lipped about it. He's got a resident army living in a compound there, and the islanders are scared to death of him. Some have paid a high price for saying the wrong things to the wrong people."

Tony nodded as if he already knew. "Okay. Now, what does your gut tell you this 'something else' is that Francini appears to be keeping from you?"

"All I know is he told me there was a bigger picture I couldn't see. And when his head thug pitched in that there were also people I couldn't see, Leo screamed at him and told me to ignore what Dingo said."

"Ray Dingo?" Vic blurted out.

Evan nodded, surprised.

"I told you I had history with that bunch."

"Quite," said Chief Manette, looking squarely at Evan. "Agent Shay was in the gun battle that took out two of her team plus Donnie Francini."

Evan stared at the frumpy woman with the silly dog and electric-fan collection as if she were an alien.

"What were the odds you'd come to roost in my back yard, Evan?" Vic asked, openly amused by his reaction. "Mighty strange, don't you think? As if someone knew you couldn't fix this thing by yourself, even though you were sure of it." She cocked one eyebrow. "Just like my husband had been sure."

She turned abruptly to Tony. "Now, I've got a pretty good notion what this 'something else' of Francini's is. It's you, Tony."

"Nothing new there," he responded without expression.

"Now hold on, Tony," Chief Manette said. "We need to assume that when Francini doesn't find Andie, he'll go after the one he *can* find. And here you are. I think we should put you under guard too."

"I won't have it," Tony declared, glancing at Warren, who had returned to the room. "I've been at this too many years to run scared now. My daughter and those dead FBI agents deserve better than that. Besides, that might not be what Francini has in mind."

"The only way to know is to let me go back to him," Evan said boldly. "And do what I've been doing for two months—pretend I'm a loyal soldier."

Chief Manette glared at him. "You have admitted to stalking, harassment, breaking and entering, and vandalism, Mr. Markham, and you expect us to turn you loose?"

"If I was a Francini faithful, why would I risk everything to run after Andie and warn her? Dingo's got people everywhere. Some of them might have even witnessed that little scene in the park and be reporting it to Leo this very moment.

"If you lock me up, you've captured a nobody. A nobody who knows nothing. If you let me continue my charade, I can uncover whatever Leo's hiding."

"No, Mr. Markham," Chief Manette answered with finality.

Evan grew angry. "How long do you think Andie can hide?" He turned from the chief to Tony. "If I don't end this, she'll never be safe. And it won't matter if you're running for governor or dog catcher. Leo's after Ryborg blood. Payment for Donnie. He'll get it if I don't stop him."

"You didn't stop him before," Manny accused.

Evan jerked his head toward Manny but couldn't summon the correct response. That would have required peeling back too many bleeding layers inside him, a piece of the truth tucked beneath each one. Instead, he answered, "You're right. I was naive enough to think that simple little plan to keep Tony Ryborg out of office would work. That Leo would back off and we could all get together for, you know, a cookout sometime. But it didn't work, and I think he's glad it didn't. Now he can play real dirty, just the way he likes."

Tony focused tightly on Evan. "What if you're right, and he finds out we brought you in? That you probably told us everything, and now you return to him a spy. We can't let you walk into that."

"It's the only option you have," Evan insisted.

"He would kill you if he knew," Vic declared.

"No, he won't," Evan answered.

"Why are you different from everyone else he's gunned down?" Vic persisted.

"Because I'm his son."

CHAPTER 21

ANDIE WAS THE FIRST to break the current of shock coursing through the conference room. "That man is your father?" she asked Evan, her eyes probing his as if a different truth were hidden there. Throughout this whole ordeal, including this bizarre gathering, Andie had barricaded herself behind an emotional wall. Hunkered down yet ready to lunge when threatened. This young man before her was the embodiment of threat, and now she understood why.

Before he could answer, the door opened and Sergeant Banks brought a file of papers in and laid it in front of Chief Manette. He opened it and began to read as the woman left and closed the door.

Evan looked down at the stack of pages. "That must be the official rundown on who Evan Markham really is," he said, his voice tight. "For those of you who didn't get a copy, it says that Evan Markham was born Evan Lansky Francini twenty-seven years ago to Nancy and Leonard Francini of Miami Beach. My father held his youngest son in his arms and marked him for all time with a name that made people shudder. Murdering gangster Meyer Lansky was my father's hero and my namesake."

A hush as dense as fog hung over the room, and something inside Andie began to uncoil.

"I didn't understand that until I was seven. Late one night, my mother woke me and told me not to make a sound. We slipped out of the house while my father and brother slept. She laid me down in the back seat of our car and we drove all night and the next day until we reached her parents' home in Tennessee. She threw away my middle and last names and gave me her maiden name. She told me never to call him *Dad* again. To forget I ever knew him."

Vic ventured the first question. "But you didn't, did you?"

Evan shook his head. "He kept showing up, maybe once or twice a year. I'd leave school one day, and he'd be standing at the curb, waiting for me."

"Were you afraid of him?" Vic asked.

"Not then. He was just a guy who told funny stories, bought things for me, took me for rides through the mountains. Mom couldn't do much about it, except call the police, which she never did."

"Why didn't she take your brother too?" Chief Manette asked sternly, still thumbing through the papers in front of him.

Evan glanced back at the file. "If you're a quick reader, you've already discovered why. By the time mom escaped her husband's violent world, my older brother had already been initiated into it. He made his first kill at sixteen and was running his own off-shore drug ring at twenty." Evan's expression grew fierce. "But he liked killing best, even helpless animals."

Andie didn't take her eyes off Evan. He'd carried her just far enough into his world to make her look hard at her own. *I'm not the only victim here. Look at him.* Evan's head was down and his mouth drawn tight. A shaft of sunlight through the window glanced off the side of his face as if trying to penetrate, to warm.

Chief Manette cleared his throat and efficiently moved on. "So, instead of entering the family business, you worked in a lumberyard for a few years, then headed to Florida State. Why there?"

Evan's eyes cut toward Andie, then back to the chief. "I don't think that's critical to what's going on now, do you?" His manner was suddenly abrupt.

"You're right," her dad allowed, glancing at the clock over the door. "Evan, it may be foolish of me, but I do believe you're trying to do what's right here. You've made some bad decisions along the way, but for some reason close to desperation, I choose to trust you. If I let you go and you run gladly back into Leo's arms, well, we haven't lost much, as you say. You've learned little from our meeting today that would be of use to you or Leo.

"If everything you tell us is true, though, we could lose a very important young man if we release you to some undercover sting to reel in your own father. You could destroy yourself doing it. Vic isn't the only one who knows what Leo Francini and his boys are capable of. And I'm not so sure his son is off limits."

Evan seemed to ponder that too. "But I have to return. There's no other way to track his moves."

"If we let you go," Chief Manette submitted hesitantly, looking warily at Andie's dad, "we'll fit a GPS transmitter to your boat and car, Evan, and give you a secure cell phone with another tracker on it. You'll use it to report to a hotline as often as you can. If you somehow lose the phone, we can still follow you by boat or car. What's the chance he'll fly you somewhere?"

"The choppers are mostly for cargo. He keeps them some-where on the mainland, I think."

"How is he planning to transport Miss Ryborg?" Chief Manette looked apologetically at her.

"She would be cargo," Evan said without hesitation.

Andie stifled a wild impulse to laugh, a long uproarious release of tension. Instead, she took a deep breath and pretended this was happening to someone else. It might well be, for the impersonal way they all spoke of her, like she was meat about to be packaged and shipped. "Before anyone else takes a crack at disposing of me, I'd like to plan my own route out of here." All heads turned toward her. "I already know the place to go."

"Miss Ryborg, we'll provide a secure environment for you," Chief Manette said. "We have such places already manned and waiting to take you in."

"Where?" she asked.

With the briefest glance toward Evan, Chief Manette answered, "I can't tell you that right now."

"He means I might tell Leo," Evan snapped. He suddenly pushed back his chair and made a move to stand, then stopped. "Do you mind if I go to the restroom? You can send as many guards with me as you want. Check the bathroom first and make sure no one's planted a weapon there for me like everybody knows gangsters do." He looked at her dad, and Evan's shoulders slumped. "I'm sorry. Sorry for everyone here."

Chief Manette looked at Manny and gestured toward the door.

FATAL LOYALTY

Andie watched Manny and Evan stand, Evan a head taller and much leaner. He wore faded jeans and a collared shirt that hung loose below his belt, sleeves rolled to the elbows revealing strong, tanned arms. The shirt was yellow, the color of the umbrella he'd left on her front porch that night, luring her inside to see how he'd torn apart her home. She couldn't look at him anymore and turned away.

When they left the room, Andie got up and walked to the window. Dark clouds were pushing up from the horizon, on time for the afternoon soaking. She couldn't see the bay but felt it tug at her. That's when she told them she wanted to spend the next two months at a house in the middle of Biscayne Bay. "Just until the election. That's as long as I will hide."

It was almost two hours before they let Evan back into the room. By then, every argument had been made for and against the Stiltsville plan. In the end, though, calls had been made, and the director of the park service had ordered one of the houses hastily, and discreetly, prepared for occupancy, though he wasn't told for whom.

From there, arrangements fell quickly into place. Vic would accompany Evan back to his boat, where he would begin the wait for Leo's next instructions. Andie was to remain at FDLE headquarters until dark. She would then be transported to the most unlikely safe house Chief Manette had imagined, yet he had admitted that *unlikely* to him might be *inconceivable* to those who hunted Andie Ryborg.

꒳

As everyone headed their separate ways, Thea approached Tony and asked, "How long will you stay in Miami?"

"Until I'm sure Andie is safely tucked away," he answered, just then noticing that Andie was following Evan Markham out of the room. "I'm speaking on Miami Beach Monday morning. Then, well, I'm not sure what I'll do." He looked toward Evan. "A lot depends on that young man."

Thea followed Tony's gaze. "Where will you stay?" she asked.

"We're booked into a hotel."

Thea seemed surprised. "But Miss Shay thinks you're in danger too. A hotel seems so public."

"She's right, sir," Warren said from his post at the door.

Before Tony could object, Thea eagerly suggested, "But I can house you and all your staff on a private estate surrounded by a high, gated wall. We've got cameras and security sensors surrounding the whole property. It belongs to my employer, who only uses it a couple of times a year. I can get his permission within the hour, and you can move right in."

Tony cocked his head at the woman as if uncertain of her motive. "Ma'am, I'm grateful for your offer and—"

"And we think it could be just the place for Mr. Ryborg to spend a few nights," Warren jumped in, obviously ignoring Tony's silent reprimand. "Of course, I'd need to inspect the property first and, uh, do a bit of a background check. Procedure, you understand."

"Yes, I understand that none of you know me, though Andie has made something of a safe haven of my home already. And I'm so pleased to offer it now to you."

That evening, Thea would lead Tony, his aides, and a contingent of law enforcement personnel to the secluded home on the bay. Against the pull of his own heart, Tony had decided Andie should remain separate from him for her safety.

ॐ

"You didn't answer my question," Andie said, coming up behind Evan. He had followed Chief Manette from the room for a debriefing before leaving with Vic.

Evan turned abruptly and looked down into Andie's face. His piercing dark eyes swept over her, and she stepped back from him, still afraid of the one who'd caused her so much torment. But there was too much left unanswered to let him just walk away.

"I asked you why my safety was so important to you," she persisted.

Evan looked at Chief Manette. "Sir, may I speak with Miss Ryborg?"

The chief didn't answer immediately, but her dad did. He'd overheard the request as he and Thea had emerged from the conference room. "If it's okay with you, Frank, let these two have their say briefly, but not alone."

Chief Manette instructed Manny Alvarez and one other officer to accompany Evan and Andie to a small, nearby courtyard.

Evan looked back at Andie. "I have no right to ask you to trust me, not after what I've done to you. But I'm begging you to. Will you go with me?" He glanced sideways at the hovering escort. "With *all* of us?"

Andie ignored the weak attempt at levity. *He asks me to trust him? How ludicrous.*

"Andie, please," Evan implored.

If this was an act, Andie thought, just one more part of a skillfully contrived charade, she was a fool to fall for it. But she wanted answers and started down the hall.

As the four entered the courtyard, she noticed her dad take a position near the glass door, the only passage to and from the small garden.

The schefflera trees ringing the concrete patio dripped remnants of the afternoon shower. An effusive cloud of steam enfolded the visitors, filling their lungs with its languid moisture. It was the time Andie usually loved best, full of primal, jungle essence that made her think on the origins of life. At this moment, though, that essence was cloying, almost suffocating.

"I didn't notice when it rained, did you?" Evan asked, leading them to a couple of dry chairs beneath a canvas awning. Manny and the officer stood nearby.

Andie followed but didn't comment. She hadn't come out here to talk about the weather, though she sensed he was just reaching for some normalcy between them.

Then he began. "I always felt it was my fault that Leo and my brother were hoodlums. That if my mother and I hadn't fled from them, I might have stopped them, changed them somehow. The few times Leo came around, I tried to persuade him to become a plumber or a car salesman, anything but a gangster. He just laughed at me."

Andie didn't interrupt.

"He'd tell me things I didn't want to know, like when he'd killed off some of the competition, other traffickers. My kid's mind reasoned that maybe that wasn't so bad. The fewer of them, the better off the rest of us were." He looked up into the trees, and Andie saw a stark sadness in his face.

"For years, I knew who he'd killed and why he did it."

"Why didn't you tell anyone?"

Evan looked at the ground, then slowly up at her. "I believed there was a special corner in hell for anyone who betrayed his father. Besides, his ramblings started sounding more like fantasy, and I didn't know what was true and what wasn't—until one day a few years ago when he told me he was going to take care of Tony Ryborg once and for all."

Andie involuntarily flinched. Evan reached to touch her shoulder. His hand was warm and gentle, but she moved away from it, at the same time signaling Manny that all was well.

"I'm sorry, Andie. I'd better not say any more." He sat back in his chair.

"No. I need to know exactly why you did those things to me." She watched him struggle to answer. "Please, forgive me."

It was raw and unmasked. She'd never seen a more honest plea. *But I can't forgive. Not now.* Then something returned to her from her mother's teaching. She'd said: "Andie, God tells us to forgive others just as he has forgiven us. And it's not just for their sake, but ours. Anger is a cancer that eats at us from inside until we forgive the one who's wronged us."

"I need to understand, Evan." It was the first time Andie had spoken his name, and it made her feel even more vulnerable.

He drew a deep breath and let it out quickly. "Leo told me how your dad had shut down one of the cartel's most lucrative networks—from the Colombian supplier, to Leo, to the street reps, all the way to the money launderer in Bermuda. Then your dad raided a nest of grow houses Leo had just set up in Tampa and carted his best boys off to prison."

Evan looked squarely at Andie. "It was Leo who sent an assassin to your home."

The horror of that night flickered like an old movie reel in her mind, and she looked away.

"Then he told me about you," Evan continued. Andie looked back at him. "Where you went to school. What you studied, when and where you studied." He paused as if to let that soak in. It did.

"They *were* watching," she whispered.

Evan nodded. "I didn't know anything about you, what he might do to you or when. I just had this crazy notion that if I were nearby, I could stop him, unlike all the times before. After the years of hiding who I was, I might finally redeem myself in someone's eyes. I wasn't sure whose."

"And you couldn't tell me then?"

"For a couple of years, he seemed to have forgotten about you and your dad. Then the ranting began again. I'd decided to go to your dad and tell him everything I knew, to risk that corner in hell. But soon after, my brother was killed, and my dad disappeared back to the islands. I thought it was over until he hatched this plan to 'just harass you,' he said. And you know the rest. I thought it would work, and he'd be out of your life. I was wrong, and I'm sorry."

Andie grew restless. She stood up and walked toward a yellow allemande vine scaling a nearby wall. Its delicate, yawning blooms drew her into their sunny hearts, and for a moment, she rested in the distraction.

"Andie?" Evan had approached her, causing both officers to draw closer. "Andie, are you all right?"

He was so close. Yet she wasn't afraid. If she didn't turn around, he would leave. But she did turn, looking at him as if for the first time. "You understand, don't you?"

Evan frowned. "What do you mean?"

"You know what it's like to hide from evil. To try to deny it's there. But all the while you watch for it, on a peaceful day under a tree in the middle of campus or walking to the mailbox in front of your home. You try not to look, but you know it's there. You can never escape it."

Evan didn't take his eyes from hers. "Yes, you can, Andie. Not all of it, not all of the time. But there's one evil I can stop."

Andie looked up into his face, resisting an impulse to touch the pain she saw there, to dispel it if she could. But why? He'd inflicted as much on her.

"Andie," he said softly, "will you trust me?"

I don't even know you. Silence was her answer.

CHAPTER 22

❧

THE BLONDE ROCKED to the rhythm of Saturday mariners steadily plying the Intracoastal Waterway. The afternoon sun glinted off the riled waters as Ray Dingo cautiously approached the same boat he'd admired when he and Leo had visited the day before. He punched in a code to the dock security gate and, after glancing quickly around him, proceeded to a set of portable stairs connecting to a gangway onto the boat.

"Come aboard, Ray," said Nick Jarvis from the deck of the boat, a black New York Yankees cap covering his bald head. The business suit Dingo had seen the man wear on the balcony with Leo had been replaced by a blue denim shirt tucked neatly into tan chinos. "It's best we sit inside," Jarvis said.

Dingo followed the man into a handsome salon of polished teak, built-in seating, navy and lime cushions, and a deep-pile white carpet. Navy curtains remained drawn over every window.

Dingo settled into a chair nearest the door he'd just entered. "We can't find her," he reported. "But we're working on it."

"We?" asked Jarvis, who had pulled a high stool from the bar and peered down at Dingo.

"Well, me and Leo's Tallahassee guys."

"And Evan?"

Dingo sneered. "That's why I wanted to see you. I don't trust him. I think he's got something up his sleeve. I'm pretty sure Leo suspects something too. Son or no son. I've been at this a long time, and I know the smell of a fake. I got a real good whiff of him."

"Does Leo know you're suspicious?"

"No way. Oh, I joke with him about the college boy getting his hands dirty, but I learned a long time ago that you don't mess with Leo's family."

Jarvis leaned back against the bar, his lips curled smugly. "Is that so?"

"You better believe it. When one of Leo's own men tried to set up Donnie Francini, I watched Leo chop off the man's toes one at a time before throwing him overboard. The idiot thought if Donnie was blown away in a bungled op, he'd be next in line for Francini's crown."

"And if he knew you were here?" Jarvis suggested with obvious pleasure.

Dingo went still, a menacing shadow stealing across his face.

"Oh, don't worry, Ray," Jarvis said in a light, placating tone. "He'll never know who you really work for. Who we all work for."

Jarvis removed his hat and scratched a spot on top of his head, then replaced the cap. "But make no mistake. If there's anyone Leo can't control—say, a son or an ex-wife—I'll do it for him." Jarvis smiled. Dingo did not.

"It's probably time I made that clear to Leo," Jarvis added in his cocky, self-assured manner. "Leo's in this too deep to get sloppy about the prodigal son he thinks has returned to his father's nest. I'll have to impress that upon him."

Dingo stood up and looked down on Jarvis, who was still perched on his stool. "Leo's no fool. He'll wonder why you're suddenly concerned about his boy."

Jarvis bristled. "I hope that's not body language you're pulling on me, Dingo. It would ruin a nice working relationship." Just then, a young man entered the salon from an adjoining room, the handle of a gun emerging from his waistband.

Dingo backed away. "I didn't mean anything by it, Nick. You can be sure of that." He glared at the young man.

"I'm rarely certain of anything, Dingo. It's the downside of dealing with my kind of clients." Jarvis stepped off the stool and extended a hand to Dingo. "Thank you for coming to share your concerns with me. When all this is over, I'll reward your loyalty." He clapped Dingo on the shoulder and steered him off the boat.

When Dingo was gone, Jarvis placed a cell call and left a coded message for someone. He waited several hours for the reply—the permission. When it finally came, he took his phone into the stateroom of his yacht. He opened the curtains to bask in the waning light and tapped in the direct number for Leo Francini. The prospect of flexing authority over the mighty Francini gave Jarvis pleasure. But when that conversation ended, he pulled the curtains back over the windows and lay still on his bed. Dingo's words suddenly returned to him: "You don't mess with Leo's family." Jarvis knew he'd probably just made the biggest mistake of his life.

CHAPTER 23

∽

"WHERE ARE MY GROCERIES?" Evan asked with a scowl.

Vic looked sharply at him. "Same place as mine. Did you expect unclaimed, open bags of food to last long in a public place?"

Evan ignored her and kept staring out the window of the old Dodge Dart. Chief Manette had sent someone to retrieve it from the market. It was now early evening and they were catching the last wave of rush-hour traffic from downtown Miami, headed back to *Misfit*.

"You know, I've got a freezer full of grouper and a nice melon at the house," Vic offered. "I might even locate some squash. You like yours fried?"

Evan glared at her. "There's a psycho drug lord running amok out there and you want to fry squash?" he said with a bite. "Besides, you stuck a gun in my face. You don't do something like that to me and then invite me over for grouper. Why did you do that?"

"Invite you for grouper or stick a gun in your face?" Vic asked with no expression.

Evan came at her again. "And where do you get off posing as some ditsy hausfrau, pretending to be my friend when all the time you're stalking me?"

"It seems entirely appropriate that I stalked a stalker. Besides, I only followed you one time, to Andie's house. And I wouldn't have done that if your visitors hadn't alerted me."

"Who were they?"

"Some vermin I recognized from old days in the trenches. Francini types, though I couldn't be sure what rat hole they belonged in now. It might have been just a friendly call, but something told me it wasn't. And by the way, I really am a ditsy hausfrau who posed as an FBI agent for thirty-six years."

"So are you retired or not?" There was still an edge to his voice.

Vic nodded. "Just a few months before you tied up at my place. But not entirely. I'm a sometimer. Sometimes I reactivate, like today. Still got the badge, the gun, and a whole arsenal of intuition. Though it didn't take much of that to know you were no novelist."

Evan finally cracked a grin. "It seems we're not the same two people who rode to the market together this morning."

Vic looked thoughtful. "But your masquerade isn't over. You're still the dutiful son come home to Papa with nothing on his mind but avenging his brother's death. Right?"

Evan watched a couple of young boys stealing one more romp before sunset. They were rolling in the grass of someone's front yard, throwing fake punches at each other while a girl in pink Crocs yelled for them to grow up.

"I'm surprised Leo hasn't questioned that part of the scenario," Evan said. "More than anyone, he knows how little I cared for my brother." He could still see Donnie pumping two bullets into the dog Evan's mother had given him. The Lab had growled at the teenage Donnie Francini one time too many.

"I'm not in favor of what you're about to do, Evan." Vic had just turned onto the gravel road to her house. "There are too many ways we could lose you."

"And more ways you could lose the Ryborgs."

"We can cover them, but not you."

Evan made a gesture dismissing concern for himself, then changed the subject. "Do you know where they're taking Andie?"

She looked hard into his face, then answered flatly, "Not for you to know. Sorry. Now how about that squash?"

Evan didn't answer. The sudden ring of his cell phone drowned all conversation.

Vic grabbed Evan's arm. "If he asks where you are, tell him the truth. They could be watching."

Evan nodded and flipped open the phone, hitting the speaker button. "Yeah."

Without preamble, Leo ordered, "I want you out of there right now!"

"What's happened?"

"They can't find her and . . . and you need to leave now!"

"Wait a minute. You haven't even asked *me* to look for her. Why not?"

"No need to. The others are."

"What others?"

"Never mind." There was a brief silence. "Evan, you could be in danger. I'll explain when you get here. Take the boat. Call me about twenty miles west of the Biminis and I'll give you the coordinates. Leave now!" Leo didn't wait for Evan to respond.

Evan and Vic stared at each other for just a moment before Vic got out and dashed for the house, ordering Evan to follow. Inside, she hastily called the bureau while loading another handgun. "Grab the binoculars on that table and go to every window in the house. See what's out there."

Thirty minutes later, Vic and Evan left the house and walked casually toward *Misfit*, Vic chatting loudly about how to fry squash. Evan carried a casserole dish loosely covered with foil. Beneath the foil lay the Glock .40 handgun Vic had just given him. Vic's sidearm was inside one of the big pockets of her dress, her hand firmly on the handle. With her free hand, she pulled a small cart with as much food and water as she could hurriedly gather for Evan's impromptu voyage.

When they reached the boat, Evan went aboard with the loaded casserole dish and food bags. Vic remained on the dock, her hand in her pocket and shaded eyes scanning for the two men Evan had just spotted in the woods behind the dock—about seventy yards from the boat, he'd gauged, even in the waning light. But so far, no movement from that direction.

As the twin diesel engines roared to life, Evan hopped back on the dock to untie the lines. "Let me know if the fish are biting," Vic said over the noise. She patted Evan on the shoulder, then in a hushed voice said, "Look for them about two miles out."

CHAPTER 24

NIGHT HAD CAST ITSELF like a black tarp over the sea. The red and green running lights of the cabin cruiser were mere Crayola specks against the dark. The occupants of the boat, a man and two women, said little to each other as they slipped into a channel angling east through Biscayne Bay. Saturday night revelers were anchored here and there in their rollicking sailboats and motor yachts. But the farther from shore, the more lonely the cruiser's quest.

A light chop had risen with the tide, and the twenty-seven-foot Sea Ray cut a smooth but slow path to its destination. Her hair tucked inside a baseball cap and a jacket zipped almost to her chin, Andie sat forlornly at the back of the boat. She looked behind her where the boat trailed a wake like a rooster tail, its wet feathers occasionally flinging sharp bits of saltwater at her. Beyond the wake lay her trampled independence, her abandoned bungalow with its starlight ceiling and caladiums, her art students who must wonder what had happened to the passionate young woman who made them see beyond the obvious. *What did happen to that person?* Andie thought, then slumped deeper into the seat.

All Andie knew was the obvious. Someone wanted to destroy her. And her dad. Back there was something she couldn't control, something she'd failed to elude. And now she was fleeing like a mindless child, tended by the man driving the boat and the woman seated opposite her.

"How much farther?" Andie called over the howl of the engine. *Just like a child.*

Sergeant Cleo Banks held up two big fists and flashed all ten fingers twice.

I guess that means twenty. Minutes? It didn't matter. Andie nodded that she understood and smiled, receiving in return only a slight spread of the lips from Sergeant Banks, now in cargo pants and a gray hoodie. The woman who earlier that day had been assigned to help make Andie comfortable was going to be her roommate. And she hadn't yet given Andie permission to call her Cleo.

Andie stood and went to the helm. She dropped into the seat beside Manny Alvarez, who gave her a brief but pleasant glance. Andie hoped he hadn't endured a superior's wrath for missing signs of Evan's handiwork. How could Manny know if she hadn't told him? And she'd been quick to hide the evidence. Besides, he wasn't supposed to be her round-the-clock bodyguard, until now.

"Manny, I'm sorry."

With his hands firmly on the wheel, dodging swells while staying on course, he grinned affably. "No problem, kiddo. If you behave yourself from now on, we'll make it through this. Don't you worry."

Without caring how it looked to Sergeant Banks, Andie threw an arm around the kindly officer's neck and hugged.

"Whoa, now." He chuckled. "You won't be liking me so much when I tell you the new rules of the house." His mood grew serious. "It's not going to be easy for you. But a whole lot safer than where you were." He pointed toward a few scattered lights on the horizon.

Andie squinted in the direction of her new home. Stiltsville. Much like a set of oil rigs anchored to bedrock in the middle of the sea. She remembered Thea's description: *like being alone in a faraway world.*

But I don't have to be alone, do I, Lord?

Andie looked again at the lights of Stiltsville, now growing larger. The night seemed not so black.

She was about to ask Manny where he learned to handle a boat when he suddenly twisted backward in his seat. Whipping back around, he caught her arm. "Andie, get below!" Then he turned again to look behind.

Before she could clear the seat, Sergeant Banks had grabbed her other arm and was pulling her forcefully down the steps into the cabin. With gun drawn, the woman hovered in a protective stance as she guided Andie inside and closed the door, then returned topside with Manny.

Only then did Andie feel the vibration of an oncoming boat. She rushed to the open starboard window of the cabin and looked out. Approaching from behind was a much larger vessel with a high bow. Andie's pulse pounded in her throat. She felt trapped and defenseless inside the cabin but knew better than to show herself. *How could anyone have followed us?* They'd smuggled her out of FDLE headquarters, wrapped in blankets on the back floorboard of an ordinary police cruiser, one of four leaving at once but in different directions to throw off anyone watching. From there, they had headed to a remote landing south of Coral Gables, where Manny and Sergeant Banks had waited in this civilian-looking boat.

The deep growl of the other boat's engines grew louder as its bow pulled even with the window. Andie crouched out of sight. She noticed that Manny didn't alter course or speed. Venturing a peak outside, she saw, to her great relief, that the boat was passing them. But a few moments later, she saw a bright beam of light rake the other boat's stern, illuminating the name painted there in tall, angular letters: *Misfit.*

The name meant nothing to her, but apparently it did to Manny. Through the cabin wall, she heard him hailing someone by radio.

"Tarpon calling base. Over."

"Base. Go ahead."

"Have Thunderhead in sight," Manny reported. "ETA thirty."

"Roger that."

Andie could no longer see the boat called *Misfit.* She opened the cabin door and peered at Manny.

"It's okay," he said, his voice calm. "Come on up."

"What just happened, Manny?" Andie blurted out when she reached the top step. She turned quickly to see *Misfit*'s wake rolling toward them.

"We didn't know who that was until I strobed the back of him."

"And . . ."

Manny turned a somber eye on Andie. "It was a young man who might as well be in a hurricane hunter for where he's headed. I don't know why we're letting him go."

Evan! "Where's he going?"

"To save the day," Sergeant Banks quipped snidely.

Andie watched the retreating lights of *Misfit* until they were just pin dots on the verge of disappearing. The prayer came unspoken: *God, go with him.*

CHAPTER 25

SHE WAS A SLOW, PONDEROUS SHIP of gangly proportions and the sweetest escape Evan knew. Even *Misfit*'s weathered old wheel felt good in his hands, and he gripped it as one clinging to the last bit of life.

As he eased the faithful trawler from the Miami River into the bay, evening winds drove a spate of sounds at him. A large catamaran ablaze with light and music was anchored near the mouth of the river, its half-naked occupants cavorting loudly across its broad deck, its tall mast rocking with the exotic Latin beat. A girl in a leopard-print bikini raised a martini glass to Evan as he passed close by. It appeared to him that she'd refilled the glass many times that evening. She called to him, "Hey, sugar. Come party with us."

Something made him think of Andie, of her courage, her selflessness. Then he looked back at the girl on the boat and silently answered her invitation. *Why would I want to do that?*

To his port side was a low-slung Cigarette the size of a stealth missile. As Evan passed, the driver gunned his ferocious engines and launched his entourage toward, well, nowhere in particular, Evan guessed. He patted *Misfit*'s wheel. "It's okay, girl," he said aloud. "It's just a lot of empty noise. But you're the real thing." And again, he thought of Andie.

As he cleared the neon baubles strung along Miami's downtown shoreline, a darker, more subtle night welcomed him into its fold. It felt good to ride the swells and taste the briny air. He wished he could change course and sail on forever, maybe south to trace Drake's Passage through the Virgin Islands. Maybe northeast to Bermuda. Or into New York Harbor. *Lady Liberty, meet Misfit. She's your kind of gal, one of your "tempest-tossed yearning to breathe free."*

Evan had seen none of those places. His mother had taken
him nowhere outside Tennessee, preferring the security of her
parents' home. It seemed the gutsy, midnight escape from her
husband's snare had demanded all she had, and there was no
more, not even for her young son. Once they arrived in Tennessee, she seemed to have cut some invisible tether between
them, letting Evan wander far from her. She'd offered him no
more shelter than her parents' stifling house, no more encouragement than the threat that if Evan ever got into trouble like his
brother, her parents would surely kick him out of their happy,
nurturing home. Because after all, he was a gangster's son. Getting into trouble was bound to happen. The whole family knew
it, she'd said. So, the first time he was expelled from school for
fighting in the cafeteria, he was booked into a military school
in the next state.

Evan had tried to call his mom several times since arriving
in Miami. She'd refused all but one of his calls. He remembered
that last conversation . . .

"If you've gone back to your father, just stay down there and
don't come home again."

"Mom, I'm not with him. I'm just trying to keep him from
hurting someone."

"Who?"

"It's best you don't know."

"Oh, I used to hear that plenty from your father."

"Mom, you know me. You know I'm not like him. Please, just
trust me."

"Your grandparents are still furious that you quit school."

"Mom—"

"They say you'll turn out no good just like your brother."

"Mom, please—"

"They say you should never come here again."

"And what do *you* say, Mom?"

"I say . . . oh, I don't know what I say, except you are my boy
and I love you. But right now, I can't talk to you anymore. Papa
might hear me. He gets so mad."

She hung up.

Evan believed that one day, he'd make his mom understand what he was doing and why. As soon as he could, he would draw her away from the paralyzing co-dependence of her family and help her live her own life. One day.

Leaving downtown Miami, the narrow bay channel ahead was clear except for one boat. Evan would pass on its starboard side. Pulling almost even, he glanced at the shadowy figure of a man at the helm. Evan appreciated the other driver's steady, unwavering pace, unlike many erratic boaters he'd encountered around Miami's teeming shore.

But just as Evan cleared the other boat's wake and nosed ahead, a beam of light strafed the back of *Misfit*. Evan pivoted quickly, shielding his face against the brazen light. *What does he think he's doing?* Then he thought, *No, it can't be them. It's too soon. Two miles, Vic said.*

Evan ignored what he believed to be just a nosy, rude boater and accelerated out to sea. He glanced to his left at the peculiar little cottages perched above the water on stilts. An impossible place to live, he thought. Lonely and vulnerable to the elements. He'd read that no one occupied them anymore, but just then, he noticed the boat that had beamed him was leaving the channel and heading straight for one of the "impossible" houses.

He dismissed its passengers as curiosity seekers and focused on what lay ahead, though he wasn't sure what that was. He had been less concerned about Leo's warning than Vic had been. Odd that she would trust what Leo said. "But I heard the voice of a father warning his son of danger," she'd told Evan when he objected to any urgent measures. In the end, she'd had her way. Evan smiled to himself. And the ways of Special Agent Victoria ("but that's too highfalutin' given my present station in life") Shay were unlike any he'd ever known.

Once she'd confirmed the presence of two visitors to her woods, Vic had flown into action. On her say-so alone, an unofficial-looking FBI boat would soon run sweep behind Evan almost to Bahamian waters. "Just in case anyone follows you from Miami," she'd explained. "From there, I'm afraid you're on your own. I don't know what's waiting for you there, son, but the only reason we're cutting the hook out of your mouth and sending you back is for information. Once we get the coordinates on Leo, we'll take care of him, with an assist from the Bahamian government. But if there's someone else out there we don't know about, we're trusting you to get us a name and address, so we can drop them a card sometime. Then you hightail it back here, and we'll talk about clearing a few charges against you."

Because it was still light when Evan needed to leave, Vic had told him of a small marina down another remote finger of the river. "You go there and wait until well after dark, maybe ten," she'd ordered. "Those two in the woods will never find you there." She'd given him money for gas and more food at the marina store. "Even shady characters like yourself have to eat."

Evan would soon reach the two-mile rendezvous with the FBI. They would signal, then fall in at a distance far enough to appear unrelated to *Misfit*, yet close enough to intercede if trouble struck.

A mile out, Evan turned and looked back at the shrinking skyline. Somewhere back there, he knew, they'd be hustling Andie to a hideout. He wished they'd told him where to find her. *She doesn't trust me, may never forgive me. I'd just like to see her again.*

Evan searched inside himself. *I've watched that girl and her father for three years, telling myself it was my duty because my father wanted them dead.* Just then, an image he couldn't restrain flashed in his head: a slain Andie crumpled on the ground, her flowing dark hair matted with blood, her eyes open and fixed—on him.

"No!" he cried to the night and loosened his grip on the wheel. An errant swell caught *Misfit* broadside, and her body pitched and rolled, nearly pulling the wheel from Evan's weakened grip. He lurched forward as if suddenly sprung from some mental crypt and struggled to regain control of his ship. A slap of seawater drenched his right side as he brought the boat to an even keel.

Clothes dripping and eyes stinging, he scolded himself. The sea on this particular night was no place to lose focus. He switched on the high-beam spot off the bow and searched for a pattern to the swells. The confluence of bay waters and open seas where currents sometimes collided could summon the unpredictable. But he was ready for what suddenly appeared about two hundred yards off his port side. Three quick blasts of light followed by one long beam. And again ten seconds later. The sequence continued until Evan answered with the same code, but in reverse order.

For the next two hours, Evan motored steadily toward Bimini, his progress digitized by beams from the GPS tracker attached to *Misfit* that were bounced to an orbiting satellite and downloaded at the FBI field office in Miami. The agents following Evan by boat kept visual contact with him all the way to the first stop in the Bahamian archipelago, reporting no hostile interception. As Leo had instructed, Evan texted his arrival in Bimini using the Bahamian cell phone Leo had given him. Leo responded in text with the coordinates of the secret Francini compound.

After shifting the boat into neutral, Evan consulted his charts and discovered his journey would take him another four hours south to a small cay off Andros Island. He logged the coordinates he'd been given into his handheld GPS, then picked up the cell phone Chief Manette had provided. It was time to transmit to the agents following him. They'd be waiting for those same coordinates. He stared down at the phone's lighted panel. All he had to do was punch in a few numbers, and that special little corner in hell would be his.

Just enter the numbers. That's all. At some point, a platoon of lawmen would swoop down on Leo Francini and end his torturous reign.

Evan held the phone tight in his hand and looked into the black that surrounded him. Onto that opaque screen sprang an image he'd blocked for so many years. It was an empty baseball field near the home he'd shared with his parents and brother in Miami Beach. The mental picture grew sharper. His dad was pitching baseballs to him from the mound. When six-year-old Evan finally connected with one, his dad ran to him cheering wildly. "It's a home run, Evan!" he cried. "Let's go, son! Daddy will run with you."

Daddy. What a travesty. Love his little boy one day, slit a man's throat the next. What Daddy does that?

Then against the same screen appeared Andie's lifeless face looking back at him.

Evan entered the coordinates into the phone, slowly and deliberately as if each number were a nail sealing the lid on a box where demons hid. Then it was over. The son had betrayed the father, and Evan knew they would both answer for their sins.

CHAPTER 26

MANNY EASED THE BOAT up to the stilt house. On the approach, Andie could see its outline against three dim spotlights. It was shaped like a matchbox, but one propped up on a crisscross network of concrete pilings. She'd seen similarly shaped pavilions at the ends of long fishing piers.

Fishing pier! With an old dance hall at the end where three kids could climb inside on a day when they should be in school. The old story her mom had told her suddenly came to life. She could see the three children steal inside the forbidden hideout, hear them laugh and dance across the rotted boards as the old transistor radio pumped fifties rock 'n' roll. She imagined her mother's childish face alight with mischief, with the flush of discovery, a teasing danger. Then suddenly, the pier collapsed.

Like the dance hall teetering over the ocean, the stilt house now loomed overhead as Manny cut the engines at the dock and hopped out. While he and Sergeant Banks tied the lines, Andie stared up at her own hideout. What discoveries awaited inside? How long before the collapse? *Trust,* she reminded herself. *Just trust.*

It took many trips to unload everything Andie, Manny and Sergeant Banks would need for their stay in the middle of nowhere. In the gear were Andie's art supplies. She would be staying here under a fictitious name and the guise of an artist-in-residence, coinciding with a real program the park service had initiated in the last year. So far, only one artist had been selected for the unusual residency, but he'd run "screaming into the night," so it was told, unable to cope with the isolation, no matter the stunning views and golden moments of quiet contemplation. One golden week, and he was out of there. Andie was looking at a month, maybe longer depending on conditions, Chief Manette had said.

Meanwhile, Manny and Sergeant Banks would rotate shifts with other armed guards, ensuring Andie fresh changes of roommates along with the linens.

The house had been built of concrete block and treated wood sometime in the sixties. An open deck with steel railings encircled the dwelling. "In the evenings, you'll want to settle on the western porch because sunset is the time of the dancing waters," the park director had said. "You'll see what I mean."

Someone had already folded back hurricane shutters from the sliding glass windows and doors. The same someone, Andie guessed, who'd left a fresh pot of pink geraniums on the open deck. She could only imagine the administrative tailspin this bizarre, eleventh-hour sequestering had created at the park office, yet someone had thought to bring flowers.

Inside, accommodations were sparse but clean. In one big room, a long, dining bar separated the living area from the kitchen. Eight wooden stools with green vinyl cushions lined the length of it, their scuffed legs and crossbars evidence of much use. In the living area sat a rattan sofa and two matching chairs, all with tan vinyl cushions, and a yard-sale assortment of lamps.

Worn, white drapes were pulled over every window and door. Each of the two bedrooms was furnished with twin beds without headboards, boxy wooden desks, stick chairs, and plain chests of drawers. Plywood floors were covered with inexpensive beige carpeting, and the walls were white-painted paneling. Electricity came from a generator, and water from the sky. Drinking water was bottled and stacked in the kitchen. The house had all the warmth of an army barracks.

But that didn't matter once Andie drew back the drapes and looked west. The skyline of Miami blazed like a giant tiara against black velvet, the sudden beauty of it snatching her breath from her. *Light against dark. Why are they always paired? Do they define each other? Would we know what good was if there were no evil?*

Andie opened the sliding glass door and walked to the edge of the deck, transfixed on the sight before her. *I'm in exile,* she whispered to the distant city that could no longer contain her. *Banished. Left to wait helplessly while others fight my battle for me.*

Something quickened inside. "God," Andie spoke softly into the night, "please protect those who stand between me and the ones who hunt me. Don't let anyone else die for my sake." She squeezed her eyes shut. "You've already done that." A wave clapped loudly against the pilings, and Andie jumped.

And one more thing: help me understand Evan Markham.

Andie looked toward the channel she and Evan had just traveled separately and remembered his boat name. *Misfit.* She smiled resignedly. *Me too, Evan.*

"There you are," Manny said, joining her at the deck railing. He looked across the vast bay at the city he served. "Look at her all stretched out there like the seductress she is," he said. "She's like one of those, you know, sirens you read about in mythology—who lure the unsuspecting, then dash them against the rocks."

He turned to see Andie eyeing him strangely. "What?" he asked, feigning insult. "You didn't think I could read?"

"Not big words."

"I see this is going to be a long, painful assignment." He turned around and glanced over the house, sighing loudly. "Here we are, sitting on poles sunk into the bottom of the bay, surrounded by sharks, and heating our pitiful frozen dinners in that tiny microwave in there. Have you seen the kitchen?" He didn't stop for an answer. "The folks who used to lease this place must have had every meal catered by water taxi. That stove hasn't seen the first batch of arroz con pollo or fried plantains. And I don't see any in our future either."

Andie patted his stomach. "Then I'd say we got here just in time, before this big thing explodes." She giggled with relief that once more, the big Cuban cop had made her laugh. "Come on, Manny. I've got a surprise for you."

She led him back into the house, stepping carefully around columns of boxes rising from the floor like stalagmites. They were full of clothes, toiletries, linens, books and games for passing the long hours, and non-perishable food. On the kitchen counter sat three coolers. Opening one of them, Andie presented Manny with a long casserole dish covered in aluminum foil. "Shrimp and scallops in dill sauce over fettuccine. Can you do Italian?"

"Who slipped that in on us?" Manny asked, reaching eagerly for the dish.

"Thea, the curious one. Manny, I've never met anyone like her. She took me into her home when she didn't even know me. And I knew nothing about her. Still don't, really."

"From her interview and the data we brought up on her, there's not a whole lot to tell," he said, placing the dish on the counter and peeking beneath the foil. "Grew up on a Miccosukee reservation, the product of a Miccosukee father and a Scots-Irish mother who died when Thea was a baby. Did all her schooling on the reservation, left in her late teens, later worked for the Blaker family for, basically, the rest of her life. No record of a husband or children, no criminal record, tax evasion, nothing."

Andie regretted that she'd exposed Thea to so much scrutiny. "There's really no such thing as a *private* citizen, is there?"

Manny considered that. "Maybe not. But this law enforcement officer would rather know more than less about the likes of Leo Francini and others who like to shoot at us. Unfortunately, we catch everyone up in our information dragnet. Never know when you'll need the scoop on the private citizen next door who likes to abduct little girls on their way to school."

"There's more to the argument on both sides," she said. "But from the way you keep looking at Thea's shrimp, you'd probably rather eat than argue, right?"

"I'm looking for a fork."

After seeing to Manny's late-night snack, Andie went to help Sergeant Banks prepare the room they would share.

"I'm happy with either bed," Andie offered, entering the small bedroom with as much cheer as she could muster. Sergeant Banks was pulling rolled shorts and T-shirts from her duffle bag, then meticulously folding and placing them in a chest of drawers as one would heirloom lace.

She glanced at Andie indifferently. "Thank you, Miss Ryborg."

Andie waited for more, but none came. She watched the woman unpack the last shirt and begin arranging her toiletries on top of the chest, from left to right in descending order of height.

Andie started filling her own drawers. "Do you like to snorkel,

Sergeant Banks? I brought some gear, which I'm happy to share with you."

"Too many sharks."

Again, Andie waited for a follow-up sentence. Still none. "Oh, I see Manny's been spreading rumors. The park ranger tells me it's just the occasional sand shark. And that there's plenty more conch, spindly sea urchins, sponges, and a rainbow of tropical fish."

No reply.

Andie turned to look at the officer, now pulling sheets so tightly across her bed, the trampoline effect would surely spring a human body onto the floor. "Sergeant Banks, I'm sorry you and Manny have been sent way out here to protect me. I always thought I could do that myself."

"I intend to do my job without complaining, Miss Ryborg."

Oh boy. Andie rubbed the back of her neck. "Would you mind calling me Andie?"

"No, ma'am. I don't mind."

Ma'am? That's worse than Miss Ryborg. Okay, here we go. "And would you mind if I called you Cleo?"

The woman hesitated. "Make it Banks. Thank you."

Andie nodded slowly. "Okay, Banks. Would you like to shower first?"

"I have to finish this, and then we'll go over rules."

A compound sentence! There's hope. But Andie wondered at the rules.

"They're simple," Manny said from the doorway. "Let's have a seat in here." He motioned toward the living room, where one lamp burned, sending a gray arc over one white wall. The room cried for color and design, which Andie planned to furnish. She would begin a new series of canvases tomorrow and pray that her "seeing" would return. *The prisoner of Alcatraz had his birds. I have my paintings.*

"Okay, Andie, we all know why you're here," Manny said, the three of them facing each other in a triangle of rattan seating. "Hopefully, it won't be too long before we bust the Francini connection and we can all go home. Or we may like it so much we'll get all our family and friends to join us out here. They can each put up their own house-on-a-stick, and before you know it, Wal-Mart will move in on a giant barge with lots of boat parking. Utopia."

Andie glanced at Sergeant Banks, who deadpanned, "If you're through with your opening monologue, can we get to the rules part of the show?"

More improvement. Andie looked back at Manny, who seemed to be struggling with a response to his subordinate officer, but not for long.

"I think mutiny probably isn't an option for you, Cleo. So just sit tight."

Manny continued his seamless discourse. "Andie, here's the thing: if you go outside during daylight hours, it has to be on the north porch. The south side of the house faces the channel. More exposure, more chances of being seen by a passing boater, even though we're a good ways off the channel. A larger boat like the one we brought here can only approach us on the channel side, which is deepest. Everywhere else, the water is only a few feet deep. Still, a small boat, even a kayak, can run close by. When you see anyone in the vicinity, come inside immediately.

"Now, anytime you're outside, I want a hat on your head and hair tucked inside. Should a boat drift a little too close, we don't want anyone recognizing you. Your dad's done a pretty good job of keeping you out of the media. In fact, I don't recall a single picture of you in the papers, but you have appeared at events with him a few times over the last few years. Oh, and sunglasses, too. Big ones."

"Question," Andie said. "How will I talk to my dad?"

"Questions are good." He held up a cell phone. "Use this one. Government issue, you see, with the right number of gizmos to squelch a foreign tracker. We can monitor your conversations and position, though we don't expect you to go anywhere. Emphasis on *monitor*. Hotline folks can pick up on your calls at any time, for any reason they think is important. By the way, your dad's got one just like it."

"Have you spoken to him tonight?"

"Just did. He's waiting for you to call him."

"Now?" she asked eagerly.

"The sooner the better."

Andie reached for the phone and stepped outside. The wind blew its raw breath laced with marine decay. In these vast underwater colonies, the dead fed the living. Andie inhaled deeply, swilling her share of nurturing vapors and daring to think of her mother's legacy. How in death, she still sustained her daughter, her voice coming quietly, even now: *Andie, don't look down into the stormy waters. But lift your face to the one they obey. And listen!*

Tony answered on the first ring. "Andie, are you all right?"

"Safe in my cocoon, Dad. But how about you? Are you at—"

"Hold it!" Tony cautioned. "Might be other ears."

Andie had already forgotten Manny's warning. "Sorry, Dad."

"Honey, I wish I could be with you."

Andie knew why he couldn't. She'd overheard Chief Manette's hushed but blunt words to him clearly enough: "*You're a danger to each other right now.*"

"It's okay, Dad. I'll call you tomorrow."

Andie flipped the phone shut and turned to go inside when she saw lights heading toward the house. She threw open the door. "Manny!" she hollered.

He sprang from his bedroom, where he'd been unpacking, and rushed to her.

"A boat's coming!"

Manny grabbed his gun from its holster as Sergeant Banks quickly appeared, gun in hand. Both raced onto the deck. A moment later, they returned. Manny laid the gun down on the kitchen counter and recovered his breath. "They're ours, Andie. Sorry. I should have told you. We're keeping a round-the-clock rotation of watchers out there. Those two must have heard you talking on the deck and moved in to make sure all was well."

Andie was embarrassed by her alarm. "I'm going to bed," she said, her voice weak. But first, she went into the bathroom and closed the door. She looked at herself in the mirror and removed the hat. Her hair tumbled onto her shoulders, a tangled mess. Fierce red splotches covered her cheeks and neck, mimicking sunburn and almost as painful. She pressed her fingers against them, feeling their heat. She took a washcloth from her bag, ran cool water over it, then held it to her face. She could smell the fragrance of detergent on the clean cloth and, at once, was by her mother's side on a Saturday morning, helping with the family laundry. Together, they would load the dryer with a fresh wet batch of clothes, but the bed linens went outside to dry in the sun—over her father's protests. "The neighbors will think we don't have modern appliances," he'd teased.

"And do we care what they think when we wrap our primitive selves in sheets that smell like the first day of spring?" With that, Jessica Ryborg had led her daughter into the sanctuary of a back yard joyfully strung with clothesline.

Andie buried her face in the cloth until the tears subsided. Then she changed into a long nightshirt and opened the bathroom door. Manny was waiting outside. Without a word, he wrapped his arms lightly around her. "It's okay," he whispered, then let her go. He turned quickly and went to his room.

The lamp was already off in her bedroom, and Sergeant Banks lay quietly in her bed. Andie tiptoed to her own and crawled in. She didn't know if the woman was asleep or not. "Good night," she ventured softly.

"Good night, ma'am."

CHAPTER 27

A COLUMN OF SEDANS from gray to black wound like a two-tone serpent down the drive and stopped in front of the grand home. In the back seat of the second sedan, Tony Ryborg pocketed a cell phone after telling his daughter good night and wondered how the coming days might forever alter their lives.

"Sir," said Warren, opening the car door. "We're keeping two men at the gate," he continued as Tony got out, "and three more patrolling the property twenty-four/seven. Miss Long was right about security cameras and electric fencing on top of the wall. Everything's in working order and, I might add, state of the art. These folks must have been sitting on a hoard of gold bullions."

Tony nodded acknowledgement of this update. He was in no mood for banter.

The front door of the house opened, and Thea Long rushed out to greet her guests. "Please come in. I know how tired you must be."

Carrying his own garment bag and a briefcase, Tony approached her. "Miss Long—"

"Thea, please," she interrupted.

Tony smiled, but wearily. "We are indebted to you for such generosity." He paused to silently admonish himself. *Talk like a real person.* "I mean, thank you for taking care of my daughter, and now me and my people here. I'm really, uh, overwhelmed."

"It's my pleasure, Tony. May I call you that?"

Tony lightly touched her arm. "Of course." But quickly, his thoughts shifted. "Excuse me, Thea." He turned and called to Warren, who was briefing the officers on the pattern of surveillance he wanted.

"Sir." Warren ran up alongside Tony. "And greetings again, Thea," he offered. She returned his smile.

"Warren, do you have the text of the speech for Monday? I can't find it anywhere."

Warren frowned at his boss. "Your speech?" he asked. "Sir, you cancelled the Miami Beach appearance."

"You only thought I did, Warren. But I'm going. It's the preamble to Wednesday's debate. Now, do you have the text?" Tony traveled with few people besides Warren, his trusted aid, sounding board, and protector. A widower with grown children, Warren left no one to fend alone at home during his extended absences on the job. Both men depended on Freda, who tended to travel-lodging-dining-transportation arrangements, made and confirmed appointments, alerted the media of keynote addresses, gathered pertinent documents, and collected all other necessary papers, including copies of Tony's speeches, which he wrote himself. She even packed his briefcase and suggested which ties to take, and which ones to burn.

"Yes, sir. But I strongly urge you to—"

"I know you do," Tony broke in, "and I appreciate your diligence in trying to keep me alive. I commend you for your success so far. Now, let's not keep this kind lady up any longer than we have to." Warren looked stunned and just a bit stung. "Yes, sir," he mumbled, his mouth tight, and fell back to help the other officers retrieve gear from the cars, including Tony's personal papers.

Tony momentarily hung his head and remembered the night a bullet meant for him tore into the chest of his faithful bodyguard. "Warren," he called. The man returned to Tony's side. "I'm sorry," Tony told him. "I'm just a crusty old codger who forgets that your job is just as important as mine. Forgive my arrogance."

"Does this mean you'll do what I say?" Warren asked.

"Of course not," Tony replied and turned back to Thea, giving her the faintest wink.

Thea ushered her guests through the front door of the home. Tony stopped just inside and tried to take it all in. A floating staircase of white marble descended into the entrance hall as if from some celestial realm. A round, Chinese rug of ebony, emerald, and cream lay at his feet, and a massive secretary of burl wood and walnut rose against one wall, its desktop open and a crystal inkwell refracting the light of a carved ivory lamp.

Warren came in behind him. After a quick look around, he announced quietly to Tony, "We're not in Kansas anymore, boss." Then he swept past Tony and entered another room through a high, arched doorway beyond the stairs. "Thea," Warren called, "where do you want us to set up?"

Tony, still processing the splendor of the home, followed Thea into what he might have called a family room, though it looked more like the inside of a posh men's club on Manhattan's Upper East Side. The smell of oiled wood and leather permeated the room. Its high walls were clad in mahogany wainscoting and sage-green grass cloth. Elaborately framed oils of heroic scenes from history hung about the room—the battle of Trafalgar, Paul Revere on his mount, and an odd pairing of two other canvases: the suicidal Jewish revolt against Rome at Masada, and the Last Supper.

Thea watched Tony study these last two paintings, hung side by side. While Warren and several FDLE officers scurried about with computers, radios, and other communications equipment, she walked over to stand beside Tony. "What do you see there?" she asked him.

He looked thoughtfully at her, then back at the paintings, studying them intently. "In this one," he finally said, pointing to the fortress of Masada, "a thousand Israelites sacrificed themselves for their country." Moving closer to the portrayal of Jesus gathering one last time with his disciples, Tony said, "And here, one man sacrificed himself for the whole world. Both events extraordinary. But only one eternal."

Tony finally turned from the paintings and saw Thea's astonishment. "I've asked that question to many visitors in this home," she said, "and no one has ever given such an answer."

Tony was suddenly embarrassed, self-conscious at probing his inner thoughts with someone he didn't know. "Well, if that's what it is, it must have come through my parents."

Thea nodded. "You were very close to them, weren't you?"

Tony looked oddly at her.

"I mean, you must have been to give them such credit."

"Yes, very close," he replied. "Excuse me, Thea. I'd better lend these guys a hand."

Something about her leaves me off balance, he thought as he walked away, hoping he hadn't left her too abruptly. But he didn't have time to worry about it. There was Andie. *She's somewhere out there with a handful of protectors and who knows how many looking for her. What have I done to her?*

"Sir, everything's taken care of, and the patrols are on duty," Warren advised. "Why don't you turn in?"

This time Tony was willing to comply. Fatigue and worry over Andie had wrestled his strength from him.

"Your things are already set up in your bedroom, first door on the left coming off the stairs," Warren said.

"Thank you, my friend." First, Tony helped Warren set up another computer on a long library table against the far wall of the room. Afterward, he was ready to retire to his room. But at the foot of the stairs, Thea caught up with him once more.

"Would you come with me a moment?" she asked him.

Tony didn't know if his limbs would cooperate, but he forced them. He followed Thea through a back door that opened onto a wide terrace overlooking the bay. Just outside was an officer who immediately sprang to alert when the two of them appeared. "Is everything okay, sir?" the officer asked.

Thea answered for Tony. "We're just going to the edge of the water. You can follow if you like." Tony noted her authoritative manner.

It was a long walk to the shore, but every step seemed to revive him. The ocean air filled his lungs and rushed through his veins, invigorating and calming at the same time.

Thea finally halted just yards from where the tide nudged the beach. "Look way out into the bay." She pointed, raising her voice over the wind. "See that sprinkle of lights to the north?"

Tony peered into the dark. "I see. What is it?"

"That's Andie," she said.

CHAPTER 28

A GUNMETAL MORNING GREETED *Misfit* as she and her captain got underway that Sunday. Through a heavy mist, the Bimini islands appeared as a gray smudge on the horizon. After receiving the coordinates from Leo and relaying them to the authorities, Evan had decided to bed down for the night and cruise the last four hours of his journey by daylight. He'd texted Leo with this change of plans.

But daylight was tenuous. Thunderclouds had gathered during the night, and a distant rumbling echoed the quaking inside Evan's troubled soul. Though he'd come only forty miles from the Miami shore, he felt as though he'd entered another hemisphere, and the only person he knew in it was the father he'd just thrown to the lions. Only they would take their time to devour him, first circling and sniffing the air for the exact moment to attack. The plan was for Evan to escape the island first, having discovered all he could about the other key players in Leo's illicit games.

But Evan didn't believe he would escape, not the island and not ever the scourge of his betrayal. He was prepared for whatever awaited him as if it were his final judgment, his due for being born of a devil.

As the mist turned to pounding rain, Evan relied on his GPS to keep him on track, turning south toward Andros Island before the Biminis ever took clear shape. Now, he could see nothing in any direction, floating in the dark with no past, no future, and only a torrential present.

Finally outrunning the storm, Evan edged from beneath the oppressive ceiling and into a clear blue run to the tiny cay called Cat's Eye. It was little more than three square miles of rugged terrain appearing from above as an almond-shaped eye lashed by native palms, wholly owned by Leo Francini, though you would find his real name on no deed.

As Evan approached the island from the north, he saw a flat plain rising to a distant ridge. In the foreground sat several encampments of what looked like cement bunkers. *Leo's army barracks, no doubt.* But as he drew closer, he noticed children playing near the beach. A bizarre thought struck: *Could Leo have sired another family?*

A young boy waved toward *Misfit* as Evan rounded the north end of the island. He returned the wave and continued, as Leo had told him, "to the eastern ridge facing the mainland. There, you'll turn into a channel that runs into a deep cove."

There it was, just ahead. If Evan hadn't known what to look for, he would have missed it. He slowed his engines and turned west into the channel, approaching the island broadside. Before him rose a steep bank densely covered in sea grape and cleft by the narrow inlet. On the sugar-white beach, coconut palms and pines stood sentinel on both sides of the cut. Evan doubted anything so lovely could be the entrance to Leo's lair until something above caught his eye. He looked up to see the sun's reflection on metal, glinting from the crest of the bank. Two men brandishing weapons watched him until he'd passed beneath their lookout and entered something he'd not expected.

A deep cove, yes. But one of such other-worldly beauty, surely this was not the place he sought. Evan geared the engines to neutral. He'd suddenly found himself in an enclosed, turquoise lagoon surrounded by a high lattice of palms and emerald vegetation bursting with blossoms. Their colors shimmered in the downdraft of sunlight through the open "ceiling," reminding him of pictures he'd seen of the Roman Pantheon and its portal to pagan gods. Only the call of birds punctuated the stillness, and if not for the one who lived there, Evan would have surely called the place holy.

But there was the dock and the boat, the drug runners' chariot of choice. Like the Cigarette Evan had passed on his way from the Miami River the night before, the high-speed racer before him was typical of the species called go-fast boats. Far at sea, they would suckle from a mother ship engorged with drugs, then race to the mainland to, in turn, feed their own flocks of dealers.

As Evan shifted into forward, his eyes followed a switchback rise of rough-hewn stairs that climbed from the dock to the highest point over the cove. There, he finally focused on a dwelling so blended into rocks and trees as to almost disappear. He chuckled to himself. *Catch me if you can find me, right, Leo?* Evan knew that even with coordinates, those who would soon follow might easily miss their target. He would have to alert them.

But first he would milk his role as dutiful son to the man now descending the steps. In a faded blue shirt and khaki shorts, no shoes, Leo hurried to catch Evan's bow line and bring *Misfit* to rest.

"Did you have trouble finding me?" Leo asked sarcastically, a wry smile on his weathered face.

"Doesn't everyone?" Evan answered, noticing how gaunt his father had grown, even in the last few days. Though the man's air was Caribbean-carefree, there was an unhealthy rigidity that even a breezy blue shirt and deep tan couldn't conceal.

"There is no 'everyone,'" Leo said smugly. "We're not on the tour of homes."

Evan lashed spring lines from the boat to the dock.

"You won't need those, you know. No wave action in here. No turbulence at all." Leo flashed a bigger, self-satisfied smile at Evan. "You're leaving that behind."

Evan understood the implication but knew better. He'd already drawn crosshairs over this island.

He hopped back on the boat, retrieved his duffle bag, the Glock handgun stowed inside it, and returned to the dock. "Lead the way," he said to Leo, looking high above him. The cliff looked like a page from a kid's activity book: *Can you find the tree house in this picture?* It seemed just the semblance of a house, its shape barely emerging from the camouflage of leaves, vines, and woody limbs.

The house appeared to be of rock and light-green-painted wood with dark green shutters, now flung open wide. It rambled along the side of the bank more than perched on top, its flat roofline obscured by the cliff-top jungle. Evan could barely detect a cement bulwark supporting the structure. This was not the commando camp he'd envisioned. Add a musical waterfall and a plastic shark surfacing at timed intervals, and it could be a Disney attraction.

Following Leo up the uneven, hand-wrought steps, Evan wiped sweat from his brow, wishing he'd shed the jeans and long-sleeved T-shirt he'd worn through the earlier, chill-blowing storm. The cove was steamy, and the heavy air almost smothering. He looked up to see Leo stopped and watching him.

"If there's nothing more suitable than jeans in that bag of yours, I'll have one of the boys bring clothes from Andros. They make a run about once a week."

"I've got all I need, but thanks," Evan said, sweat dripping from his chin.

"Your mother and I pegged you as the stubborn one before you were out of diapers."

Evan recoiled at the notion of Leo and his mom together. Nancy Markham, in Evan's mind, was Leo Francini's perennial victim. Even now, she struggled under the oppressive weight of those years as Nancy Francini. The Tennessee family that had harbored her and her child after their escape from "the mob," as they called it, only compounded the guilt already infesting his mother for bringing two children into a fractured marriage and a lawless home. Her parents had been vehemently opposed to the marriage and fairly gloated over its failure. Twenty years later, they still dangled its charred remains in his mother's face as their proof that she could never again trust her own judgment. So she hadn't.

Like a penitent pilgrim, Nancy Markham laid every decision in life before her parents. They, and frequently her older siblings, decided that she and "the boy," as they most often referred to Evan, would remain in the family home. They decided when and where Evan would go to school, how he should dress, whom he should and shouldn't associate with, and when it was permissible for Nancy to travel alone with her son. She was allowed to work only part-time as a bookkeeper in her father's accounting firm, where he could keep a steady eye on her. No fraternizing with the opposite sex. There had been enough of that, he determined. So there was no more.

Now, uncomfortably in step behind the man who had caused it all, Evan continued to climb until they reached a wide deck cantilevered over the edge of the cliff. Its coarse plank floor and heavy-rope railings seemed to grow from the side of the bank, meshing with verdant colonies of overhanging ferns and fronds from palms rooted some twenty feet below.

Leo paused on the deck. "Want coconut juice for breakfast? Just reach out and grab some." He demonstrated, plucking one of the coarse fruits from a cluster, hacking it with a nearby machete, and pouring its nectar into a sky-blue glass, one of several placed upside down on a small, outdoor dining table. He held the glass out for Evan, who accepted it hesitantly, swirling it around in the glass.

"Fruit of the gods, Evan. Drink it and live forever." Leo poured some for himself and made a show of savoring its sweet yet deceptive promise.

Despite himself, Evan welcomed the smooth-flowing drink down his parched throat. "Thanks, Leo. But do you have anything really cold and lots of it?"

"Beer?"

"Ice water."

A shadow passed quickly over Leo's face, momentarily dispelling his light mood. "Sure, Evan. I'll get you whatever you like."

That was out of character, Evan thought, and followed Leo up a few more steps to another landing, the last, it appeared. The sun struck at a bold angle, casting all colors more brilliantly than they appeared below. Evan looked down into the pool where *Misfit* and her flashy dock mate waited. He could see fish and a few manta rays chasing about in the crystalline waters.

"Come inside and cool yourself, Evan," Leo said.

Evan turned and stepped through a garage-size opening into the house. Its doors slid back on both sides, revealing one vast room which, like a cave, reached deep into the cliff with recesses Evan couldn't see. The living area sprouted wicker furniture with deep cushions in a tropical print. Tables nested here and there, each one bearing a candle. A few lamps, one or two plants, and an enormous oil of a sunset at sea completed the room, almost. One more thing snagged Evan's attention. On a narrow wall at the far end of the room was a family portrait. Evan moved just close enough to see the long-ago image of his parents, his brother, and himself at age seven. He knew exactly how old he was because the picture had been taken just days before he and his mother fled.

"I still have a family, you know," Leo said as if justifying the picture. He set a tall glass of ice water on a nearby table.

Evan didn't respond but picked up the glass and drained it. "You want to tell me why I'm here and why it was so urgent?" he asked abruptly, ignoring the reference to family.

"Because of that," Leo said, pointing back to the portrait.

Evan glared at him. "What? The family you *think* you have?"

Leo colored and spun toward Evan. "You want to tangle with me? You want to get me down and stomp on me because you still hate me? You do, don't you? Say it!"

Evan went rigid, his sweat-wet body suddenly chilled. He regretted his outburst. Why had he done it? He was here to do a job, not drag out the family corpse. "I'm sorry I said that."

Leo stepped back and stumbled over an ottoman. Evan reached to steady him, but Leo pushed him away. "Don't!"

He took Evan's glass and walked to the kitchen. He returned with a full glass and the unruffled, stone-cold countenance more familiar to Evan. *He's a master at that. The instant switch—emotions on, emotions off, like nothing was ever said. Just as well.*

"You're here because I've made an unwise liaison with someone I can no longer trust," Leo said, handing Evan the water.

"Who?" Evan asked, setting the glass down.

"Always quick with the questions. That's okay. But you don't need to know that. Just that there are some who don't trust you." Leo looked sharply at Evan. "They think you might have an agenda separate from mine. Imagine that, Evan." Leo held Evan's eyes for a moment, then walked to the open door and looked down at the lagoon. "Imagine a father not able to trust his own son." Leo quietly studied the water, the pause seeming deliberate.

Does he know I was at police headquarters? Evan fretted. *Or is he just baiting me for the sport of it?* "Yeah, imagine that, Leo. Especially a son who's given his father no reason to doubt him." *If he knows, now is the time he'll pounce.* Evan braced for it.

Leo turned slowly and seemed to reach some resolve within him. "Suspicion is an infectious thing, Evan. One gets it, and it spreads. But even at this point in our relationship, I choose to trust you because I couldn't bear not to. You see, by the laws of my world, betrayal is a capital offense."

Evan managed an expressionless face.

"No matter whose son is guilty," Leo added, walking closer.

Evan wildly conjured the image of a trap door opening beneath him, jaws snapping in some murky hole below. *Steady!* he warned himself. "I've pictured you as many things, Leo. But not a bully."

"A compliment, I'm sure. But understand, I'm not the one threatening you. And your mother."

"Mom? What are you saying?"

Leo seemed unusually agitated now. "I'm going to deal with this."

"With what?" Evan fairly shrieked. "I'm tired of no answers. Is Mom in danger?"

"You're going to stay on this island until the threat is over. That's the way it's going to be. I'm not losing another son."

You did that a long time ago.

"So I have to stay in my yard until the bogeyman goes away? Is that it, Leo? Until you've wiped out yet another enemy on your turf?"

"It's not about turf. Not this time. Not when they target my family."

Something told Evan to stay quiet.

"That's when everything changed." Leo began to pace. "You don't threaten my wife and kid and expect business as usual." He paced faster. "No more deal. They were stupid enough to poke the cobra, then turn their back. Now, I strike."

"Why haven't you warned Mom?"

"What's she going to do? Hide under the covers? She wouldn't listen to me anyway."

"Then I'll tell her."

"No, no. I told you I'll take care of this."

"Is this why men were watching my boat?"

"When?" Leo asked sharply.

"Late yesterday."

"He didn't waste any time," Leo said, more to himself, but Evan heard it.

"Meaning?"

"Yes, that has everything to do with why you must stay here."

"And what about the Ryborgs?"

"They're still looking for her, but she's of no use to me anymore."

"Who's looking?"

Leo snickered. "The bogeyman."

CHAPTER 29

❧

FROM THE HIGHEST POINT on the island, Evan gazed at a sea-scape that didn't seem real. Aquamarines, pinks and lavenders shimmered too brightly. *If someone were to paint these colors the way they are right now,* he mused, *people would say the artist exaggerated.*

As the thermals stirred, he caught an evocative scent. Searching for the source, he noticed a bloom-engorged frangipani tree, its bulky, gnarled limbs incongruent to the grace of its flower and fragrance. Another time, in the company of a tamer soul, he might have enjoyed this respite in the Caribbean. But seated in an open Jeep waiting for Leo, Evan felt only dread. At this hour before Sunday's sunset, Leo had insisted on taking him on a tour of the island, though Evan wasn't in the mood to be a tourist.

"You might want to buckle up," Leo advised, hopping into the driver's seat and turning the key.

Evan eyed him blankly, making no effort to comply. He felt like a pouty kid made to accompany a crazy uncle to visit the relatives. Only these relatives all toted automatic weapons, Evan was certain.

After the opening salvo of their morning reunion, he had retreated to his assigned bedroom, wondering whether to risk a cell call to the FBI hotline. But he had nothing to report. There was promise, though. Just an hour earlier, Evan had seized the opportunity to search the house after Leo announced he was going on an errand and would return shortly. It had been a short but productive search. In Leo's bedroom, Evan found a file box inside one of several old trunks, its rusty padlock open. He'd just begun to search a stack of papers inside when he heard the Jeep coming up the hill to the house. He'd quickly returned the papers to their trunk and raced into the kitchen. He was standing at the open refrigerator when Leo entered the room. That's when the tour was announced.

Now, bumping along a two-rut lane running a zigzag pattern down the slope, Leo's erratic driving finally made Evan belt up, which elicited a satisfied smile from Leo.

"Those are the solar panels that help power the island," Leo said, pointing to the top of a distant rise. "We've got a bio-diesel generator as backup." Evan listened carefully, not knowing what information might serve him and those waiting to raid the island.

At the bottom of the hill, Leo turned north onto a roadway of hard-packed sand. It wound through a scrubby thicket of under-growth spread like kudzu over the rolling terrain. Topping a small hill, they descended into the semblance of a village, the same Evan had seen on his approach to the island.

"These are my loyals—bodyguards, gardeners, the occasional cook, repairmen, fishermen, and militia when they need to be." He pointed to a young man sitting on the stoop of a bright blue house, a rifle laying across his lap. Noting the weapon, Leo explained, "He heard the Jeep, saw someone he didn't know sit-ting next to me, and was ready for you." Evan met the flinty eyes of the young soldier. No greeting was exchanged.

"You see, when I bought the island, word spread to parts of the mainland that a rich American was paying top dollar for peo-ple to work it. In time, though, they found out that the American was very particular about what information was channeled off Cat's Eye. It only took a few of them disappearing to get my point across. Now, they're so fat and happy with what I pay them, I don't have to lift a finger to punish the loose-lipped among them who threaten their good fortune. They do it for me."

Evan counted about seven well-kept houses, even a small schoolhouse and a nurse's station bearing a crude red cross over the door. A few more people wandered out of their homes to see who had arrived in their little compound. With them came more guns. Leo looked at Evan and laughed. "You'd better watch your-self around my, uh, subjects. They'd shoot first, then apologize for killing my guest." Evan didn't share his amusement.

"That's our water supply." Leo pointed to a large, capped well.

"It's shallow but delivers the sweetest water, especially after it passes through our filtration system."

Just then, a few young children ran from behind a long, low house made of coquina rock. From the multiple front doors, it appeared to house more than one family. Its yard was well tended with beds of yellow hibiscus and bright coral exora. The children chased a small dog that had made off with a baseball mitt. Evan recognized the young boy who'd waved to him earlier. *Get out of here*, he wanted to warn him, making a mental note to alert the FBI that there were children in the compound. Vic had told him little of their plans for taking the island, and he hadn't cared how they captured Leo. But now he knew innocents were in the line of fire.

They were back on the road to the house. As the Jeep lumbered up the hill, Evan noticed a large, warehouse-like building about a half mile away. "What's that?" he asked.

"Storage."

"What kind?"

"Why do you want to know?"

"This is a tour, right?"

Leo studied the road ahead. "Just storage." He said nothing else until they reached the house.

"You're welcome to join me for dinner on the porch, or you can eat alone," Leo offered brusquely as they entered the house. "It doesn't matter to me."

"I have another question," Evan ventured, despite Leo's sullen mood.

"Shoot."

"Why do you live alone?"

"I don't." Leo cast a smug eye on Evan. "You probably noticed a few gents on the cliff as you entered the cove this morning. They bunk just below the house near the dock. If I hadn't told them you were coming, they would have blown you and *Misfit* out of the water. Then asked who you used to be." Leo shot a swagger of a grin.

That night, Evan endured an awkward dinner with Leo, who was unusually quiet. They ate fresh conch grilled with mango and peppers, a melon, and fried plantains, which Evan knew to be a Cuban delicacy. Leo told him his housekeeper and cook had escaped from Havana.

After dinner, Leo headed for the long stairs down to the dock. "Need to check on things," he told Evan. "I'll be awhile."

A few minutes later, Evan heard Leo talking with some of his men on the dock. Now was the time to search the file box. He slipped quickly into Leo's bedroom, a small flashlight in his hand. In no time, he had an assortment of papers spread before him on the bed. But after skimming each, he'd determined they were mostly invoices for supplies, a bill of sale on the go-fast boat, which Evan guessed was registered to a fictitious company, a copy of a *Miami Herald* article on the death of Donnie Francini and a few torn scraps of paper. *There has to be more.*

He returned to the trunk where he'd found the file box in case he'd missed anything else. Nothing. He poured through the other two trunks, dresser drawers and closet shelves, careful to return them to their original order. He'd found nothing but personal effects of no interest to him. He was replacing contents in the file box when one of those torn scraps of paper caught his eye. It was a Ft. Lauderdale address written in Leo's chicken-scratch hand, the one Evan had read in the occasional letters and cards Leo had sent throughout the years, none of which had been answered.

Evan knew it might be nothing but would call it in to Vic anyway. He pocketed the small note and replaced the box in the trunk. As he hurried back to his room, he heard the loud bantering of men's voices below. They were laughing at something. Evan guessed Leo was enjoying the company of his soldiers far more than his son's. He quickly punched in the hotline number on the cell phone Chief Manette had given him. The agent who answered took down the Ft. Lauderdale address Evan had just found, then patched him straight to Vic's cell.

"Evan, you okay?" she asked.

"Got an address, and that's all," he said, slipping the note back into his pocket.

"Can you uncover anything else? Or is it time for us to move?"

"Not yet, but when you do, you need to know there are children in the village on the north end of the island."

"Roger that. What's the head count at Leo's place?"

"Hard to tell. Maybe six, seven at the house. More in the village."

"When it's time, how quickly can you leave? We want you out of there before we come in."

"I'll signal when—"

The blow to his head knocked Evan to his knees and the cell phone from his hand. As he fell, he knocked over a lamp, sending it crashing to the floor.

"Evan!" came Vic's voice from the phone as it slid across the tile floor.

A hand reached down and picked it up. "Who may I say is calling?" Leo snarled.

There was no reply.

A young man wearing a bandana held a gun on Evan, who tried to stand up, but the pain in his head stabbed so hard, he crumpled back to the floor.

᠅

Leo ended the call and pocketed the phone. "Sit him on the bed." Miguel tucked his gun away and heaved Evan off the floor.

Slumped onto the bed, Evan moaned and held his head. With a nod toward the door, Leo commanded Miguel again, "Bring him some ice, then leave us alone."

Leo said nothing until Miguel had reentered the room, handed an ice pack to Evan, and left again.

As Evan shoved the ice pack aside, Leo caught him glancing at the duffle bag in the corner. Moving quickly toward the bag, Leo dumped its contents onto the floor. His instincts were rewarded as a gun thudded loudly onto the tile. Leo bent to pick up the weapon. "Well, well. The boy who refused to carry a gun got himself a new play toy. Or was this government issue?"

No response.

Leo shoved the Glock into his waistband, retrieved ammunition packs from the bag, and turned back to Evan.

"It's really over now, isn't it?" Leo said, keeping his voice low, controlled. "We can finally put this father-son masquerade to rest."

With great effort to appear casual and unfazed, he slowly pulled a chair beneath him, leaned back, and crossed first his legs and then his arms. His body language masked the rage he felt over his son's bitter betrayal.

Still reeling from the blow Miguel had delivered, Evan struggled to sit upright on the edge of the bed.

"Pick up the ice and hold it to your head," Leo ordered. "You won't die. There are deadlier things than a pistol butt to the side of the head." Evan did as he was told.

"Who was it?" Leo demanded. "FBI? Did they really believe you'd turn on your father? Because I can't. Suspected it, yes. But refused to believe it."

Evan stiffened. "You surprise me, Leo. All those years, I'd never given you any reason to think I'd ever join your ranks. Why did you believe I had?"

Yes, why? "Because I wanted to. How's that for a candid answer?"

"Did you really believe I wanted to harm that girl to get even for Donnie's death—when it was *you* who made him die? Who raised him to die the way he did!"

Leo jumped from his seat and came at Evan, fists balled. But something stopped him. Something from long ago when this boy was the only decent thing in his life. Hovering over Evan, arms flailing, Leo screamed, "Why did you do it?"

"To save the girl. You've done enough to hurt the innocent"— Evan finally looked him dead in the eye—"like Mom."

⌣

Leo's body seemed to go limp. Evan felt no pity for him, but something was there, like a weak signal from somewhere beneath the layers of contempt. It was no more than a dim pulse, but a persistent one, and Evan finally read it for what it was—the last shred of a son's love for his father. Not summoned, not wanted, but still there.

Evan wanted desperately to break through to the heart of Leo Francini, in whatever condition it was in. To say or do something that would bring the man back to life, out of the howling pit he lived in. Was there no remnant of the man who ran with his young son around the bases, all the way to home plate?

Evan opened his mouth to speak, but Leo threw up a hand to silence him. "No more!" he growled, his hand shaking, eyes wild. He left the room, locking the door from the outside.

Evan sat in the dark holding the ice to his head and fingering the note in his pocket. He felt certain Leo knew nothing about it. If he'd heard Evan report it to the agent, Leo would have searched the room for what else there might be.

Of more concern to Evan was escaping. He glanced around the windowless room, his thoughts turning possibilities when he heard Leo's own cell phone down the hall, its sharp ring-tone insistent. He heard Leo pick up, then walk quickly outside. It was a long time before he returned, in a frenzy and hollering for his men. Moments later, Evan heard the Jeep lunge to life and speed down the hill.

CHAPTER 30

❦

SUNDAY MORNING CAME too swiftly for Tony Ryborg. After talking to Andie the night before and praying for her safety, he'd dropped into a hard, dreamless sleep. Now, the invasive light of day reminded him that no one was ever completely safe. It was a mind-set he'd lived with for so long, he'd begun to despair, to doubt his chances of ever stemming the tide of deadly narcotics arriving every day in his beloved state. *Jess, I miss your strength.* But he suddenly knew how she would respond to that: "*You can do all things through him who strengthens you.*"

I can almost hear you say it. And I remember that it's true.

He rose from the old feather bed in this well-appointed bedroom of the Blaker mansion and phoned Manny Alvarez. All was well in Stiltsville, came the report. Andie was still sleeping, and two patrol boats were in place.

Tony dressed quickly and went downstairs. Thea was cooking bacon, waffles, and poached eggs. The table was set with a vase of fresh flowers and thermal decanters of hot coffee. Warren and a few officers greeted him.

"Mornin', fellas," Tony returned, looking over the cheerful, domestic scene. "I don't know what any of us have done to deserve such a gracious hostess."

Thea turned and smiled brightly at him. "I hope you slept well, Tony."

After a round of pleasantries, Thea served breakfast and turned on the television wedged into a hutch near the table. "Tony, you might be interested in this morning's guest on *Sunday Wrap,*" she said.

When she turned up the volume, Tony heard a familiar voice: "Throughout his terms as attorney general, my esteemed opponent's whole platform has been a fist-pounding crackdown on crime in our state, and I applaud him for that."

"Sure you do," Warren shot back to the round, fleshy face of Bill Neiman, looking particularly dapper for the camera this morning in a navy pinstripe suit and pastel peach tie. His heavy thatch of gray hair played well against the bronze of a perpetual tan.

"But there's more to the role of governor than that," Neiman continued. Settled comfortably in an overstuffed chair opposite the news show's host, he was the image of relaxed confidence.

Tony raised a coffee cup to his lips as he listened.

"Our citrus industry is in shambles following a string of record freezes, and those growers need help. Our schools are struggling under the weight of an exploding populace, and we need more facilities, more computer labs, and pay raises for our teachers. Yes, Tony Ryborg has taken on the high cost of pre-scription drugs our elderly are forced to pay, but how about the medical resources to keep them healthy so they don't need so many drugs?"

"And maybe a tax break for people with tans?" Warren chided.

Unresponsive to Warren's quips, Tony quietly ate his eggs, but his eyes remained on Neiman.

"This state is already bursting at the seams with baby boomers coming to enjoy their golden years on our shores. Yes, they bring their money with them, but also their growing needs. It'll take more than a gun on his hip to meet the needs of these and all our citizens."

"Oh, yeah. We're getting a little testy now," Warren said. "Looks like he's the one doing a bit of gunning for the debate on Wednesday, don't you think, sir?"

"It's okay," Tony said. "Just listen." He knew something more was coming. It was time.

"And it'll take more than one family's tragic experience with drugs to equip the next governor to lead this state through a whole gamut of problems," Neiman declared.

I was wondering how long it would take you. Tony felt the glances of those in the room dart his way. But his cold, rapt stare at the television discouraged comment.

"What are you referring to specifically, sir?" asked the show's host.

"Well, many of us heard the speech the attorney general gave a couple of days ago in Orlando, in which he clearly acknowledged that striking back at those responsible for his wife's drug habit— God rest her soul—and others like her, of course, is the chief reason he wants to be governor."

Forgive me, Lord, for doing this to Jessica.

"He twisted it to suit himself, Tony," Warren said scornfully when the interview ended. "Ignored everything else you said in that speech and went for what he thought would hurt you most."

"No, Warren," Tony said. "This is a victory for Jessica. She conquered an enemy far greater than Bill Neiman."

After breakfast, Tony went straight to that place near the water where he could see Stiltsville. A powder-blue haze hung over the bay, seeming to separate him even more from his child. Then he looked beyond, to the horizon where a lone young man had crossed into certain danger. Because of him, Tony knew where to find Leo Francini, having received the coordinates as soon as Evan relayed them to the FBI. An invasion force was gathering even now to sweep down on the compound as soon as Evan gave the signal, as soon as he discovered who else had Andie Ryborg in their sights.

꒰꒱

That evening, as Warren and his security team swept the Miami Beach hotel where Tony was to speak the following morning, Vic relayed news of her aborted phone conversation with Evan, leaving everyone to guess at his fate.

In the quiet of the Blaker den, Tony prayed for Evan's safety and for the collective wisdom of the law enforcement team now assessing his situation. *How much more, Lord? Give me strength to face whatever comes.*

Now, he must polish his speech for the morning. That it would be given on Bill Neiman's home turf of Miami Beach would be justice of some kind, he thought. But he wasn't looking to counter

Neiman's televised remarks that morning, only to expand on them. He would simply complete the story Neiman had begun, drawing the focus away from the battle of the candidates and into the real-life struggles of those listening.

When he was satisfied with the remarks he would give, he trudged up to his room and went to bed. But moments after he switched off the lamp and settled under the covers, his cell phone rang. It was Warren.

"Sir, the FBI has just received a warning they are taking very seriously."

"Go on," Tony replied wearily, raising up on one elbow.

"It came in just moments ago. An unidentified man said, and I quote, 'There will be an assassination attempt on Tony Ryborg tomorrow morning on Miami Beach.'"

There was silence.

"Sir?"

"I heard you, Warren. Why does this particular message raise more concern than usual?" Tony had spent too many years fending off threats to be easily alarmed.

"The man told them something he shouldn't have known."

"What?"

"Where Andie is."

Tony sprang from his bed and stalked to the window facing Stiltsville. "Get her out of there now!"

"We already have, sir. She's here with me at FDLE headquarters."

"I'll meet you there in thirty minutes!"

"No, sir. That's not advisable. We're locking down the mansion right now and treating this as a viable death threat against you. I'm afraid you have to trust me to look after Andie. I've sent SWAT and surveillance reinforcements to the mansion. They should be arriving shortly."

Just then, Tony heard the rumble of cars entering through the front gate and, he was certain, the percussion of rotors growing louder over the treetops. "They're already here," he told Warren. "Chopper, too."

"Sir, there's something else. I think we've got a mole in FDLE."

"If that's true, Andie shouldn't be there."

"It's still the safest place for her right now, sir."

"I want her with me," Tony said firmly. "You've turned this place into an armed camp that should be sufficient to protect us both. I've allowed my child to dangle out there by herself long enough. Now, I want her here."

Warren drew an audible breath. "We'll transport her within the hour, sir." He paused. "And Tony, our girl is something else. Six of us bruisers sped out there in a loud boat, stormed into the house, scooped her out of her bed and told her the location had been compromised and that it was urgent she leave with us immediately. You know the first thing she said?"

Tony listened, his hand squeezing the phone.

"'Is my dad all right?'"

There was a long silence before Tony could speak. "Thank you for that, Warren. Bring her to me."

"Yes, sir."

Before he hung up, Tony asked, "Warren, didn't Manny and the other officer know you were coming?"

"No, sir. We didn't know who had leaked Andie's location. You understand."

"Surely you're not suggesting that—"

"Chief Manette is investigating everyone who had that information."

꒰ꙫ꒱

Minutes later, someone knocked at Tony's bedroom door. He quickly pulled on a robe and opened it to find Thea, swaddled in her own thick wrap. "Has something happened to Andie? The house is full of policeman asking for you."

"No, Thea. She's okay." He debated trusting her with the information, but realized she'd know soon enough. Just then, three officers topped the stairs and headed in their direction.

"Everything's secure up here, officers," Tony reported. "I'll come down as soon as I'm dressed." He looked into the old woman's face and led her to a couple of chairs in the broad hall- way, where ornately framed portraits of the Blakers and their

ancestors lined the walls. He imagined them looking on in horror at what was taking place in their family home.

Tony told her about the FBI warning and why Andie would
be arriving soon. The news of this most recent development
seemed to have stricken the woman, draining the color from
her face. "Thea, I'm so sorry you wound up in the middle of this,
and I don't think it's wise for you to remain here with us any
longer. Is there someone you can stay with until we can relocate
to Tallahassee? I realize how brazen it is for us to take over your
home, then ask you to leave. But it should only take us a day or
so to vacate."

Thea seemed not to hear him, as if she'd suddenly departed
into another realm of thought that had nothing to do with his
question.

"Thea."

"I'm sorry, Tony. What did you say?"

"I asked if there was someplace you could stay for a couple of
days, somewhere safer than what we've turned this home into,
I regret."

"Uh, I'll see."

Tony looked at her warily but said nothing more. He would
see that she was taken to a hotel, if need be.

❧

Tony was downstairs in the den, looking over the speech he
wouldn't be giving on Miami Beach the following morning, when
he heard someone call, "Tony, we got your girl."

He rounded the doorway to the entrance hall and saw Andie
standing next to Vic Shay, who had finally forsaken the housedress for FBI-marked fatigues. "See there," she told Andie as Tony
approached. "Told you he was fit as a fiddle." Then she stood back
and watched the reunion of father and daughter.

"Dad, what's happening?" Andie asked when Tony released
her from a smothering bear hug he didn't care how many officers witnessed. "Who do you think warned the FBI that you
would be—"

"Assassinated?" Tony finished the sentence for her, then waved it off. "Honey, it's just more of the same." He tried to comfort her.

"No, it isn't, Dad. Warren wouldn't tell me everything, but he said enough to make me know this is different. Now, what's going on?"

"Well, Andie," Vic weighed in instead, "your dad doesn't know any more about the source of tonight's warning and the leak of your whereabouts than the venerable bureau to which I pledge my troth, so to speak. That means, let's just batten down and wait for answers. I guarantee you, there'll be no sleep for many of us tonight. I just left a wad of our agents plus Chief Manette and your own Warren Jacobs with heads together over this." At Tony's request, she didn't tell Andie that Evan's cover, most likely, had been blown wide open.

Vic looked up to see Thea standing midway down the stairs. "Evening, Miss Long. You must think the cavalry has arrived. My apologies."

Tony and Andie turned toward Thea. Tony was surprised to see she had already dressed and now carried a small suitcase.

"Thea, where are you going?" Andie asked with mild alarm.

"I decided to take your father's advice and get out of your way for a couple of days."

"Where will you go?" Tony asked remorsefully.

"My nephew is picking me up in just a minute. I'll stay with him and his family on the reservation. I'm overdue for a visit with them anyway. So please don't worry about me."

"You're leaving your home because of us." Andie said. "I feel awful."

But Thea seemed too preoccupied with other thoughts to respond much at all. She waved a dismissive hand in Andie's direction. "I have a few things to tend to at the boathouse, and I'll be gone." She left quickly through the front door.

Vic instantly disappeared into the den, where Tony saw her talk in hurried tones to two of the officers. When she returned, she announced she was leaving but would stay in touch with Tony. "Andie, don't let him get into any more mischief. I'm too old for all this. Night, folks."

"Vic left in a big hurry," Andie noted.

Shortly afterward, Tony was seated near a front window of the house looking over more surveillance reports when he noticed a set of headlights moving toward the boathouse. He watched as Thea emerged into the faded wash of a spotlight and climbed into a pickup truck, which then headed toward the main gate. At that instant, he saw one of the plain sedans parked at the side of the mansion ease from its spot, lights off. As it passed beneath another spotlight on the front drive, Tony saw Vic at the wheel and two officers with her. As the pickup disappeared down the lane to the main gate, so did the sedan.

CHAPTER 31

❧

JUST BEFORE MIDNIGHT on Sunday, the Jeep returned and Leo entered the house yelling. "We're ready!" A few seconds later, the door to Evan's room burst open. Leo filled the doorway, his head almost touching the upper door frame. He stood looking at Evan for an awkward time.

"You never told me what college was for," Leo said dryly. "What were you going to do with yourself?"

Evan could almost believe his dad really wanted to know. With no pretense, no emotion, Evan answered, "I wanted to be a doctor."

Leo blanched. He stared into Evan's expressionless face until an engine revved loudly outside. He turned sharply toward the sound, then slowly back at Evan.

"Time for us both to go. Me first. The feds will be here soon for you." He stepped back into the hallway, retreating into shadow where he lingered for just a moment more. Evan didn't move or speak. Without another word, Leo left by the back door.

When Evan heard what sounded like a couple of Jeeps tearing off down the hill, he ran out the back door, and saw taillights bouncing against a moonless night, growing smaller and disappearing over a rise. He'd have to hail the FBI boats immediately, but he couldn't imagine Leo had left him any means of doing that. He'd taken the hotline phone with him. But Evan had left the phone Leo gave him in the cabin of the boat, which he'd locked. Then he thought of the keys. He'd dropped them into his duffle bag.

He ran back into the house and searched the contents Leo had emptied onto the floor. No keys. A lightning search of the house turned up nothing. Just then, he thought of the marine radio at the helm of *Misfit*. He needed no keys to reach it. He rushed to the front door, overlooking the lagoon, then stopped, slid it open carefully, and stepped quietly outside to listen. Nothing. No one. Just the gentle lapping of sea water against *Misfit* and the abandoned go-fast. Evan rushed down the steps toward the dock.

⌇

On the other side of the island, on a pad behind the concrete warehouse, a Bell helicopter was stripped of its camouflage netting. Seven armed men jumped inside and Leo, at the controls, flew off the island that had been his refuge.

He banked steeply over the lagoon and hilltop dwelling, seeing no one about. After hovering briefly, he headed north to the Florida mainland.

Leaving his son behind, he had one pervading thought. *A doctor?*

⌇

Evan had just boarded *Misfit* and found the cabin door unlocked when the thrashing beat of a helicopter advanced suddenly over the hill. His whole body jerked at the sound as he trained his eyes on the running lights now bearing down on him. He lunged into the cabin and hid as the chopper made a pass over him and paused, its lights sweeping the dock. Then it was gone.

Evan nodded in defeat. *Of course. Just storage, right, Leo?*

The feds had missed their man, but Evan still had to make contact. Inside the cabin, everything had been tossed about in a careless search. He spied the phone, its battery removed and no more to be found. He raced up the steps to the helm and discovered the marine radio also disabled. There was nothing left to do but get out of there. He hurried toward the house to search again for the keys.

He had just topped the steps when he heard the rumble of an approaching vehicle. He ran through the house to the back door and peered out. Headlights bobbled over the rough road as an oncoming pickup truck slowly took shape beneath a spotlight some distance from the house. *It's got to be from the village.* He remembered the dead-on eyes of the man at the blue house.

The truck stopped and two men got out. They slipped into a line of trees leading to the house, and Evan knew with certainty that he needed to disappear quickly.

He locked the door, and as he raced back to the front door, his eye caught something at the far end of the living room. On a narrow wall. Hanging from the corner of the framed photograph of his family. A set of keys clipped to the bright orange bobber he'd used to keep them from sinking. *Leo! You haunted man!*

Evan dashed across the room and grabbed the keys, refusing to look again at the faces of his pretend family. As he slid the front door closed behind him, he heard the back door burst open. *Who are they?* He knew he wouldn't make it down the steps to the dock before they spotted him.

He heard them rampage through the house, yelling for him. "Leo's little boy! Come out and play with us!" one bellowed. They laughed as they threw open doors and pounded fists against walls.

A thick vine snaked down from a nearby tree branch, then looped beneath the steps closest to the house. Evan grabbed it, hoisted himself up and over the railing, then, hand over hand, lowered himself to the underside of the front porch. From there, he scrambled over the rocks and wedged himself against the concrete bulwark supporting the house.

In seconds, the broad, sliding front door zinged across its track, and the men stepped onto the wide planks of the porch, just a foot above Evan's head.

"He said the kid was still here," one of them said.

"How did he know that?"

"One of Leo's men phoned him just before they flew out."

"Who? Miguel?"

"Naw. Miguel hates Dingo. He wouldn't tell him anything."

Dingo? Evan didn't understand.

"Let's check the boat."

As their voices trailed down the steps, Evan heard one more thing.

"It's not gonna be me who pops Francini's kid. You'll have to do it."

When the two men reached *Misfit* and went inside, Evan moved slowly from beneath the porch and cautiously worked his way across the steep bank toward the far side of the cove, clinging to vines and tree trunks as he crawled beneath the concealing undergrowth, hoping nothing gave way with him. His only escape was his boat. When they didn't find him there, they'd come back to the house. Evan intended to be as far away from there as possible, and as close to his boat as he could get.

The men moved quickly from *Misfit* to Leo's racer, then headed back up to the house. When they disappeared inside, Evan eased from under the dense foliage and, fingering the boat keys in his pocket, silently slipped into the water. He swam just beneath the surface, rising for quick gulps of air and his bearings. He wished he'd removed the heavy jeans, which slowed him down. At least, dry clothes were on board.

When he reached the boat, he waited in the water until he heard the pickup crank and lumber off down the road. Were both men inside? Had just one left to get others for the search?

Not waiting another second, he climbed the ladder at the stern of the boat, cast off the lines, and sloshed his way to the helm. But before he turned the key in the ignition and announced his location, he found himself doing something he hadn't done since he was a child. He prayed. *God, I don't know you, or if you're really there. But if you are, please help me. I don't think I can do this by myself anymore.*

When he turned the key, *Misfit*'s growl echoed throughout the cove. Cringing at the sound, Evan spun her away from the dock and shoved the throttle forward, willing the sluggish trawler to get up and fly. He had just cleared the bottleneck of the cove when the first shot rang out from the house, lodging somewhere in the boat's stern. *Please, God!*

Another shot clipped his antenna, and two more found what sounded like the cabin door. Bursting out of the inlet, Evan swung the boat into a violent left turn, her port side plunging almost into a dive as the starboard reared up, perilously close to flipping the boat. Though she was too old and out of shape to be treated like this, *Misfit* dug in and held the turn long enough for Evan to gain the cover of shoreline trees and pull out of the turn. Still, he demanded more as the boat strained for optimum speed. He was grateful for calm waters that offered little resistance. Finally, the bow dropped onto plane, and *Misfit* found her stride. Evan turned only once to look back at Cat's Eye, as if the whole island had given chase. Nothing stirred behind him.

Avoiding his earlier route that hugged the north-end village, he headed due east, speeding out of firing range before turning north toward the open sea.

ᨬ

"Go ahead," the FBI hotline agent answered.

"You boys can go on in now," Leo called over the roar of the helicopter. "I left a few beers for you in the fridge. And, oh yeah, you take good care of Evan Markham. He's waiting for you at Cat's Eye. You know where that is. Everybody knows where that is now. Besides, I'm sure this little phone you gave my son has been sending all the signal you need. Have a safe trip." He opened the window and tossed Evan's phone into the Atlantic.

CHAPTER 32

A CROWD HAD GATHERED behind the Excalibur Hotel on Miami Beach where a state medical convention was kicking off a three-day run. Its milling throng covered the back terrace of the elegant hotel, which was feting them with a tropics-flavored breakfast buffet and a steel-drum band.

Also gathered that Monday morning were news crews from two local television stations and a battery of newspaper reporters. Tony's speech in Orlando and the fire it drew from Neiman had been gasoline on what had been a slow-burning campaign. Neiman had repeatedly tried to draw his opponent into battle, but Tony had preferred to campaign as if a lone candidate, just laying out his agenda, and his alone, before the public for their endorsement.

He had won the Republican primary handily, while Neiman had fought long and hard over contenders for the Democratic slot. The senator seemed unwilling to lose that confrontational momentum, and that made for promising news days.

Weaving inconspicuously through the crowd was a surveillance team of FDLE officers and FBI agents, men and women dressed like everyone else that breezy morning near the surf—linen slacks and chinos, loose sleeves or no sleeves, unbuttoned collars and slip-ons from Birkenstocks to Italian sandals.

From a first-floor balcony above the terrace, Warren, in a Miami Dolphins cap and running clothes, and two similarly attired detectives stood with coffee cups in their hands, casually soaking in the morning rays, or so it would seem to anyone glancing up at them. Behind dark glasses, though, their eyes were systematically scanning every face below them, searching for something familiar or incongruent.

"He's here somewhere," Warren said under his breath. "Right now. Waiting to take his shot."

Beyond the terrace was the usual contingent of beach-goers in various pursuits. Guests of the hotel lounged beneath umbrellas, reading or watching children romp in the waves. Some in partially enclosed cabanas slept or played cards. Shellers carrying buckets and mesh bags formed bent-double silhouettes as they picked through the bounty deposited by retreating waves. Habitual strutters, with no notion of weekend or weekday, never let anything stop their display of skin as they passed in review up and down the famous beach.

Offshore, a couple of sailboats and other small craft cruised the shoreline. With binoculars, Warren swept the decks of those boats, noting who and how many were aboard and what their interests seemed to be. On a bright morning full of southeasterly wind to billow their sails, what else might those interests be but the leisurely pursuit of pleasure? And how unlikely that someone could steady a shot from a bouncing boat. Still, Warren watched. A white sloop with three or four aboard bobbed along a northerly course. A small J35-class sailboat with a green hull and three bare-chested guys already downing brews passed the sloop heading south. A couple of supple-bodied young girls ripped wakes with their Jet Skis, wet hair flying behind them and hardly a glance toward the terrace. *Why would they?* Warren thought. The world was theirs already.

Besides Warren and the rest of the law enforcement team, only the hotel manager knew that Tony Ryborg, the featured attraction at this morning's campaign-stop breakfast, had cancelled his appearance, though the manager wasn't told why. But he *was* told to announce that cancellation to no one, not even his crew now setting up the podium and microphone. Before the FBI's warning of an assassin, Warren had instructed that the podium be placed deep under the wide awning along the back wall of the terrace and not in the open. The most likely vantage point for an assassin would be one of the ocean-view rooms, each with an open balcony and sliding glass doors. At the time, though, there was no certainty that anyone wished Tony harm. Now, there was. At least, that was the collective opinion.

The tipoff late last night had changed everything. With Tony and Andie now under guard, Warren and his team had hustled to set a trap for the assassin. Warren hoped that he, or she, was unsuspecting and maybe a little brazen. That would make him easier to detect, if he didn't first sniff the disguised officers placed about the building.

Instead of emptying all ocean-front rooms, which tight security might have dictated, officers were placed in various costumes up and down the hallways feeding those rooms. Anyone leaving the area in any suspicious manner or carrying questionable baggage would be stopped and searched.

In swimsuits and loose-fitting shirts to conceal their weapons, officers patrolled the beach, watching those in cabanas, under umbrellas, offshore, and just strolling by carrying anything that would conceal a weapon, even another blousy shirt.

Warren had asked the bewildered manager to move the podium from under the awning to a wide-open spot by the steps to the beach. To insure the manager's silence and to monitor anything the man thought unusual, like an employee he'd never seen before, one agent remained with him throughout the morning's preparations.

"Sir, when was Mr. Ryborg supposed to speak?" one of the detectives on the balcony with Warren asked.

"In an hour, but they won't announce until it's already apparent he's not going to show. Meanwhile, keep looking. I'm going down there. And use your earpiece discreetly. We don't want him spotting us first."

As Warren walked away from the two detectives, he felt their eyes on his back. Ever since he'd stepped in front of the last bullet meant for Tony Ryborg, he'd had to weather a celebrity he found distasteful. Too many of his fellow officers had set him apart, unabashedly proud of him, but at the same time fearful they might be incapable of rising to that kind of bravery, that unspeakable sacrifice. Some just thought he was crazy, which he preferred.

On the terrace, Warren passed through the crowd and headed for a palm-shaped shadow on the beach. From there, he studied the bank of windows on the back of the hotel, then focused on the breakfast crowd. He alerted his team through the wireless, Bluetooth-type fittings on their sunglasses. "All team: Watch for anyone who frequently looks up at the building. There may be a spotter in the crowd who'll signal to the shooter. Pay close attention when the announcement is made that Tony has canceled. That should prompt a clear signal. Those of you in the garage and on the street, check all cars parked or idling with a lone driver for any length of time. Officers on the beach, watch those boats and cabanas. Anyone making a sudden move, grab 'em and hold 'em. Out."

Warren quickly returned to the balcony. The buffet line below had wound to an end and nearly all the convention guests were seated at tables spread over the terrace. The news crews hung back and waited. None of them seemed to mind the sun, still low in the sky, its September heat buffeted by a steady breeze off the Atlantic.

At the podium, a man introducing himself as the convention director greeted his guests and invited them to take their time over breakfast. He acknowledged that Tony Ryborg had not yet arrived at the hotel, but assured them the candidate would take the podium momentarily. As if to fill time, he offered a protracted review of the convention's agenda with profiles of its research presenters and other guest speakers, notice of forums and receptions hosted by pharmaceutical companies, and a list of enticing options for spending their off time.

"Sir," came a voice to Warren's earpiece, "two o'clock to your position. The guy in dark green polo shirt. Seems interested in a spot about the fifth floor, to your far left."

"Roger that. Keep watch." Warren alerted the officers on those floors and studied the man in question. After a while, though, Warren decided the man was too chatty with others he obviously knew—not the profile of a lone signaler who'd somehow finagled his way into the event.

"Got one," came another transmission. "Blue Hawaiian shirt seated your left of podium, midway back, facing south. No sunglasses. Crew cut. Definitely fixed on a window about a third way up, to your right."

"I'm watching," Warren replied. From the tight fit of the man's shirt across his shoulders and the display of tanned arms now casually folded across his chest, Warren could see he was well-built. But what locked him on the man was the way his eyes kept lifting toward the building, always the same place—and the way he talked to no one at his table, as if he didn't belong.

"Everyone hear that? Keep scanning, but pay particular attention to blue Hawaiian ten yards left of podium, facing south." Warren then reissued an alert to all hallways on the south wing.

It was fifteen minutes past Tony's expected arrival time. Many had finished their breakfast and begun to fidget. The director approached the podium again, his brow creased with displeasure.

"Here it comes," Warren alerted. "Listen and watch." Warren's voice was low but urgent. "This is the announcement we've been waiting for."

"Ladies and gentlemen, I regret to inform you that our featured speaker, Tony Ryborg, will be unable to address us this morning. He sends his profound apologies to . . ."

The arms came off the chest of the man in the blue Hawaiian shirt. His head shot upward and, in the most unmistakable fashion, moved side to side.

"Fifth floor!" shouted an agent on the ground. "Drapes just swung shut behind an open door. No ID on suspect."

Outside room 550 on the hotel's south wing, a maid was folding towels on a laundry cart when the door to the room opened and a man in light blue shorts and a white golf shirt calmly walked out. He smiled at her as he shouldered the strap of his golf bag and closed the door. As he headed toward the elevators, the woman reached beneath the towels and pulled out a handgun. Between her and the elevators, a man vacuuming the carpet also reached for a gun, then yelled, "Miami Police! Stop!"

The man in the golf shirt suddenly bolted for the stairwell behind him, threw open the door, and plowed into a snare of six beefy arms and a pair of ready handcuffs. After reading the man his rights, one of the arresting officers bent to search the golf bag, which had fallen to the floor during the scuffle. Inside was all the firepower and other proof the courts would need to judiciously remove one more assassin from polite society—and someone's payroll. But whose?

In the service alley to one side of the hotel, a squad of unmarked cars awaited the transfer of two suspects to FDLE headquarters. Only one of them, though, was ready to go. Back on the terrace, Warren and three FBI agents were discreetly following the man in the blue Hawaiian shirt as he hurried, not back into the hotel lobby like the other guests, but down a sidewalk to the parking garage, where Warren had stationed another team.

In minutes, the suspect was in handcuffs and escorted to one of the waiting cars. "Surprise is a wonderful thing, don't you think?" Warren taunted as he pulled the suspect along.

"Shut up!" the man seethed.

"There you are enjoying a relaxing moment in the sunshine, and the next minute . . . you're meat on a hook!"

When they reached the car, Warren firmly pushed the man's head clear of the car roof and delivered him inside, slamming the door after him. "Take him!" he ordered.

❧

The arrests were made so smoothly, the removal of suspects so quickly, no one from the media knew anything untoward had happened until one steward on the hotel staff, eager for an on-air interview, alerted the press.

Afterward, the local networks buzzed with speculation on what might have happened at the Excalibur Hotel that morning, though the hotel manager offered no comment. The steward knew only that two men had been arrested, nothing more. Still, it was one more incendiary incident in a campaign the national media was beginning to court.

❧

When Warren reached headquarters, Chief Manette snagged him. "I've uncovered our mole," he told Warren. "Come with me."

Warren followed him down a hallway to a series of interrogation rooms. In one of them, Manny Alvarez and Cleo Banks sat opposite each other at a table. When the chief and Warren entered the room, both officers stood. "Sit," the chief snapped.

A sick, incredulous feeling swept over Warren as he stood looking down at the two.

"Sergeant Banks, tell Captain Jacobs about your encounter Saturday afternoon."

Cleo Banks sat hunched in defense mode. She glanced quickly at Warren, then at Manny, then back at the table. In that brief exchange, Warren read two things in Manny's eyes that somewhat relieved him: compassion for a fellow officer and disappointment, as from a father, for that officer's misbehavior.

"I was hurrying to gather my things for my assignment at Stiltsville with, you know, Miss Ryborg," she began, "when someone stopped me near my locker and started asking questions."

Warren quietly pulled a chair up to the table, but the chief remained standing. Sergeant Banks looked nervously from one to the other. "Go on," the chief ordered.

Cleo swallowed hard. "She wanted to know where they were taking Miss Ryborg. And, well, I told her."

Warren slapped his hand against the table, making the woman jump. "Why? And who was it?"

"It was because of *who* it was that I told her," Sergeant Banks replied, her voice rising. "Lizzie's been a dispatcher here for a long time. Everybody knows her, and no one would dream she might be, you know, bad." She paused. "I sure didn't." She stared back at the table and kept talking. "She knows most everything that's going on, anyway. She has to. It's her job."

"And it was your job to keep the whereabouts of Miss Ryborg confidential, knowing her life depended on it," the chief snapped. He turned to Warren. "I'll fill you in on the rest." He left the room, and Warren followed, not looking back.

"It didn't take us long to get a confession from Lizzie Stafos," the chief said. "She's Leo Francini's plant. There's no telling how many busts of his operations she foiled. Knowing when and where we were headed, all she had to do was signal the alarm.

On those raids, we got the goods but no personnel. He paid her handsomely. We've already tapped her bank accounts. Had that in hand before we questioned her.

"And guess who her handler was?"

Warren leaned in.

"One of the guys you just brought in."

"Let me guess. Blue shirt, stubby hair."

Chief Manette nodded. "Name's Ray Dingo."

CHAPTER 33

᪷

As the Excalibur Hotel operation was reaching its climax, lieutenants Paul Rivera and Bill Levitt arrived at the Ft. Lauderdale address Evan had provided the night before, after his search of Leo's file box.

Cross-reference and background checks found the owner to be an independent yacht broker named Nick Jarvis. He'd moved to Florida six years earlier from his home state of New Jersey, where he'd once been indicted for racketeering but escaped conviction after two key witnesses changed their testimonies. Since then, his record had been clean.

"Maybe Francini's just buying a boat from the guy," Levitt suggested.

"Could be," Rivera said as he stopped the unmarked car at the palm-shrouded entrance to a low-rise condominium building. As they got out, they could see the Ditch stretched behind the building. To many East Coast boaters, the Intracoastal Waterway was as much a monotonous straightaway as I-95, broken only occasionally by an alluring strip of real estate such as this.

The two officers parked in front, entered the glass-walled lobby, and took the elevator to the third floor. They knocked and rang the doorbell at Nick Jarvis's apartment, but no one answered. A moment later, an older gentleman stepped off the elevator and was about to head in the opposite direction when Rivera stopped him. "Sir, may we ask you a question?"

The man turned and frowned at the pair now approaching him. Noting his apprehension, both officers produced their badges, and the man visibly relaxed. "Do you happen to know Nick Jarvis?" Rivera continued.

"Oh my, yes," the man answered with an English accent. Everyone here knows Nicky."

"How so?"

"Well, he's a most likable fella who rather dotes on his neighbors, throwing elaborate parties on his vessel and whatnot."

"Do you know where he might be?"

The man brought a hand to his chin and considered. "Well, I did see him leave yesterday with a bit of luggage, so I would say he's on holiday. Or off to one of his other homes."

Levitt raised his brow. "Where might these other homes be, sir?"

"Perhaps I shouldn't be answering so many questions without knowing why you're asking them. Is Nicky in some sort of trouble?"

"We just need to ask him a few questions about some people he might know. It would help us with an investigation we're not able to disclose."

"Oh, right. I understand. I just hope nothing has happened to him. Well, let me see. He's mentioned an apartment in Manhattan and some sort of residence in Monte Carlo. And of course, he spends a lot of time on his vessel."

"And where might that be, sir?" Rivera asked.

The man chuckled softly. "Oh, I should say you'll have no trouble finding it. Out back there on the waterway. Nicky named it *The Blonde*. Isn't that delicious? Well, I must be going."

"Thank you, sir," Levitt called as the man abruptly walked away. "May we get your name, sir?"

But the man didn't stop to answer.

"We can find him later if we need to," Rivera said. "Let's check out the boat." But that proved as unyielding as the apartment: curtains drawn, no one about. The officers were about to return to the building to question more residents when Rivera's cell phone rang. He listened intently, then shot his partner a "you won't believe this" look. "Yes, sir. We'll wait for them." Then to Levitt, "That was the chief. He's sending a warrant and a search team. It seems Tony Ryborg nearly got himself assassinated this morning, and the chief is real interested in our 'likable fella' here."

Leo was on U.S. soil again, at a new base camp in the Keys. It was a crude installation he kept for fall-back times such as this. No one but Miguel and the small band of soldiers with him knew about it. Not even Dingo.

Later, one of Leo's cell phones rang. He checked the incoming number and smiled, then quickly plugged the phone to a tiny digital recorder and answered. "Too bad you missed your man this morning," he said to Nick Jarvis.

"Too bad for you. It's going to cost you plenty."

Leo didn't respond.

"I know it was you," Jarvis said. "No one else could have tipped him. I'm just not sure why you did it. Was it because I threatened your kid and his mom? The same kid who nearly brought the cops down on your head? I just don't know, Leo. But I tell you what: no more threats. You broke the rules, and I don't punish with mere threats. Know what I mean?"

"No, Jarvis, what do you mean?"

"Uh-oh, you broke another rule. No names, remember. You're getting sloppy. Bad things happen to sloppy people." The call ended.

CHAPTER 34

༃

ANDIE SET HER HALF-EATEN BAGEL back on the plate and walked outside. "I'll be on the porch, Dad," she said to Tony. A cell phone snug to his ear, he smiled faintly and kept talking with Warren, who had just arrived at the Excalibur Hotel that crisp Monday morning, on the cusp of a dragnet. The warning call they'd received the night before had ignited a fury to catch an assassin. Tony had been up since dawn, camped in the kitchen with several officers monitoring communications from Warren's team at the hotel.

The grim mood inside followed Andie to the porch. She leaned against a column and gazed at the hazy yellow orb lifting from the horizon, turning clear water to polished sapphire. *How can something so grand be eclipsed by what lurks in the small, dark mind of a man? Someone out there wants to kill my father on this beautiful morning.* She squinted at the horizon. *Someone else out there is risking his life for me, and I repaid him with my contempt.* She eased into the wicker chair behind her. *And now, we've run Thea from her home after she took us in.*

After following Thea the night before, Vic had reported that the older woman had gone to the reservation as she'd said. "It's just those crazy hunches I get sometimes," she'd told Tony in her call to him earlier that morning. "One hit me hard last night when Thea announced she was leaving. There's just something about that nice old woman that makes me want to scratch, you know? But I'm not sure where the itch is."

Hearing about that conversation from her dad had made Andie smile for the first time that morning. *But what makes Vic suspicious of Thea?* Andie squeezed her eyes shut and pictured her friend preparing food for everyone, making up beds and putting out clean towels, washing clothes, and all the while quietly offering encouragement. Who was taking care of her now?

She sat for a long time, praying for Thea and Evan until the back door opened. "Andie," her dad called, "come inside. We've found a note."

As he held out the small envelope to her, he explained, "It was propped on a table in the upstairs hall." The note was addressed to "Tony and Andie" in a neat, flowing hand. Andie opened it quickly and found a single piece of stationery and a key. The note read:

> Dear ones,
>
> Take this key to the boathouse and go inside. I have left something for you on my bed. Andie, you remember which bedroom is mine.
>
> This isn't the way I intended it. But I pray you will understand.
>
> May God bless you both.
> Thea

Andie answered the unspoken question in Tony's eyes. "I don't know, Dad. Let's go."

Followed by two armed guards, Tony and Andie crossed the side lawn to the boathouse. Tony had not been near it but now admired its quaint charm. They used the key and went inside. At once, he was struck by the same things that had captivated Andie on first sight. The vibrant paintings of young children playing in bright sunlight and the many sculptures of trees and animals. "It's a happy kind of place, isn't it?" Andie said.

But Tony was fixed on just one spot. One painting. In it, three little boys in Cub Scout uniforms sat on a wooden floor playing Jacks. One little boy with jet black hair sat with his back to the viewer. The other two boys had light hair, one with a cowlick in the front. Tony slowly approached the painting and stopped before it, mouth open, eyes locked on the image.

"Dad, what's wrong?"

He pointed to the dark-haired child and said, "That's me."

Andie stared at the painting, then back at her dad. "What do you mean? You can't even see the face. It's—"

"That's me with my friends Joey and Bruce from next door. Mom took the picture and framed it." He spoke mechanically, as if dazed. "It sat on my dresser for a while, and I don't know what happened to it. But this was painted from that photograph."

He looked more urgently at Andie. "Where's her bedroom?"

She led him into the room with the pretty blue and white toile wallpaper, and the first thing she noticed was pictures hanging where there had been none before, just two hooks on an empty wall. But now, two faded portraits hung side by side. In one, her dad wore a graduation cap and gown. In the other, her parents stood in front of a Christmas tree, her dad holding his baby daughter. Andie's hands went to her cheeks, hot and flaming. "Dad, this can't be."

They finally tore themselves from the photographs and focused on the old suitcase in the center of the bed. "Go ahead, Andie," he said softly. "Open it."

He stood over her as she unlatched the top and opened the old case, groping its contents with her eyes before touching anything. Finally, she lifted the gourd. It was just like the one in her dad's keepsake box. Small and brightly painted. She looked up at her dad and saw the sweat on his brow. He reached for the gourd, turned it over in his hands, then shook it. He sat heavily on the bed and picked up one of many albums stacked inside the case. He opened it, flipped through its pages, then moved to the next album, and the next. They were all filled with photographs, copies of graduation announcements from kindergarten through college, awards, news clippings—all copies because the originals were in his home, left him by his mother. They were the paper trail of his young life.

On the bottom of the case was a large brown envelope. Inside was a binder of legal papers. Tony withdrew them and read, the papers beginning to shake in his hands. When he was finished, he handed them to Andie and left the room. She heard the door to the porch open and close.

They were adoption papers documenting that Paul Everett and Isabel Andrea Ryborg had taken legal custody of a baby boy, born out of wedlock to . . .

Andie gripped the side of the bed, digging her fingers into the soft quilt. She couldn't think what to do, how to feel. She stared down at the papers unable to collect all their implications, fingering them as if she might coax some explanation from them. It was then that she saw the letter, tucked in a plain, sealed envelope, her dad's name on the outside written in the same hand as the note just found in the house.

When she reached her dad, he was sitting quietly on the porch, staring out at the sea. He seemed not to notice when she opened the door. "Dad," she said hesitantly. He turned to her with weak eyes, his face pale. Andie handed him the letter.

He ran his hand over the writing on the outside, then gave it back to her. "You read it."

Andie removed two typewritten pages from the envelope and began reading aloud:

> It's true, Tony. You are my son. I just couldn't know you. That was your deliverance from my broken world, I thought, and my punishment.
>
> Days after your birth, I gave you away because I was without faith, without hope, but mostly, without a husband. Your father was an English artist named Ian Strathmore, who visited our reservation one summer. We fell in love. He was a charming but reckless man who soon returned to England, where he was killed by another inmate in prison. He'd been sent there for a crime I never knew about. It wasn't important what it was. He died soon after you were born, never knowing he'd become a father.

When my own father discovered I was with
child, he banished me from my home and the
Miccosukee Indian Reservation to which we
belonged. I was four months pregnant and an
outcast with nowhere to go.

But Paul and Isabel Ryborg, through a ministry to
unwed mothers, helped me find a job and housing.
They were with me when you were born. They
wanted me to keep you and trust God to take care
of us, but I didn't know God then, and I didn't trust
myself to give you the life I wanted you to have.
What could an outcast Indian mother offer you? I
knew Paul and Isabel would cherish you as I would.
They were childless. It was perfect. I just didn't know
how tormented I would remain for the rest of my life.

Though your parents sent me most of the things
you see in these albums, I made them promise
never to tell you who I was. After Paul was gone
and Isabel knew she didn't have long, she wanted
someone to be the keeper of our secret. So she told
your Jessica about me. Your wife was thrilled to
know of your biological mother. She was coming
to see me the day she died. We were to meet in
Asheville, where I was vacationing alone in the
Blakers' mountain house.

I knew that one day I had to make my peace
with you, Tony, or at least try. I had to know my
granddaughter. When one of her paintings showed
up at Randall Ivy's gallery and he told me Andie
was teaching classes, I believed God was finally
opening a door for me.

I regret that this comes at such a difficult time in
your life. But I couldn't wait any longer to tell you

that I have loved you your whole life. Forgive me
for not being there.

Your mother,
Thea Long

Andie reached for her dad's hand. He gave it a squeeze but
wouldn't look at her.

As father and daughter rested on that wind-swept porch by
the sea, it occurred to Andie that she had the answer to her question: How can something so grand as creation be eclipsed by the
evil in the small, dark mind of a man?

It can't. Something she'd just read in Scripture returned to
her. Jesus told his disciples, "In this world you will have trouble.
But take heart! I have overcome the world."

And all the evil in it.

CHAPTER 35

LATE THAT AFTERNOON, the gates at the Blaker mansion opened and yet another unmarked sedan entered the long drive. When it emerged into the head-on light of a dropping sun and came to rest at the front door of the house, Tony Ryborg was there to greet it.

The back door of the car opened. Evan swung his long legs out and stood up. His jeans were baggy but his cotton T-shirt stretched tight across his broad chest. They were the only clothes he had, the only ones from the boat that he hadn't packed into his duffel bag and, later, left behind at Cat's Eye.

Tony's strong hand gripped Evan's shoulder. "I know it's been hard, son."

Son? The familiarity caught Evan by surprise.

"You had a tough time on that island. I just got the FBI's preliminary report. That tracker they put on your boat before you left was the only way they found you last night."

Evan shrugged. "I would have made it back on my own."

"But without you safely in their grasp, they wouldn't have gone through with the raid." Tony eyed him carefully. "You once told us you were a nobody, remember? I hope you now realize how mistaken you are."

Evan looked quickly at the ground, not knowing how to respond. Being a nobody had always been easier. But he was growing sick of it. Sick of the pity he'd heaped on himself, the blame he'd hurled at his mother and grandparents. He'd convinced himself it was their fault he was a nobody, son of a murderer. He was tired of it.

"You haven't had much sleep, have you?" Tony asked.

"Just a little on my boat coming back. One of the agents drove."

Tony looked thoughtful. "You know, after they sent you and your security detail back to Miami and went on with the raid, they and the Bahamian police uncovered quite a stockpile of weapons and drugs in that village. The whole place was corrupt, and here's what you need to know: because of you, we saved the lives of some little kids. They were living with parents who had no business bringing children into that kind of world. But now those kids can know a better life, if they choose to."

Evan met Tony's direct gaze and understood exactly what he meant. *If Evan Markham chooses to.*

"Now," Tony said brightly, as if to dispel any tension, "until this thing comes to a head, you'll be camping here with us. I hope that's all right."

Evan looked up at the fine home, catching a flutter of curtains from one of the upstairs windows. She was there, and something inside him lurched. The curtains closed, and he looked back at Tony. "Why is Andie here?"

Tony glanced at the window and back at Evan. "Someone found out where we'd taken her. The same someone who warned me that I was to be, uh, eliminated this morning during my speech on Miami Beach."

"What!"

Tony patted his shoulder. "We'll tell you all about that later."

"But sir, I want to know—"

"And I will tell you after we've settled you in. Andie and I are fine, so don't worry."

Don't worry? Mad men are out there hunting for us all, and he says don't worry. What is the man made of?

Tony led Evan into the front hall of the house. Evan quickly scanned the sumptuous home, its impact clear on his face.

"Humble digs, I know," Tony said, "but we've come to think of it as home. For longer than we thought. Come into the kitchen, and we'll fix you a sandwich."

This isn't the reception I thought I'd get, more like a boot from behind and a "get out of our lives." I don't know what to make of this. "If you don't mind, sir, I'd rather get cleaned up a bit."

"Sure, that's fine. Oh, and you'll find some clothes in your room. Vic saw to that. She said you'd left the island in too big a hurry to pack." He smiled kindly, then summoned one of the officers to show Evan upstairs.

His room was at the opposite end of the hall from where he'd seen Andie. *That's strategic.* He shut the door behind him and went straight to the private bathroom off what must have been a young boy's room. Framed pictures of Roger Maris and Mickey Mantle hung on the wall, and model airplanes dangled from the ceiling.

After a long, indulgent shower, he went to the closet and found several pairs of new pants and some shirts of different styles. *No pink flamingos?* He smiled to himself as he pulled on blue jeans and a white cotton shirt, tails out and sleeves rolled to the elbows. He slipped back into his boat shoes and left the room. A sandwich seemed a good option right now. He'd almost reached the stairs when she called to him.

"Come talk to me," Andie said.

Evan spun around and saw her sitting in an alcove off the long hallway, which ran the length of the house. His pulse pounded as he approached. He didn't understand his reaction to her. He'd only wanted to redeem himself by protecting her. Nothing more. So why did the sight of her do this to him?

She stood up. "Out here." She led him to an upstairs porch overlooking the bay. When she opened the door, he caught the clean, earthy scent of her on the sudden draft. He followed her across the deep porch, watching how easily she moved in the long, summery dress, its light skirt ruffled by the wind.

She went to the railing and rested her arms on top, gazing out to sea. He awkwardly joined her. "I saw you out there the night you left," she said, her eyes still on the water. "You and *Misfit.*"

"Where?"

She pointed toward the channel. "Out there near the stilt houses. You passed us."

Evan suddenly remembered. "Was it you who flashed the light across my boat?"

"That was Manny. He told me it was your boat. I watched until I couldn't see you anymore, going where you shouldn't have

gone. And I was sorry." She turned to look at him, a long strand
of hair blowing across her face. She pulled it aside and tucked it
behind one ear.

Evan saw the tiny seashell earring. So delicate. But he knew
she was not. He knew there was steel beneath that soft exterior,
and he was grateful. It had sustained her. "I don't know what to
say to you, Andie. I shouldn't even be here."

"Where should you be?"

It was his turn to look to the horizon. "Maybe back at school,
putting Leo Francini back in his box. I don't know."

"You were pre-med, weren't you?"

"How did you know?"

"Don't think for a second that every data bank with your name
in it hasn't been raked by every law enforcement branch out there
by now. Maybe you can go back soon."

That amused Evan. "Tell me you haven't forgotten who they
handcuffed and hauled in for stalking you and vandalizing your
house. What I did deserves—"

"What you did, Evan," she interrupted, "was save my hide and
sabotage this outrageous plot. I know that now, but I'm not sure
you do. I think you've been feeling sorry for yourself for so long
you don't know when to stop."

Evan bristled. "And you can say such a thing because you know
me so well. Right?" *But she is right.*

"No, I just listen well, mostly between the lines." She sighed,
looked out at the water, then turned quickly back to him. "But
I'm sorry. I didn't mean to be so harsh. I brought you out here
to tell you I understand what you did. And to thank you for *why*
you did it."

The same lock of hair escaped from behind her ear and blew
into her face again. Before Evan knew what he was doing, he
reached for it and tucked it gently back in place, lightly brushing
her cheek as he withdrew his hand. He was suddenly embarrassed at this impulsive act, one that seemed to catch them both
off guard.

Andie didn't move, her eyes steady on his. *Whatever this is, it
isn't supposed to happen,* he thought, fighting a sudden impulse

to gather her into his arms and wrap her tightly against a dangerous world. He wanted to press his cheek to the soft curls of her head and linger there. Instead, he stepped back. "You're welcome, Andie." He didn't know anything else to do but turn and walk away.

He closed the porch door behind him and started back to his room to sort through all that collided inside him. But when he reached the door to his room, he stopped and looked back toward the entrance to the porch. No movement, no sound. *She's still out there, still a Ryborg. And I'm a Francini. And that's that.*

Just then, hunger struck Evan with gnawing force, and he realized he'd eaten very little that day. After leaving *Misfit* at police docks that morning, he'd been taken to FDLE headquarters and questioned most of the afternoon. They'd wanted to know all he'd seen and heard on Cat's Eye. Now, he turned and headed down the stairs, almost laughing at himself. *When life hangs in the balance, go fix yourself a sandwich.*

As he entered the kitchen, Vic turned and greeted him. "Well, here you are," she chirped. She regarded him carefully for a moment, then walked up to him and gave him a quick catch-and-release hug, which took him by surprise.

"Oh, now don't get bashful on me," she teased. "You just looked like you needed it. Fresh from trying to kill that giant all by yourself." She fixed a knowing eye on him, then turned to the group. "Now, everybody sit down here, and let's see where we are."

Senior Special Agent Vic Shay held court. "Tony, of course, knows more than I can tell the rest of you, but Evan, that little snatch of address was a coup, perhaps even worth letting Leo get away from us, for now. I can't divulge what all we found inside the Ft. Lauderdale condo this morning besides one mother lode of computer files naming folks Jarvis liked to do business with. The bureau's in a cross-matching frenzy looking for three of the same fruit to line up across our screen. At this moment, we're also searching the contents of that little dinghy tied up behind Jarvis's place."

Tony sat quietly.

"As for our two hotel hoodlums, the trigger man doesn't know who hired him. The assignment came through a killers-'r'-us kind of network based in Amsterdam, its tentacles spread around the globe." She cut her eyes quickly at Tony, then back at the others gathered around the kitchen table.

"But the signal man on the ground is another story. Ray Dingo isn't talking."

"Dingo!" Evan groped for the missing link.

"At this point, Evan, we're not sure if Dingo is still Leo's man or not," Vic said. "We can't be sure your dad was behind the assassination attempt." Evan felt the chill through his limbs. "But if what you heard from those two men on the island indicated that Dingo is in someone else's camp, then it's someone who wants to get at Leo by killing you. At this point, I doubt Leo ordered the assassination. Not this time."

"Then who did?" Evan asked.

Before Vic could answer, Andie walked in and motioned her dad aside. He got up and went to her. Evan overheard something about Thea returning soon. But he didn't understand the intensity on Andie's face. *What's going on?*

Andie moved toward the refrigerator, glancing at Evan, then the others. "I'm pulling out leftovers and sandwich stuff. Help yourselves."

Evan watched her as she busied herself with the food. She'd caught her hair up in a clasp and pulled on a loose sweater.

"Evan, we don't know who's running Dingo," Vic continued. Then she put a plate of food down in front of him and ordered him to eat. Evan complied. As he dug into the ham and cheese on a soft roll with a side of potato salad, he watched Andie and her dad take their plates to the back porch. No one followed them.

It was soon dark, and no one had come in from the porch. Evan remained in the kitchen. He'd almost come to welcome his time with Vic, even though she'd recently held a gun on him. There was something strangely reassuring about her. Almost nurturing. He asked with genuine concern how Elvis was. That launched an expansive tale about the little dog's confrontation with a wild parrot, the same one, Evan guessed, that had once buzzed *Misfit*. In the middle of Vic's animated story, Tony returned from the porch, alone. Evan wondered where Andie was and if she'd ever want to talk to him again. When Vic had to break for a call, Evan seized the opportunity to walk outside. Andie wasn't there.

Spotlights around the house made it hard to see beyond. He strolled into the back yard, stopping to inhale the salty rush of air and focusing on tiny lights from boats in the channel—night fishermen heading to sea. He longed for the freedom he felt at the helm of *Misfit*, plying the ocean with nothing but the moon and stars as crew. Then he remembered the loneliness of it. *Fighting giants all alone.*

CHAPTER 36

ANDIE WAS GLAD for the sweater she'd slipped over her dress. She hadn't planned to come this far from the house, not in the chill of night. But now that she was here by the water's edge, she was happy to remain for a while longer. She took off her shoes and sank her toes into the sand, almost luminous under a full moon.

Noticing a bench a few yards away, she wandered toward it. She brushed the sand from her feet and tucked them beneath her on the sagging wooden slats, then gathered her skirt around her. Swaddled and warm, her thoughts turned to Evan, as they did so often now. This enigmatic young man who'd entered her life—both predator and protector—had shaken her to the core. Because of him and his father, she and hers were now captive, quarantined from the rest of society for the peril they attracted.

Still, she was drawn to him. Why? Did she feel responsible for the trouble he was in? Indebted to him? When he touched her cheek, why did she shiver?

Lord, should I run from him? If so, then take away this longing to be near him. I don't understand it. It may only be gratitude for the risks he took for me. Maybe it's because he's so alone and wounded. Andie instinctively wrapped the sweater tighter. She lifted her face to a caressing wind. *Make him know you.*

Suddenly, she heard footsteps in the grass behind her. She jumped to her feet and saw the white of his shirt.

"Andie, it's Evan," he called. "Don't be afraid."

She didn't move as he slowly approached. "You shouldn't be out here by yourself," he told her with a trace of scolding.

"I'm not."

He looked at her oddly.

"Let's walk, Evan." They started down the beach. He seemed content to just stroll quietly beside her, but Andie couldn't rest until she'd spoken what pressed so insistently upon her. She wasn't used to speaking as she was about to. It wasn't comfortable. But at that moment, with that one person beside her, she believed it was critical.

"Evan, I don't know you and may never see you again after all this is over. I don't even know where either one of us will be tomorrow."

He said nothing.

"But I do know that, well, that I care about you." She could feel his eyes on her, but she wouldn't look into them, only at the moonlit beach spread before her. Though she trembled inside, her voice was steady. "Evan, all those nights when I lay awake wondering who might be outside my window, I did the only thing that brought me peace. I prayed."

Evan abruptly stopped and turned toward her. Only then did she look up at him. "I talked to God all night, Evan. Have you ever done that?"

He ran his fingers through his hair and gazed beyond the shore. When he turned back to Andie, he said, "Last night, I asked him to help me escape the island alive. It was the first time I'd prayed since I was a little kid. Every Christmas, my mom would take me and my brother to church. I didn't know how to pray, but I tried. I just didn't think anyone was listening."

"And last night?"

Evan shrugged. "I don't know if the prayer saved me or not. I'm not sure God's even there."

Andie responded immediately. "Do you trust me, Evan?"

His eyes seemed to take her in and hold her. "I want to."

She reached for his hand and held it gently. "Trust this, Evan. When I pray, he answers. When I'm afraid, he comforts. When I'm in need, he provides. If you don't know him, it's because you haven't asked to."

"Andie!" came the call. They looked to see two men heading toward the beach. One of them was Manny Alvarez. She released Evan's hand and waved both arms. "It's okay. We're over here."

"Back to the house," Manny called.

CHAPTER 37

THAT NIGHT, ANDIE COULDN'T SLEEP. Just before midnight, she pulled on a pair of jeans, a sweatshirt, and old sneakers and went to the back porch where she and Evan had talked earlier. After quietly closing the door, she was startled to see a figure at the railing. *Evan.*

They stood facing each other for a moment, surprised that the other was there. Then he motioned for her to join him. "Come look at this big white pizza someone hurled into a tree." He turned back and pointed to a flat-looking moon perched like a Christmas-tree topper on a soaring pine.

When Andie reached him, she looked into the sky and giggled. It was just a silly thing, but it soothed her to think of something lighthearted.

Then Evan's mood changed. He turned his back on the moon and focused only on her. "I came out here to clear my head, but I'm not sure I did." He shoved both hands into his pockets and lowered his gaze to the floor. "You've filled it too full. It feels like bumper cars gone haywire in there."

Andie hardly blinked as she watched his face.

"I just did something I've never done before, Andie." He glanced at the rooftop. "I just spoke to Jesus like he was standing right in front of me. I'd like to think he was."

Andie's breathing grew shallow.

"I mean, I've never thought of him as anything but a figure in stained glass or someone slumped on a bright gold cross hanging so high in a church you couldn't reach him. That's the religious icon part, I guess. And what you're trying to tell me, I think, is that it's not about religion. It's about him and me. Just the two of us. Me asking, him answering. Is that how it goes?"

She couldn't speak. She just took his hands in hers and laid her cheek against them.

Without another word, he pulled her gently to him. Feeling his arms tighten around her, she rested her head against his chest, inhaling the warmth of him. In the light of new understanding, two young people, both prey to the scheme of man, rested in each other's embrace.

Andie lifted her face to his. With her eyes, she traced the line of his jaw and mouth. Then she closed her eyes and felt his lips brush softly against hers.

He raised his head and looked at her, his arms still snug against her. "If you don't want me to fall in love with you, you'd better say so now," he whispered.

She pulled back from him and looked earnestly in his eyes. "I have a question."

He let his arms fall limp to his sides. "Well, that wasn't the response I was looking for, but go ahead."

"Why didn't you ever speak to me at school?" she asked.

"And kindle a relationship that was impossible? The attorney general's daughter and the son of public enemy number one?"

"And is it still impossible?"

Evan answered by reaching for her again. This time, Andie let the fullness of his kiss engulf her. How could something so tender weigh so powerfully upon her? It seemed every loose tendril of her life had been caught up and secured in this one moment.

He tucked her to his side and turned them toward the bay. "And here we are, the Capulets and the Montagues," he teased. "But maybe, my Juliet, we'll override Shakespeare and write our own ending: we will be revived, and while the families scramble for justice, we'll sail away."

Andie laughed. "Where?"

"Where there are no drug lords, only beautiful skies for you to paint and lots of villagers who need a doctor." Evan suddenly looked wistful.

"Then, it *is* possible," she declared.

He kissed the top of her head but said nothing.

CHAPTER 38

𝕏

AFTER STOPPING FOR GUARDS to search the pickup, Thea's nephew drove down the long drive. Before reaching the Blaker house, though, the truck veered left toward the boathouse. Thea got out and retrieved her bag from the back of the truck.

As the old truck rumbled away that Tuesday morning, Thea went inside her house to prepare for that moment she'd dreamed of her whole life. After unpacking her small bag, she took a seat in the living room and waited, picking nervously at the loose weave of her turquoise tunic.

In a little while, the front door opened, and Andie and Tony stepped inside. Ordinarily, Thea would have jumped to greet guests to her home, but this morning, she didn't move from her chair. Her eyes swept back and forth between her son and granddaughter, searching for a sign that they either welcomed or rejected her. No one said a word. No one approached the other, but Thea saw a terrible conflict in Tony's face. She'd expected it. If he'd rushed to her, thrown his arms around her, and called her *Mom*, it would have been a lie.

And Andie. Was that sorrow Thea saw in her?

Finally, she stood. "I have asked God to forgive me for how I failed you both. And I believe he has. But he never took from me the consequences of my actions. I thought I had done what was best for you, Tony. I knew your parents loved you as their own. And you them. I could only rest in that, knowing it was too late to do anything different. But I longed to hold you and call you my own."

Andie reached for her father's hand. He gripped it tightly, but his eyes never left Thea.

The old woman moved slowly toward the painting of three little boys playing jacks. She looked at it and smiled. "I'm sure you recognized this image of you and your friends. Your mother sent me the photograph along with many others. I painted them all." Her voice caught for just a moment, but still focused on the painting, she continued. "I could recreate you on my canvas with my brushes and colors, and then I could keep you."

"These are *your* paintings?" Andie asked excitedly, breaking away from her father and moving closer to Thea.

"Yes," Thea said.

"*You* are Joch?"

"For Jochebed. Do you remember her?"

Andie's face brightened. "The mother of Moses!"

Thea looked back at Tony's solemn face. "Jochebed set him adrift in the Nile to save him. I don't presume to be so noble. There was no threat of death hanging over my infant son. Just my own fear that my indiscretion, my exile, and poverty would ruin his chances for happiness. I didn't know that God could restore what the locusts had eaten."

"Where are the other paintings?" Tony finally spoke.

"In a storeroom on the reservation."

"Why not this one?" he asked.

"No one would know it was you."

He moved closer to the painting, passing in front of Thea but making no motion toward her. "I would like to see the others," he said flatly.

"Then my nephew will bring them to you."

"You mean . . . my cousin?"

Thea nodded sadly. "Yes."

"I would like to meet him. Are there any other family members for me to know?" His tone lay empty, passive. Thea had not anticipated what seemed to be indifference.

"There is only my nephew, a niece, and their father—my brother, who is ailing."

"One day I would like to meet them all."

Andie looked into his troubled face. "Dad?"

"It's okay, Andie." He looked back at Thea. "I respect and understand your decision to give up your child for adoption, and I thank you for choosing godly, loving parents for me. But I know only one mother, and she is gone. If I am to know you at all, it must be as a kind and brave friend, which you are." He looked down at the floor and said nothing more.

I am not ever to be his mother? Only his friend?

Andie walked up to Thea and wrapped her arms about the thin body. "Give him time to absorb this," she whispered.

But Thea wasn't finished. "There's something else you should know, Tony." She returned to her seat and looked up. "Please sit down, just for a while."

Tony and Andie settled onto a small sofa opposite Thea.

Nervously, she began. "Though I haven't lived on my reservation since I first left it in my teens, I have returned often, staying with my nephew and his family. I am close to my people and try to help them in any way I can. Several years ago, I discovered one of them selling drugs in our village. He was a man I knew well. I confronted him and made him tell me where he got them. It was from Leo Francini's camp in the Everglades."

Tony leaned forward in his seat.

"The man told me where it was. So I went there."

"You . . . did . . . what?" Andie sputtered.

"I couldn't allow that to happen," Thea continued. "I had to make them leave our village alone. The man told me when Leo would be at the camp."

"Wait a minute," Tony said, his eyes narrowing to a squint. "You thought you could just walk into the middle of a cartel and ask, pretty please, would they stop selling drugs?" His tone was incredulous.

Thea didn't react. She was expecting worse. "I guess they were too shocked by an old woman alone on an airboat, daring to approach them. When I told them I had important information for Leo, though—and after they quite roughly searched me—they led me to him."

Tony and Andie stared at her in disbelief. "*You* had important information for Leo Francini?" he asked.

Thea nodded. "I knew his location, so I . . . sort of made a deal with him. I wouldn't call law enforcement if he kept away from my people."

Tony raised a hand to the side of his head as if it needed prop-ping up.

"I knew I was wrong to do it. It was as if I didn't care if he infested someone else's village or home or school, as long as he kept away from the reservation." She looked out the window. "I've asked God to forgive me for that, especially now." She turned back to them. "Look what that man has done to you and Andie."

"He could have killed you on the spot!" Andie scolded.

"Yes. But I told him if he harmed me, there were others who would lead the authorities to him. I asked if he was prepared to kill us all to keep that one decrepit camp."

"And he said . . ." Tony prompted.

Thea grimaced. "Actually, he laughed. He was quite amused. He said they'd be breaking camp soon anyway, and he'd see that no one trafficked in our village again."

"Just like that?" Andie asked.

"Just like that," Thea agreed. "But they came back. After that shootout with the FBI, after you lost those men, Tony, and I watched you on TV, promising to bring Leo to justice, they came back to a place they knew had been compromised. They must have thought I was just a crazy old bird they needn't worry about. But I had to do something, especially when I discovered they were dealing in the village again. I doubted Leo would be at the camp, but I was going to find out. So I went back."

Tony leaned back hard against the sofa and murmured some-thing to himself, something Thea couldn't hear, but she could read the bewilderment on his face.

"What did you hope to gain?" Andie asked.

"If I'd found Leo there, I was going to appeal to him again or say whatever I had to say to get away and call the police as quickly as I could. But he wasn't there—just a ragtag band of thugs. So I told them I'd had a deal with Leo, and they had broken it. That I'd already called the police and they'd better get out."

"And they let you go?" Andie seemed painfully confused.

"They knew I'd given them time to run. My shameful attempt to spare the village their revenge. The fact was, I didn't call the police until after I left camp. I had to be sure Leo wasn't there. I would risk retaliation to bring him down, but not for just a few of his men. Either way, I would get rid of them." She smiled awkwardly. "As for shooting me? One of them called me an ugly old woman not worth a bullet. I was glad for that."

Tony shook his head and crossed his arms over his chest. He looked at the ceiling and exhaled what seemed a long-held breath. "Is there anything else?"

Thea fumbled with the thread of her tunic again, then looked up. "I have lifted great burdens from myself, Tony, and placed them on you. What you do with them is your choice. And I will understand."

His look pierced her to the core. But she had laid her heart bare and could proffer no more. Finally, he got up to leave. Andie joined him, reluctantly, Thea thought. She followed them to the door, stopping just short of it and wondering if this was the end of it all.

As Tony held the door open for Andie to pass, he turned back to Thea. "You and I have missed a great deal by not knowing each other. But now we do."

CHAPTER 39

༄

TUESDAY AFTERNOON, Tony and his advisers had retreated to the living room to prepare for Wednesday night's debate. It had been moved from Palm Beach to the University of Miami, not far from the Blaker estate. Though Chief Manette and Vic weren't at all comfortable with Tony making any public appearances until they'd apprehended Nick Jarvis and knew who else they were dealing with, they determined that keeping their fearless candidate down was a losing battle. He would, however, wear a bullet-proof vest, and the campus would undergo a thorough security sweep. But they couldn't handpick the audience—only search them and detain anyone who looked like Jarvis. Tickets to the debate would be available to the public.

"Sir, they'll be drilling you on the economy and immigration," said one of his aides. "Here's a list of possible questions and the answers we recommend."

Tony was slouched deep in a wingback chair with his reading glasses perched on the end of his nose and a binder of debate notes in his hand. Something caught his eye from outside a window next to him. He saw Andie and Evan round the front corner of the house and head across the lawn that swept to the side cove and the boathouse, where all of Tony's thoughts had been trained since the morning's visit with Thea.

He feared his abrupt departure from her had sent a signal he hadn't intended, like slamming a door on something he'd secretly longed for—the truth. But once confronted with the facts, he didn't know what to do with them. *How do you process a thing like that? Work it into your schedule like one more news update? File it and move on? And the timing, what did that mean?* The morning he'd discovered the beginnings of his life was the same morning he'd been marked for death. *Just a coincidence?*

He watched the two young people on the lawn, almost playful in their animated conversation. He hadn't missed the stolen glances between them that day, but this was the first time he'd seen them together. How could Andie not find a handsome young man of such intensity irresistible? And there was Tony's answer: Evan slipped his hand around Andie's as they walked, and she briefly leaned her head into his shoulder. Then she glanced quickly toward the house, apprehension on her face.

Yes, my child. I saw that. And it's okay. Sometimes when the world attacks, God shields us with human love. Tony dropped the papers into his lap, halted by the implication of his words. *An assassin and a mother, arriving in his life at the same time?*

ᴄᴏ

"I think I saw this place in a Grimm's storybook," Evan said when he and Andie arrived at the boathouse.

Andie knocked on the door. As they waited for it to open, Evan wove his fingers into the wavy strands of hair falling about her shoulders. She'd answered the gesture by reaching an arm around his waist when Thea opened the door. Abruptly, the couple disengaged, embarrassed.

Thea beamed at them. "Come in, children."

Andie gave the old woman a hug, then turned to Evan. "I want you to meet my grandmother." Andie's smile was triumphant, but Evan's slid from his face. "Yes, it was a shock to me too," she said. She pulled him down on the sofa next to her and invited Thea to tell her story again, even of her association with Leo.

Afterward, Andie pointed out the paintings to Evan. "Thea . . . oh, I guess I'll still call you that, if it's all right?"

"I like it fine," she answered.

"Anyway, Thea painted all these marvelous canvases. Look at them, Evan. They're brilliant. The composition and layering, the texture and tones. And I actually offered to give her art lessons. Do you remember that, Thea?"

Thea nodded and laughed softly, but Evan saw sadness in her face. He wondered if it had anything to do with how Mr. Ryborg might have received her announcement. He marveled at the woman now chatting easily with her granddaughter about pigments and glazing. To walk so bravely into Leo's den and declare her demands on him was more than Evan could fathom.

He thought of his own mother and how she'd allowed herself to become the perennial victim, first her husband's, then her parents', now her own. How he'd love for her to know these two women. He looked from one to the other, and his heart swelled. Here in this cottage by the sea with the sun shining through the red bougainvillea at the window, and the gentle goodness of these women so near him, something suddenly resonated in him. Something that felt pure and undefiled. Hope. Evan could almost feel its pulse.

He opened the door to the porch and wandered outside. The cove sparkled with emerald reflections of the mangrove across the way. He leaned over the rail and looked at the water lapping against the rock wall below. There, he saw his own image tossed about in the waves. The more he stared into his reflection, the more fractured it became. Then he looked up at a giant royal palm overhanging the boathouse. He scanned the length of it from its spiking fronds down its solid trunk to the bulbous mound shooting roots into the ground, fortified against the storms.

He closed his eyes. *God, if you can anchor a tree, surely you can ground me in something. In you.*

The porch door opened, and Andie came up beside him. She tucked her arm under his, and his heart raced at the nearness of her. He knew that he loved her. But she didn't know him, not really. He believed the feelings she showed for him were probably temporary, just her need to hold onto someone while she weathered her own storm. But when it was over—and it would be over—she would shed him along with every other entanglement to this madness, glad to be free of it all. Like his mother had shed his father.

"I've talked Thea into going back to the house with us." She tightened her grip on his arm.

He smiled down at her, grateful that for now, she was beside him.

Later, the three of them had just entered the front door of the house when the phone in Evan's pocket rang, the one Leo had given him. He looked quickly at Andie. "That can only be one person," he said, then rushed toward the back of the house where he heard Vic's unmistakable voice. Entering the kitchen almost at a full run, he jumped into the middle of her conversation with Tony to announce. "It's Leo!"

Vic responded instantly. "Speaker phone, then pick up."

Evan gathered his thoughts, assuming the casual demeanor that was his defense against the embroiling attachment to the man on the phone. "Nice of you to call," he droned.

"Of course it is," Leo said. "I'm all soft in the middle. Few people see that, though. By the way, greetings to those gathered around Evan's phone. I can almost hear the hum of the tape recorder, so here's what you need to know. My business is with Tony Ryborg and him only. Tell him to call me back at this very untraceable number. Tell him to—"

"I'm here," Tony snapped. It was the first time he'd ever spoken to Leo Francini.

There was a moment of dead space before Leo finally responded. "Evan, I know this is a preposterous question, but can I rely on you to tell me the truth?"

"Yes, sir."

"Was that Tony Ryborg who just spoke?"

"Hard to believe, isn't it, Leo?" Tony answered instead. "After all these years."

"Well, what do you know? The man, himself. The one who once told the good people of Florida that he would make Leo Francini pay the severest penalty. My, my, how the tables do turn. It seems I saved *you* from paying the ultimate penalty."

"What do you mean?" Tony demanded.

Leo chuckled. "Oh, this is very rich stuff." He paused. "Who do you think warned you away from Miami Beach and told you your little girl's hiding place had been blown?"

Tony was too startled to respond.

"Evan, you there?" Leo asked.

"Why did you do it?" Evan struggled to grasp a motive.

"Oh, you'll know in time."

"What do you want?" Tony snapped.

"What? No 'thank you'? No offers to repay me?"

"How are you going to repay the families of those FBI agents your boys killed?"

Silence. Then, "You lost agents. I lost a son." A long pause. "I'm not going to lose another one. So here's what we're going to do. You take that phone, Mr. Ryborg-for-governor, cut it off speaker, and talk to me one-on-one. Can you do that?"

⌁

Tony walked to the back porch and closed the door behind him. "Say what you have to say, Francini."

"Okay, we're going to take this a step further. I want to meet. Tonight. If you mess it up trying to take me in, you'll lose the one who's after both our kids. The same one who might be arrogant enough to try another shot at you."

CHAPTER 40

By NINE O'CLOCK TUESDAY NIGHT, two boats were tied up at the concrete pier on the landward side of Dutch Key, their silhouettes faint against a fretful sky. On this remote, abandoned island off the Florida mainland, only a pale wash of light escaped the cabin of an FBI cruiser. The other boat sat darkly, its high, tuna tower swaying fitfully against a blustery front moving in from the east.

Throughout the long, bloody conflict between Tony Ryborg and Leo Francini, never had there been a more bizarre moment. The two men sat alone in the cruiser, facing each other in the dimly lit cabin. Each had brought only two aides to this tenuous, secret summit. Warren, Miguel, and their drivers were topside, watching each other with equal intensity. Just offshore were the troops, the outer wall of defense for both sides. More boats, more arms—assurance that neither Ryborg nor Francini would be taken against his will.

Leo relaxed against the cushions of a built-in booth wrapping around three sides of a small dining table. On the opposite side, Tony sat straight, body language suggesting that the meeting be opened and closed with efficiency.

Leo removed the baseball cap from his head and plopped it on the table. "You've been an enormous pain in my rear."

"Get on with it, Francini. What do you have?"

Leo smiled thinly. "Like a hand of cards? You wonder if I'm bluffing? Do you think I would be here if I didn't have a hand I was sure of?"

"Then show it!"

"Oh, let's play the game awhile before we cash in. We may never have another opportunity like this."

"To do what? What is this all about?"

Leo looked down at the table, then back at Tony. "You know, it was just business."

"Having a problem with your conscience, Francini? All the lives you've ruined beginning to weigh you down?"

Leo seemed unfazed. "I never sent my condolences when your wife died."

Tony clenched his fist under the table.

"You don't have to believe me," Leo continued, "but I really was sorry to hear about that. I lost a good woman, too. My fault. Business again." He shook his head. "And here's something else. All that stuff with your little girl—just mischief to get you off our backs."

"*Our* backs?"

Leo grinned. "We'll get to that later. You see, I plan to drop from sight pretty soon. Time to retire and never surface again. And you're going to help me do that. You're about to cut a deal with me, and you'll do it gladly once you hear what I've come to tell you."

"What do you want, Francini?"

Leo fiddled with the curtains at the window, then looked sharply at Tony. "I want my son to be a doctor. I want you to help him get a loan, a scholarship, whatever it takes, because he'll accept no money from me."

Tony listened.

"I want all charges against him dropped. And he's not to know where I am, ever."

Tony wondered what powered the shifting, seismic plates inside this man who at once was both unconscionable gangster and caring father. How did the two live in one body, and would one destroy the other? Tony wondered which. "In exchange for what?"

Two hours later, both boats left Dutch Key, heading in different directions. As the cruiser raced for Miami, Tony stood near the stern of the boat, a tight grip on the side rail. Impervious to the rough seas, he allowed the occasional spray to catch him full in the face, welcoming its sobering sting. For as deep as the years had plunged him into the dark of the criminal mind, he hadn't been prepared for what he just heard.

CHAPTER 41

ༀ

"WE HAVE JUST CONFIRMED that the debate between Attorney General Tony Ryborg and Senator Bill Neiman will take place as planned tonight at seven in the Heigel Auditorium at the University of Miami," reported a local television news anchor during a morning broadcast. "It will be the first time Ryborg has been seen in public since his Orlando campaign stop last Friday.

"In a related report, it is still uncertain what charges have been brought against the two men arrested at Miami Beach's Excalibur Hotel on Monday. You'll recall that incident coincided with a scheduled campaign address by Tony Ryborg at the hotel the same hour the two men were taken into custody. At that time, however, Ryborg had already cancelled his appearance, claiming an unavoidable conflict in scheduling. Still, the incident raises speculation that Ryborg may have been the target of an attack by the two men and that the attorney general may have been isolated and under guard since Monday."

Warren Jacobs chewed vigorously on a muffin while watching the newscast. He was due to return to the auditorium, where exhaustive security measures were underway. But first, he would brief his boss one last time.

"You through with that?" he asked Vic, hunched over a blueprint of the auditorium, which had been spread on the kitchen table for a growing number of agents and officers to study, along with photos of Nick Jarvis, still at large.

"Yep. Know it like my own house."

Warren walked to the back door of the Blaker house and called for Tony to come inside. He'd been talking with Andie and Evan on the porch.

"Something's up," Evan said after Tony excused himself and hurried inside the house.

"What do you mean?" Andie asked.

"I mean just hours from putting on a bulletproof vest and marching off to one of the biggest nights of your political career, you don't concern yourself with how some guy you hardly know is going to pay for medical school. And he refused to comment at all on what's got to be one of the strangest meetings in law enforcement history. Not one word on what the top cop and crazed criminal talked about in private." Evan squinted toward the house. "No, Miss Ryborg, something is definitely up." A vague shape of it had already begun to form in Evan's mind.

He looked back to see worry etched on Andie's face. He reached for her hand and pulled her up. They ambled toward the beach.

"We've been ordered to stay here during the debate," Evan said, staring at the ground as they walked. "But I have to get inside that auditorium tonight."

"Why?"

"There's something going on between my dad and yours, and I believe it has everything to do with tonight. Will you help me get away?"

"Only if I go too."

"Would it do any good to say no?"

Andie shook her head and broke into a run for the boathouse. "Come on," she called behind her.

Evan took off after her. "What are you doing?"

"I know how to get out of here."

෴

When they reached the boathouse, they slipped around back and took the stone steps to the water's edge. "Thea is still back at the house," Andie said, trying the lock on the small, side door to the old boat shed. "I'll have to get the key." She let herself into the house using the spare door key Thea kept in a garden shoe. Moments later, she returned. "I don't like sneaking into her house like that," she told Evan, producing the key to the boat shed that she'd taken from a hook on a kitchen wall. "Granddaughter or not, I have no right."

"Then tell her what we're doing and ask her forgiveness. Otherwise, she'll freak out when she finds the boat gone. And you with it. It's best someone knows you haven't been kidnapped."

Andie worked the lock and threw open the creaking wood door, suddenly flooding the dank, watery cavity with sunlight. When they stepped inside, Evan whistled through his teeth. "Look at that!" Cradled in a lift about five feet off the water sat a gleaming wooden boat from another time. "That's a Chris-Craft runabout, about 1948, maybe '50. A classic!"

"Teak?" Andie asked.

"Mahogany and well pampered, it seems. Look at the varnish on that thing." He turned a quizzical glance on Andie. "Surely not Thea."

"And why not? She's an able captain, and captains like to maintain their boats."

Evan noticed the control box for the electric lift and opened the metal door. "I think I can get this thing in the water. Running the lift shouldn't make much noise, but this little piece of boating history isn't known for its quiet engine." His eyes slid the length and breadth of the boat, noting its double cockpit with turquoise upholstery, the brawny steering wheel that looked like it might have come off a Duesenberg touring car. "She's a treasure. No telling what she's worth. It'll be like riding on the back of a Stradivarius. I hate to do it."

"But short of climbing the electrified wall and hitchhiking, it's the only way out," Andie confirmed. "How long will it take us?"

Evan fiddled with the controls to see if they were getting juice. The metal slats supporting the twenty-foot boat suddenly ground into action. Evan quickly reversed the movement. "How about the door?" he asked, pointing to the wide, garage-like door at the end of the shed.

Andie looked on the wall behind her and noticed a switch. She tested it, and the door lunged to life, raising slowly and, they were glad to discover, quietly.

"I'd say we can get underway in fifteen minutes," Evan said, peering anxiously into the boat's cockpit. "Assuming you can also locate the ignition key, we should make the Coconut Grove Marina in about thirty minutes. From there, we'll take a cab to the university." He ran his hand along the polished wood of the boat, still figuring time and distance in his head.

"Working backwards: the debate's at seven," he said. "I want to arrive no later than six. Let's leave here about four thirty." Not hearing a response, he looked over his shoulder at Andie. In the slant of light through the small door, he caught the sheen in her eyes. He turned from the boat and held his arms out for her. She moved into them and looked up.

"What's wrong?" he asked. The painful wrenching he'd known so long, the one that came at every sight of her tore at him even now, even with her in his arms. How long would she stay there? Until she no longer needed his help, his comfort? *She must look at me and see only a diseased family tree that could bear no fruit, no future for her.*

Andie shook her head. "Something's very right." She lifted her hand to his face and lightly ran a fingertip over his mouth, then touched it to her own. "I've waited all my life to love you." She pulled his face to hers and kissed him.

"Andie." But he could say no more. His arms tightened around her waist, and he suddenly lifted her, clutching her to him as if her heart had to beat for them both. He buried his face against her neck, in the softness of her hair, and just held on. When he finally released her, he found his voice. "Stay, Andie. We'll find our way."

CHAPTER 42

JUST BEFORE SHE WAS TO MEET Evan at the boathouse, Andie stuffed a jacket and hat into a knapsack and headed downstairs. When she opened the front door, she saw Tony and Thea walking toward the house, together.

Her surprise made her forget the telltale knapsack on her back.

"And where are you off to?" her dad asked.

"Oh, I'm, uh, just going for a walk around the property." *Change the subject quickly.* "Thea, I've hardly seen you all day." After testing the mechanisms for launching the boat, Andie and Evan had spent most of the afternoon on the beach with a couple of officers in tow. Since her dad's meeting with Leo Francini the night before, an even closer guard had been kept on the men's offspring, though she didn't know why.

"She spent a lot of it with me," said Tony. He and Thea exchanged a quick glance. To Andie, it seemed a signal of reassurance.

"We have come to terms with who we are to each other," Thea offered.

"Andie," Tony said, "I have traveled through many emotions since you and I discovered that suitcase on Thea's bed. I have always prayed for God to do his will in my life and I believe he has done that at every turn. His is always the perfect plan. And now, undeniably, that plan includes . . . my mother." He looked at Thea with what Andie believed was admiration. Affection, she hoped, would come.

Tony cleared his throat and glanced at his watch. "Now, you'll excuse me, please." He patted both women on the back and hurried into the house.

"And there he goes." Andie laughed as she wiped moisture from her eyes. "Cut to the point and clear out. Thea, he's always been like that. But you'll get used to it." She felt the tug of the knapsack. "And now, there's something else you should know."

When Andie confessed the plan to sneak off to the debate that night, Thea grinned and withdrew two keys from her skirt pocket. "I always place this house key in the left shoe." Her eyes flashed at Andie. "Not the right one, where I found it earlier this afternoon. And this key to the boat shed always hangs at the back of the hook, not in front of the other keys, as I found it, too, earlier this afternoon."

Andie grimaced. "Evan said I would need to ask your forgiveness. I guess this is a good time."

"For tonight's mission, you're going to need more than forgiveness. You need a driver."

"But Evan can—"

"No, Evan can't. There's a tricky gear shift to this boat that old Mr. Blaker installed to prevent theft. You and Evan would have realized that too late. I'm sorry, dear, but you have no choice. When do we leave?"

"Why, you sly fox. The genes are beginning to emerge." Andie stared at Thea with new appreciation. "We meet Evan in ten minutes. He's going to love this."

♒

Thea scribbled a quick note telling the guards that she had taken Evan and Andie for a cruise and that they would return. All truth. All deceptive. She felt a pang of guilt, but if the two young people were determined to go where they had been ordered not to, it was best she went with them. She also suspected her good judgment had just failed her.

Grabbing her bright blue backpack stuffed with food, water, a light jacket, and a canister of Mace, Thea hurried down the long staircase of the Blaker house, where she had moved back in temporarily to help care for her guests.

She propped the note up in the empty kitchen and left by the back door. When she reached the boat shed, Andie and Evan were waiting for her. Evan looked less than amused. "I'm not trying to spoil your fun, Evan," Thea said. "But like it or not, you need me to operate the boat for you." She kept talking as she unlocked the small side door and hit the button to raise the main door at the end of the shed. "I used this boat to ferry Mr. Blaker's kids back and forth between the house and the weekend place at Stiltsville."

"Yes, ma'am," he said dryly. "But maybe you could just show me the trick."

"We don't have time, son." She started the lift, and they all watched the boat descend slowly to the water. Evan helped Thea down the steps and into the boat first. Andie followed, needing no assistance.

In no time, the rumble of the inboard motor cut the stillness of the cove as the sleek racer and its three passengers backed from the shed, cleared the cove, and accelerated over the bay waters heading north to Coconut Grove Marina. Passing boaters gawked not only at the vintage boat, but also at its elderly female skipper holding her own against the brisk chop on the bay, a broad-brimmed hat tied securely with a red bow beneath her chin.

Thea was pleased to see that her passengers seemed to relish the ride as much as she did, the wide-open sky and water evoking a sweet release from the nightmare they'd all been living.

When they arrived at the marina and securely tied down the boat, Evan tipped a young dockhand twenty dollars to keep a close eye on it, promising another twenty if they returned to find that no one had tampered with it.

"Let's go," he said, ushering Andie and Thea to the closest cab stand.

CHAPTER 43

Heigel Auditorium rose beside a stream on the University of Miami campus. Its modern facade peaked and plunged in great walls of red granite and clear glass. Inside, the acoustics were pitch perfect, thanks to the architect and a sound team borrowed from Lincoln Center in New York.

High in the booth, technicians rotated, flipped, and massaged switches to funnel voices from the stage to every rounded surface of the landmark building's interiors. In just over an hour, the doors would open to a capacity crowd drawn by the drama of this provocative gubernatorial race.

On a low platform in front of the stage, Channel 5 anchor Kay Landrum prepared for her duties as co-moderator with *Miami Herald* columnist Greg Silvera. Their aides fitted microphones, tested the cameras, shifted chairs, arranged notes, filled water glasses, and waited for the candidates to arrive.

"Greg, look at this brief," Kay said, sliding a memo across the desk. "Ryborg will be wearing a bullet-proof vest. Makes me feel real safe."

"This bothers you? In a city where they stake out the mafia at the local bagel shop? Go ahead and bail, Kay. Your peers will be lined up to fill your chair."

She was about to respond when voices erupted from the back of the hall. One rang above the rest. "One candidate down, one to go," she said to Greg as she turned to greet the man leading an entourage toward the stage. "Good evening, Senator," she called to Bill Neiman. He responded with a jaunty salute to her and Greg.

"And a fine one it will certainly be, Miss Landrum." He drew close enough to take her hand, kiss the back of it, then turn snappily toward Greg. "Silvera, it's about time the *Herald* recognized your acumen beyond the printed word. This show of face tonight promises to win you and your paper a bevy of new readers, wouldn't you say?" He leaned toward them both and affected a stage whisper, "Especially if your challenges are courageous." He looked pointedly at them both, then bounded onto the stage to huddle with his advisers.

"What was that about?" Kay asked.

"I think the senator just suggested we move aggressively against his opponent."

"Oh, the Jessica Ryborg issue. *Courageous* meaning take the risk of being battered by sympathetic viewers." She thought a minute. "I can do that."

⌇

Evan, Andie, and Thea bumped along Dixie Highway in the back of a cab whose seats had long ago parted ways with their inner springs. The three had the look of shipwreck victims washed onto a strange shore, watching something hidden yet moving in the underbrush.

"We'll try to slip into the auditorium," Evan advised, his voice low despite the driver's blaring radio, over which he would hardly hear a word from the back seat. "Maybe have to buy tickets, I don't know."

"I don't think so," Thea said, a look of apology on her face. "I've done a terrible thing by bringing you both into the open. I should have tried to stop you. But now, the least I can do is see that you're protected. I want us to announce ourselves to Tony's security people and let them take us where you both will be safe."

The ensuing discussion ended with Evan and Andie yielding to Thea's request. "As long as I'm close enough to see," Evan said.

"See what?" Thea asked. "Why is it so important for you to be here?"

"Just a feeling," Evan replied. "That's all."

The cab stopped in the parking lot beside the auditorium. The lateral trajectory of rays from a sinking sun caught them full in the face, and seconds later, so did a familiar figure. Special Agent

Vic Shay moved in quickly as if she'd been lying in wait for them. With her were three fellow agents. "Well, who do we have here? Let's see. I count two runaways and, uh, Thea, are you the willing getaway driver?"

"Guilty," Thea said, clearly chagrined. Andie took her grand-mother by the arm in a gesture of solidarity.

"You knew we were coming, didn't you, Vic?" Evan said.

"Some of my hunches hit the mark, that's true. One of our agents found Thea's note and reported seeing you head out of there to the north, and, well, here you are. Now, let's get you out of here."

They moved as a tight group through the back door of the audi-torium, where Warren's team had just delivered Tony Ryborg. Vic had already told him of his daughter's escape.

Andie broke away and rushed to him. "Dad, don't be angry."

"Too late," he scolded. "Why did you disobey me?"

"I'm sorry. Evan and I just had to be here tonight."

"And Thea?"

"Our fault again. She didn't want us to come alone. We'll be okay."

Tony looked over her shoulder to see some of his security detail already hustling Evan and Thea into a wing off the stage. "Go with them, and stay put," he ordered firmly.

"Dad, I'm sorry."

He hugged her tightly, then sent her backstage.

Just then, Warren appeared at a small side door of the audito-rium and motioned for Tony. One of the candidate's bodyguards accompanied him to the open doorway.

"Everyone's in place, sir," Warren reported.

Tony looked past him to a plain white Suburban with dark-tinted windows parked outside. "You understand exactly what has to happen, right?"

"We do, sir. But a few reporters are showing way too much curiosity."

"You're sure they're reporters?"

"Yeah, a couple of capital boys."

"Sniffing out an exclusive for the *Tallahassee Democrat*?"

"No, sir. They're from the *Washington Post*."

"Oh."

"You underestimate the reach of your celebrity," Warren teased beneath a somber expression.

"As a no-show for an assassination?"

"Something like that, though the media can only speculate about what happened Monday morning."

"Let them speculate all they want; just keep them away from that van."

"We will, sir. Did I just catch a glimpse of Andie?"

Tony rubbed his forehead and sighed deeply. "You did. Evan and Thea are with her."

"But how did—"

"A story for another time," Tony interjected, then turned to leave.

"One more thing, sir. Does Evan know what's happening?"

"No."

～

When the house lights came up and the audience was seated, Kay Landrum welcomed those present and the television viewers to the night's debate and explained its format. Behind their podiums, the two candidates scribbled last-minute notes, sipped from water glasses, and nodded toward familiar faces near the stage. The auditorium had filled quickly, with most tickets having been sold in advance. From their vantage point tucked behind the heavy drape, Evan, Andie, and Thea could see only Tony. No one could see them, not even Bill Neiman.

The first question of the evening was for Neiman. Greg Silvera asked the senator how he would address the escalating rate of insurance fraud, especially in his South Florida district, which included Miami Beach.

Next, Kay Landrum asked Tony what considerations he was prepared to offer citrus growers whose crops were destroyed by weather and/or pestilence.

Later, both candidates weighed in on issues such as beach erosion and laws governing property taxes for homeowners whose beachfront properties gradually slid into the ocean, illegal

immigration, water purification and conservation, appropria-
tions for education, hurricane preparedness, and advancements
in emergency relief efforts.

When it was Kay Landrum's turn again, she looked over the
top of her glasses at Tony and asked, "If you were governor, Mr.
Ryborg, how much of your time would be devoted to fighting
drug traffickers?"

Greg Silvera issued a faint groan over the blunt question.
Neiman furrowed his brow and turned bodily toward Tony. The
senator was the image of one anxious for the answer to what he
apparently considered a critical question.

The weight and heat of the vest beneath his shirt had begun
to wear on Tony. But he knew if he mopped sweat from his face
now, it would appear that the question had made him nervous,
when in fact, he was fully prepared for it, or something like
it. As calmly as he could, he addressed the issue in the same
way he had in his Orlando speech. But then, he took his reply
further.

"If my wife can defeat addiction, anyone can. We need programs to counsel those already in the grip of addiction. But more
than that, we need to so inundate our children with opportuni-
ties to succeed, so occupy them with pursuing what's uniquely
good and promising about each one of them, that they wouldn't
dream of wasting their lives on drugs. That's the fight! And
every parent in this state, elected official or not, needs to spend
as much time as it takes to save our children."

That brought the first standing ovation of the night. During
it, Tony slipped a handkerchief from his pocket and wiped down
his face. He drained his glass of water and turned for someone
offstage to refill it. Still, the audience applauded.

When they finally settled back into their seats, Greg Silvera
delivered the next question. "This is for you, Senator Neiman.
With regards to local drug trafficking, do you have a plan for curb-
ing its relentless proliferation throughout the state?"

"I'm glad you asked that question," Neiman responded. "As a
matter of fact, I have put together what I consider to be an ambi-
tious proposal for after-school programs aimed at educating

our children to the dangers of drugs and how to identify and run, I mean *run*, from dealers who hang out near our schools."

"Have you ever personally encountered a drug dealer, sir?" Greg asked.

Neiman held his head high and proclaimed, "I have never knowingly been in the presence of such a person. I would never—"

"Hello, Bill," a voice called from the side door of the auditorium. Leo Francini emerged from the shadows of the balcony overhang and started down the aisle. His hands cuffed, he was accompanied by two uniformed police officers.

Bill Neiman stepped back from the podium. "I . . . I don't know who—"

"Oh, sure you do, Bill. You and I go way back." Leo walked slowly, deliberately, a menacing smile on his face.

While news crews scrambled to close in on the evolving spectacle, Tony slipped quietly from the stage. Neiman looked after him with what appeared to be the dawning of horror in his eyes. Then he looked back at Leo, standing beside Greg Silvera, who'd already signaled the cameramen to cut, over Kay Landrum's objections.

"Don't you have anything to say, Bill?" Leo taunted.

Neiman took another step back and stumbled. He grabbed the drape to keep from falling and pulled it from its frame, exposing Evan, who had jumped from his seat at the sound of his father's voice.

"Evan!" Leo cried and lunged toward the stage.

Neiman gaped at Evan, his eyes blazing. "You're Leo's boy?" The stunned audience seemed to hold its collective breath as the senator lost his statesman's bearing. "You're a dead boy," Neiman growled. "I'll see to that!" He rushed from the stage but didn't get far. Chief Manette and his team were waiting for him. They had been all afternoon.

"Get your hands off me!" Neiman screamed as officers cuffed and arrested him. Tony, himself, delivered the statement of his rights. "Ryborg, you've got nothing on me. But this will ruin you and your kid too!"

Tony signaled for Neiman to be taken away. It gave him no pleasure to watch the downfall of one who'd succumbed to his own power, one who'd hired an assassin to eliminate the man who was not only Neiman's political opponent but the one who most threatened Neiman's long-entrenched under-world empire.

In the last few weeks, the polls had clearly indicated that Tony was the frontrunner by a wide margin. If he were to be removed from the race, one way or another, an eleventh-hour appointee to take Tony's place would most certainly fare poorly in a race against Neiman.

But now, in hours of testimony taped just that morning, Leo had provided enough to indict the senator for drug trafficking and attempted assassination. Still, Tony had wanted to lock down a conviction by prompting Neiman to incriminate himself. Greg Silvera, recruited earlier in the day, had aided that effort by ask-ing questions supplied to him.

As a stunned crowd poured from the auditorium, and media crews plunged into near breathless reports on what had just hap-pened, Tony followed Chief Manette into a private office back-stage. Inside, Leo squirmed on a small, straight-backed chair. After dismissing the two officers guarding him, Chief Manette and Tony closed the door and sat opposite Leo, who was no lon-ger wearing handcuffs.

"What was Evan doing here?" Leo growled. "You're supposed to be guarding him!"

"He slipped away from us," Chief Manette admitted.

"Well, get him out of here."

"Calm down, Leo," Tony said.

"We have a deal, Ryborg. Remember?"

"That's why we're here."

"That's why I shouldn't be. Now that my part in this sting is over, let me go."

"We'll arrange that shortly," Chief Manette said, "but first we want to make sure you understand what will happen to you if you are caught anywhere in the U.S."

"Something about extradition back to Dade County where the full weight of the law would come to rest on my sorry head. Is that about right?"

"Fairly accurate," Tony replied sullenly. "Remember, we have your signed confession, not to mention Ray Dingo's testimony against you, Neiman, and Nick Jarvis. So prosecuting you would go quickly."

"And wouldn't you enjoy that?" Leo smirked.

"I think we've said enough here," Chief Manette cut in. "You'll stay here until the crowd has cleared out and we think it's safe to move you."

"Safe? Me?" Leo straightened in his chair. "What about my boy? And why did he come?"

"Evan knew nothing about your being here," Tony answered. "He and Andie—*our* children, Leo, and that is rather bizarre—came just to watch the debate."

"Well, until you've got Jarvis in hand, Evan gets full protection at all times. You hear me?" He paused a moment. "And don't forget who gave you the tape of my last conversation with Jarvis. That'll be enough to lock him down too."

"What about Neiman?" Chief Manette asked Leo. "What's to keep him from ordering payback on Evan from prison?"

"Do you have any idea how much Bill Neiman loves himself? And do you have any idea what I can do to him even from exile?"

Chief Manette and Tony looked quickly at each other.

"Well, he'll find out," Leo answered himself. "Sometime after he's locked away, he'll receive a very personal message from me, a reminder that I have people everywhere, especially in prison."

Tony was the first to rise. "I don't think threats against anyone will serve you well. So I suggest you sit here quietly until we're ready for you."

Tony was headed for the door when he stopped and looked back. "One question, Leo. Why *did* you warn me about the assassin?"

"When I figure that out, I'll let you know."

CHAPTER 44

❧

By the time Leo was led from the building to a waiting car, the parking lot was nearly empty, and the news crews had given up on interviewing authorities that evening. The night had grown heavy with the kind of humidity that fed the subtropical plants but sapped the human body. Though advised not to, Tony had rid himself of the vest and had left the collar open on his damp shirt. He was walking beside Leo when they heard a voice from the back door of the auditorium.

"Dad!"

Leo turned to see Evan running toward him. Something else caught Leo's eye. The briefest flash from a stand of trees behind the parking lot. Instantly, he heard the bullet ping off a sign behind Evan's head. There would be another, he knew. "Evan! Get down!" But words wouldn't save his son, still running for him. Leo jerked free of the officer's grip and ran at Evan, hurling his whole body against him as the next bullet found its mark.

Leo slid to the ground, and Evan crumpled on top of him. The bullet had passed through the father to the son.

Vic and three officers raced into the trees as tires squealed just beyond them. They unloaded their weapons at the escaping car, bringing it to a halt halfway down the bank of the stream. Slumped in the front seat, Nick Jarvis was dead.

As radios crackled and sirens split the night, a human shield was thrown around Leo and Evan, with Tony closest to their bleeding, but still-breathing bodies. "Lord, please don't let them die!" he cried.

Andie ran from the building. "Dad! Evan!" Thea ran down the steps behind her, reaching arms blindly into the dark. Then she lost her balance, and her body slowly folded toward the pavement.

Andie didn't see her, but one of the officers did, reaching Thea a second before she hit, catching her around the waist and rolling with her into a patch of grass.

Andie's screams brought Tony to his feet. "Grab her, and get her down!" he yelled even as he lurched forward to intercept her himself. But Andie evaded them all and broke through to the bodies on the ground. Evan and Leo were soaked in blood, neither one moving.

Andie dropped to her knees over Evan's still body. "No! Oh God, no!" With violently shaking hands, she cupped his ashen face. "Evan!" she sobbed, "Don't go! Please don't go!" Her fingers flew to the hole in his side and plunged into it to stop the bleeding, but the damage was too great. Tony tried to lift her off Evan, but she fought him. "No, Dad!" Minutes later, paramedics had to pry Evan from her. They rushed him into one ambulance and Leo into another.

"Wait!" Warren called from the other side of the parking lot. Only then did Tony realize Thea had been hurt.

The officer who'd grabbed her was carrying her to one of the ambulances before they closed the doors. "I think she's okay," he told Tony as they loaded her inside with Leo. "Just shaken up and bruised."

"Tony," Thea called weakly. "This is my fault. I should never have let them come." But the doors closed on her before he could respond.

Tony broke into a run, hollering for Warren. "Get us to the hospital!"

CHAPTER 45

❧

THROUGH THE NIGHT, surgeons fought to save Evan, though they lost his spleen. Early in the morning, he was moved to intensive care. His condition still critical, he remained under heavy sedation. By day, Andie never left his side, though she wasn't allowed to stay overnight.

From things Evan had told Andie about his mother, she was located and summoned, but she chose not to come when told her ex-husband was in a nearby room. She asked that someone keep her informed of Evan's condition. Then she sent a huge bouquet of flowers, which wasn't allowed in ICU.

Thea, who recovered quickly from her mild cuts and bruises, rotated her vigil between Evan's room and Leo's. "There's no one for him, Andie," she'd said of Leo.

"I don't care. Because of him, Evan could die!"

"If not for Leo, Evan would already be gone."

"What?"

"You didn't know? Leo threw himself in front of Evan, blocking the bullet."

Andie stared blankly at Thea, then her eyes narrowed. "But it's his dad's fault they were shooting at him."

"Yes, I know. And so does Leo. He's a broken man, Andie. And if we can't forgive him, why should we expect God to forgive us?"

"I've never killed anybody."

"Have you ever hated anyone?"

"I hate Leo Francini!"

"Then in your heart, you have most certainly killed him."

Andie stared incredulously at Thea.

"Oh, yes," Thea answered the unspoken challenge. "The book

of Matthew quotes Christ saying that while anyone who murders must be judged, the one who harbors anger toward another must be judged as well. The Apostle John also warns that anyone who hates his brother is a murderer."

Andie visibly recoiled, rejecting the notion, but Thea continued.

"Sometimes the Bible tells us things we don't want to hear. But we must listen and understand why God says such things." She paused, searching Andie's downturned face until it finally lifted to her. "To hate is to kill even the good inside another person. Inside you, Andie."

⌇

Later, Thea sat with Leo, who sustained entry and exit wounds in his side. Though serious, the injury was less severe than Evan's, and Leo's body was mending. But Thea knew the inner man was shattered.

Though his eyes were closed, Thea whispered to him. "Leo, let God restore all of you. It's not too late." He turned his head from her. "You have a very fine son," she persisted. "I believe he wants to reconcile with his father. You saved him, you know. You were willing to give your life for his. There's no greater thing a person can do."

Leo turned a patronizing look on her. "I'm sure the irony of that bullet passing through me to my son wasn't lost on you. Sins of the father and all that. No, Miss Thea, the less I have to do with Evan, the better off he is."

Thea placed her hand on his. "You are a tough one, Leo. In need of tough forgiveness. God has a huge capacity for that. You can ask for it, if you like. If not, you'll never be healed."

Leo was about to speak when Tony Ryborg entered the room.

"Oh, the man of the hour has come," Leo quipped. "Is it with pity for his torn and wretched prisoner? Or pride over his astounding catch? Why, even the national media are in a frenzy over what you just pulled off. Bagged two bad boys and killed another in one night."

"How are you feeling, Leo?"

Leo shook his head in mock dismay. "Look at this, Thea. He won't even allow me the pleasure of sparring with him. I guess he would have to stoop too low to do that."

Tony walked closer to the bed, continuing to ignore the jibes, and lightly touched Thea on the back. "You okay?" he asked her.

She nodded and smiled back at him, grateful for his affectionate touch. He had forgiven her for allowing, even driving, Evan and Andie into harm's way.

"Thea, would you excuse us, please?" Tony said.

As she closed the door behind her, she heard Tony say, "As soon as you can make it alone, we'll get you out of here."

CHAPTER 46

ॐ

LATE THAT NIGHT, the door to Evan's hospital room opened. A young female nurse wheeled Leo inside and up to the bed. The officer who'd been standing guard outside Leo's room now waited in the hall with another stationed outside Evan's.

"Please leave me for a while," Leo whispered to the young woman, whom he'd begged to bend the rules and allow him this visit alone with his son.

When she'd gone, Leo rolled himself to Evan's side. He looked into the colorless face, eyes closed in sedated sleep, tubes and bandaging exposed upon his wound and fresh incision. The only sign of life was the slight rise and fall of Evan's chest and the blip of his heartbeat marching across the monitor.

Leo looked down at Evan's left hand, limp against his thigh. Leo reached between the railings of the bed and spread his own hand over his son's, gathering it wholly within his grip. He hung his head and wept, the mournful sobs wracking his body.

Then, Leo released his son, grabbed the railing of his bed and slowly stood, ignoring the searing pain in his side. Wobbling slightly, he laid his hand on Evan's head. "Why did you give this boy to me?" he whispered. "Look what I've done to him." He labored to breathe. "I'm no father. Why give me sons to destroy?" Leo felt faint and struggled to keep standing. "Save this boy. He's yours. He was always yours. I never—"

Suddenly, a vile pain tore through his head, and his body slid into the hemorrhaging vortex of the aneurysm. In his last moment, he looked into the face of his son, and it was over.

ॐ

Frantic voices raised Evan from a numbed sleep. He opened his eyes for the first time since the shooting and tried to focus on what was happening near his bed. A nurse quickly positioned herself in front of him, blocking his view. "Try to go back to sleep," she coaxed.

Someone was lifted from the floor and placed on a gurney. Someone who looked just like . . .

"Is that . . . my . . . dad?" Evan slurred.

He tried to lift himself up from the bed, but the nurse gently restrained him. "Mr. Markham, please don't try to move. We'll take care of this, and someone will come talk to you a little later."

Evan ignored the nurse and tried to push against her. "No . . . now."

Another nurse entered the room and added something to the IV tube running into Evan's arm. In seconds, he returned to sleep.

The next morning, he awoke to find Andie, Tony, and Thea standing beside his bed. Andie pushed a damp lock of hair off his forehead and kissed his cheek. "Welcome back," she said.

As he fought to pull himself to full consciousness, a dim vision surfaced in his mind—his dad running toward him and yelling. But why?

He tried to move, but a wrenching pain stopped him cold.

"Whoa," Tony said, quickly placing a steady hand on Evan's shoulder. "You don't want to do that."

Evan looked down at the bandaged wound, then back at Tony.

Tony answered the question he saw in Evan's eyes. "You were shot, Evan. You and your dad."

"Dad?" Something stirred inside him, a faint memory of voices, something urgent in the night. He focused on the faces of those who stood before him, and his dulled senses quickened. He tried to sit up but fell back on the pillows.

"Now, son," Tony said firmly, "don't do that anymore." He strengthened his grip on Evan. "We'll tell you what you need to know."

But Evan knew his dad was dead before Tony told him that Leo had survived his gunshot wound only to suffer the fatal burst of a cerebral aneurysm. The shapeless truth of it had already risen from the fog of recall and clarified itself. Evan was certain he had seen Leo lifted from the floor in the night.

When Tony explained how Leo had slipped into Evan's room, something else rose from Evan's subconscious. He interrupted Tony, saying, "I heard crying."

They all looked at him in surprise.

"When?" Andie asked.

"Last night. And I heard someone talking. Close to me." Evan looked into Andie's fearful eyes. "It was Leo. I know that. But I don't know what he was saying." Evan looked past them. "Nothing makes Leo Francini cry."

"Except burying another child," Thea said confidently.

"You don't know him," Evan responded.

"You're right. I don't think any of us did. But I know this: he loved you enough to give his life for you."

Evan blinked hard, not comprehending.

"Leo saw the gunman first," Tony explained. "The first bullet missed you. Before the second one hit, your dad threw himself against you. But he didn't count on the bullet passing through him to you. It was a .22 rimfire from a .38 revolver with a silencer. You would have died instantly if he hadn't shielded you."

No! Evan cried silently. *He wouldn't have done that. Not for me. Not for anybody.* But Evan could still feel the impact of his father's body against his.

"The gunman is dead," Tony continued. "It was Nick Jarvis, the guy who ran Neiman's drug network while the affable senator played politics. Jarvis was after me the night of the debate."

"He was in the auditorium?" Andie asked.

"In disguise. We found a wig pulled into a ponytail in the back seat of his car, and part of a fake beard was still glued to his face. He must have freaked when he saw Neiman implode, so he slipped out of the building. The rest was a vengeful rampage. Our background checks indicate Neiman didn't pick the coolest head to be his second in command, and Jarvis knew we were already on his heels."

Tony could tell he'd unloaded too much on Evan at once. He would wait to tell him about the deal Leo had made with the state prosecutor, about why Evan had seen his dad in handcuffs. "I'm sorry, Evan, for the trauma you've been through. But I couldn't be more proud of you if you were my own son."

Evan looked startled.

"And if you were my son, I'd be taking you home with me when you leave this place. So, that's exactly what I'm going to do. You need time to recuperate—and someone to tend to you." He slid a quick glance at his daughter.

"But I can't just—"

"Yes, you can, Evan," Andie insisted. "Dad and I want you to come home with us to Tallahassee, and when you're well again, you can go wherever you like."

"You're going back?" Evan asked Andie.

"I promised Dad I'd come home until after the election in November. The Democrats will have to name someone to run in Neiman's place, so the race is still on."

Evan seemed to drift somewhere else. Tony guessed it was to his home in Tennessee. But he had already spoken with Evan's mother and not been encouraged by the reception Evan would receive from that household. Where would the boy go if not home with him?

"Please, Evan," Andie implored. "Come home with us."

CHAPTER 47

ༀ

Vᴵᴄ ʜᴀᴅ ᴠɪꜱɪᴛᴇᴅ Eᴠᴀɴ every day since the shooting, mostly watching him sleep, talking in hushed tones with Andie, and conferring often with the doctors about his progress. She'd moved lightly about his room, not wishing to disturb him. But this morning, she entered the room like a locomotive, flung open the curtains, and pulled the blinds as high as they would go, flooding the room with sunshine. "Evan, this is the day to begin the rest of your life."

He and Andie, who had been at his darkened bedside since early morning, squinted irritably at her.

"See that bright light?" Vic asked, her voice just as radiant. "There's lots more where that came from, and you're about to walk into it."

Evan rubbed his eyes and struggled to a sitting position. Andie helped him.

"You're leaving here day after tomorrow," Vic announced. "And since you're going to be in Tallahassee anyway, it's time you got back to school. I came here to tell you that and cheer you on your way. Besides, I might need some free medical care one day."

Just then, Vic's cell phone rang. She stepped outside the room to take the call. A few minutes later, she rushed back into the room and turned on the television. "Look at this!" she said, flipping to a live news report:

". . . and firemen have now been dispatched to a fourth house fire in Dade County, this one just south of Homestead in a citrus grove nearly destroyed by Hurricane Andrew. The house had been abandoned since the 1992 storm, or so it was thought." The camera panned the scene of a raging fire, attended by multiple fire units. "As with the other three houses—we repeat, all in Dade

County—hundreds of hydroponic marijuana plants were discovered growing in pots crammed into every room. Sources tell us the fires were deliberately set in close succession. Investigators are scrambling to link the fires and determine the ownership of these grow houses, as they are called."

Vic turned the volume down. "We already know who owns them."

"The late Leo Francini?" Evan asked.

Vic nodded and turned the volume back up.

"We have just now received news of two more fires," the reporter continued, "this time in Broward County near Ft. Lauderdale. Our affiliate station there will soon . . . oh, here it is." The scene shifted to a warehouse engulfed in flames. "This is a live feed from an industrial park west of Ft. Lauderdale where fire units, as you can see, are just beginning to battle yet another blaze. The count is now up to six buildings, all full of hydroponic marijuana. Let me add that it seems no one was living in any of these structures at the time of the fires. But inside was millions of dollars worth of the plants that produce the high-potency drug that sells so rampantly on the streets of Florida. Stay with us as we monitor this strange story."

"It's about to get stranger," Vic said to the screen. She turned to face Evan. "Leo's island house on Cat's Eye just burned and fell into the water."

Evan seemed to lean into that news. "What's going on?"

Vic stared out the window as if her answer were lodged in one of the trees outside. "Here's what I think," she said. "By the time Leo got to the auditorium that night, he knew he was headed into exile and would never return. I think he set a few things in motion before that night. He probably left a handsome payment for some of his men to carry out his orders, one of them being the wholesale destruction of his operation."

"But why?" Andie asked.

Vic looked thoughtful again. "It's just a hunch, but you know how they used to burn down the houses where people had died of bubonic plague or typhoid fever?" She turned soulful eyes on Evan. "I'd like to think Leo was just sick of being . . . sick."

Vic approached the bed. "So how about we burn up a few things of yours, Evan? Like the charges pending against you. You're free to go."

"Was that another part of my dad's deal with the state?"

"You got it." Vic patted his arm. "Now, excuse me while I go tackle all the paperwork you created for me." She headed for the door, where she paused and looked back at Evan. "Of all the people I've arrested, I like you best."